TROUBLED WATERS

Gillian Galbraith

First published in 2014 by Polygon. This
paperback edition published in 2015 by Polygon,
an imprint of Birlinn Ltd
West Newington House
10 Newington Road
Edinburgh
EH9 1QS

www.polygonbooks.co.uk

ISBN 978 1 84697 316 1
eBook ISBN 978 0 85790 818 6

British Library Cataloguing-in-Publication Data
A catalogue record for this book is available from the British
Library.

Most of the places mentioned in this story are real, but all
persons described are entirely fictitious. Any resemblance
between characters in the story and any real persons, living or
dead, is purely coincidental

Set in Italian Garamond BT at Birlinn Ltd

Printed and bound in Great Britain by
Clays, Bungay, Suffolk

ACKNOWLEDGEMENTS

Glenys Andrews
Colin Browning
Martyn Clark
Douglas Edington
Lesmoir Edington
Robert Galbraith
Daisy Galbraith
Diana Griffiths
Tom Johnstone
Mr E. Macdonnell
Roger Orr
Aidan O'Neill
Dr David Sadler
David Watt

DEDICATION

To Robert and Daisy
one each now –
with all my love

I

An accident, that's what it had been, just a horrible accident. No more than an accident. His mind was chaotic, thoughts barging in, swirling, colliding, chasing each other, disappearing, and all without his volition. In the maelstrom, all he felt was panic, a tide of fear rising, threatening to engulf him. He could not breathe.

Trying to calm himself, he slackened his grip on the steering wheel and looked into the rear view mirror. Behind him, the girl was busy picking at the dry flakes of skin on her upper lip, as she tended to do when anxious. He watched her for a few more seconds before, unable to bear it any longer, he exclaimed, 'Stop it, please. Just stop it, will you?'

It came out more sharply than he had intended. Like a startled deer, she glanced up, meeting his eyes before lowering her gaze to her lap, chastened, her right hand now wringing her left as if in mute appeal.

Looking ahead again, he followed the narrow road round into Kirk Street, braking hard as he noticed a one-way sign coming up and just managing to take the sharp right into the lane leading back to Leith Walk. As he turned the steering wheel, he felt his car slewing sideways on the snow-covered road, and heard a dull thud as something hit the inside of the boot, followed by a slight intake of breath from behind him. Glancing at her reflection again he sighed; she was at it once more, only now

1

with renewed vigour. At one side of her Cupid's bow lips, the carmine merged into an inflamed, angry pink at the side of her mouth, a testament to her obsessive picking and a visible reminder of his impotence. There was even a bead of fresh blood. By now, she ought to know that it was forbidden. By now, a dumb beast would know that.

'Stop it!' he shouted, and this time felt a surge of shameful pleasure in seeing her petrified expression as she jumped, dropping her hand as if it had touched an electric current. Frightened, she blinked repeatedly before closing her eyes, shutting out the world and everything in it.

In repose, he thought, stealing a few additional glances at her as the engine idled at the traffic lights leading into Great Junction Street, she would pass as normal. Her condition manifested itself, not in her features, which were regular and well-proportioned but in her incessant, maddening tics. No wonder she was so thin, with one or more of her muscles always busy, propelling this limb hither or thither, working a tendon or bending a joint, and all to no useful purpose. Sometimes it was as if the Almighty was some sort of puppeteer, pulling her strings simply to test that they were still attached. Yet, when relaxed or asleep, at rest, she would pass for a beauty.

A red light on his dashboard began to flash, attracting his eye, warning him that they were all but out of fuel. By good fortune, no, likely by Divine Providence, a garage was within sight, on the other side of the bridge. Turning in, he began to apply the brake gently, over-sensitive now to the risk of skidding on the icy tarmac. All the pumps were busy, and as he waited he drummed his fingers manically on the steering wheel. Three minutes later, he drew up opposite the last pump in the row.

Turning round to face her, and fixing her in the eye as if she were a dog, he commanded, 'Stay!'

Satisfied by her meek, nodded response, he managed to still his trembling fingers, undid his seatbelt, and clambered out of his Mazda 6 into the cold air. For a second he stood gazing up at the sky, transfixed by the innumerable flakes of snow as they poured down, every one revolving in its fall, every one illuminated by the forecourt lights. Digging his hands deep into his pockets, he fingered the two crisp twenty-pound notes. They would get him fuel enough. As he yanked the nozzle from its holster, he noticed the man in front of him doing the same thing and automatically speeded up, determined to reach the cashier first and settle his business. His need was greater.

———

Once he was in the shop, the girl took her chance. Opening the door as quietly as she was able, she crept out, marvelling as snowflakes landed on her face and melted there. Instinctively she extended her tongue, allowing them to land on it, before, lizard-like, withdrawing it at speed.

Excited by her freedom, by the unfamiliarity of the place, by the spiralling snow and the bright lights of the cars, she began to walk along the very edge of the pavement, arms out for balance like a tightrope walker. Teetering to one side, she caught sight of a narrow lane, signposted Prince Regent Street, ahead of her, righted herself and headed for it, dragging her feet through the fallen snow for a while simply to experience the sensation. It was like walking on solid clouds.

Lights were on in many of the windows she passed and, unselfconsciously, she pressed her face against a few of them. In one house, a man was watching a television, its unnatural glow reflected off the bridge of his nose and his sharp cheekbones as he sat open-mouthed before it. Next door, a couple of small children appeared to be dancing, each of them holding something in their right hands. They, too, were facing the screen and seemed entranced by it. As she rose onto her tiptoes to get a better view of what they were looking at, she felt something snuffling around her skirt, poking her knee. A bony dog, apparently ownerless, had its cold, wet nose against her flesh, exploring it insistently as if she was as inanimate as a side of beef.

With stiff, frightened fingers, she pushed it away but it resisted, its head returning to snuffle her thigh again. Hysterical, unnerved by its boldness, she ran away, abandoning the dancing children and looking back at the stray, fearful that it might follow her. In her absence, its attention had turned seamlessly to a piece of grease-stained newspaper, flapping and pinned by the wind to the front of a nearby wheelie bin.

Shaking her head at the sight, she blundered on, blinking as snowflakes hit her eyes. The wind had risen, changed direction, and a horizontal stream of thick snow blew directly into her face. A young couple passed, their arms linked, talking and laughing together as if they were alone in the world. Glancing back down the street and seeing the dog staring at her, she became fearful that it would follow her after all and started to jog again, legs and arms flying in all directions. It would bite her this time. She had seen its teeth. That was what dogs did.

In her terror, she veered off the pavement and all but collided with the wing of a passing car, catching the blare of its indignant horn as its brake lights receded and merged into the red lights of the T-junction ahead of her. A cyclist, having to swerve to avoid her, hurled abuse at the top of his voice. Something in her mind began to scream. Standing still in the gutter, feeling the world racing around her, spinning out of control, she bent over, covering her eyes with her hands.

'Breathe in, breathe out. Breathe in, breathe out.' That was what Mrs Smollett had said the last time in the games room. On that occasion, one of her teacher's manicured hands had been pressing on the small of her back, and the woman had been inhaling and exhaling in time with her, sounding like a steam engine. But it wasn't working. Not here and now. Not without Mrs Smollett.

'You all right, dear?' a stranger asked, coming towards her and bending over slightly to reach her level, to be face to face with her.

She said nothing, relieved when she saw the woman's companion, a little boy on a scooter, wrinkle his nose and incline his head, signalling that they should move on, mind their own business. The scent of stale coffee tainted the woman's warm breath. Suddenly, alarmed by the uninvited proximity, the girl stood up straight, crossed her arms against her chest and walked off, eyes looking directly ahead as if she had heard nothing, seen nothing. The mother and son might have been as insubstantial as ghosts for all the notice she took of them.

Through the constant drone of the Leith traffic she could make out snatches of music and, hardly conscious of what she was doing, she began to search for the source of it. Having adjusted and readjusted her course innumerable times, she eventually found herself opposite an open doorway at the far end of Madeira Street. Standing outside it, peeking in, she blew on her fingers, her whole body chittering with cold. Then, drawn by the light and the sound of piano music streaming from the door, she walked inside.

Everywhere there were people, all talking, all laughing, and every one of them seemed to be holding a glass. A woman, much of her tanned flesh on show, glowered at her as she pushed past, their buttocks touching in the closeness of the crush. Observing them both, an old fellow winked at her. Someone had dropped a packet of crisps on the floor and she could hear them crackling as they broke under her feet. Accidentally she jostled a plump lady's elbow, making her spill her drink over herself and curse out loud in annoyance. Burrowing on, she lowered her head and kept pushing through the crowd until, unexpectedly, she found herself in a corner. Turning round she spotted a small alcove with a table and two chairs in it. There was even an open packet of nuts. Following the wall with her hands until she reached it, she sat down, now eye-level with the surrounding shirts, ties and blouses.

'Like a wee drink?' a smiling man asked her, tapping the side of his wine glass as if to show her what a drink was.

'Donald!' The white-haired lady beside him said, frowning.

'What?'

'She's a child!'

'No, she's not, she's a young lady. Well, what's she doing in here if she's a child, I'd like to know?'

'Leave her alone!'

'I am. I was only asking if she'd like a drink, for Heaven's sake! There's no harm in that, is there, Hilary?'

'Yes. There is.'

The girl was no longer listening to them or to anyone, anything. She was gazing out of the window, watching the snow pouring from the sky like water in a waterfall, hypnotised by the perpetual movement. A young man had taken the only other seat and was glancing at her, taking an occasional gulp from his beer glass as he did so. Had he chanced upon the crock of gold at the end of the rainbow he could not have looked more pleased. After a couple of minutes, he plucked up the courage to speak to her.

'D'you like the snow?'

Hearing his voice, she turned to face him and, for the first time, he saw just how extraordinarily beautiful she was. Her dark, long-lashed eyes met his and as they did so, she shivered and a slight tremor started up in her right hand. To stop it, she slapped her left over it, trapping it.

'You cold?' he asked.

'You're wasting your time, boyo,' Donald said to the youth. 'She's probably foreign, immigrant Polish or something. She doesn't say anything, she doesn't understand.'

'Just because she didn't answer you!' his wife snapped, putting her empty glass on the table and waiting, expectantly, for her husband to do the same. His was half-full of gin but, smiling at her with his mouth only, he obeyed.

Listening to the background music, the boy sat with the girl, getting no reply to any of his questions, collecting more drinks and, after a while, staring at her openly as if she was an object. She ate the peanuts in front of her, singly and slowly, and then, unselfconsciously, licked the inside of the packet. His eyes always on her, he stacked and restacked his pile of beer mats. Twice while they sat there, he had to fend off the attentions of drunken men, telling one of them that she was his sister and giving the other, more insistent one, a shove. He, his balance long gone, careered into another customer, getting a hard stare for his pains and quickly retreating back into the anonymity of the melee for his own safety. Under the table, the boy slid his foot beside the girl's, feeling the warmth of her flesh through the leather and heartened that she made no attempt to move it away. They had an understanding, wordless, but real.

Twenty minutes after going into the BP kiosk, the man hurried out of it. He was jingling his small change in his pocket, whistling as if he did not have a care in the world. Once he had done his belt up he glanced into the mirror, expecting to see the girl's familiar, anxious face behind him. But there was nothing. He could make out the road beyond, the cars zipping past, the buildings and pavement, but no human being. Maybe she was kneeling down for some reason? Was playing Hide and Seek, larking about, making a fool of him? Now, of all times!

Feeling his heart speeding up, rapping against his ribs, he ripped off the belt and climbed out of the vehicle. He grabbed the back door and yanked it open. Nothing: there was nothing there. He got in, knelt on the seat, looking forward as if, somehow, she might have concealed herself in the foot-well of the passenger seat. No one was there either. Under the seat? Not a dickey bird. Heavens above! She had done it again, scarpered into the night, and dropped him right in it. This time, Lambie might not forgive him.

Breathing rapidly, too shallowly, he clambered out of the Mazda and began looking about him. Snow was still falling all around, disorientating him and making

8

everywhere appear strange, new and other. Even the sounds of the traffic seemed muted. No footprints were visible on the garage forecourt. The queue in the kiosk had been long, certainly, but not that long, surely? He should not have gone to the Gents, too; that was it. That had been silly, added another five minutes to his total. Undoubtedly, the bloke with the wrong credit card had done the bulk of the damage, but the queue, the Gents, it all added up. She had probably stayed still for quarter of an hour or so, then lost all hope, and gone in search of him or something. The stupid, stupid little ninny. On her own, outside the car, she was as vulnerable as a snail without a shell, as a new-born baby on ice. Anything could happen.

Panicked by the thought, he raced back down Great Junction Street, accosting people as he passed them, demanding to know if they had seen her, getting strange stares, shakes of the head and, from one, a mouthful of foreign curses. In case she had doubled back, he looked again at the car, illuminated brightly within the distant forecourt lights. A youth was ambling next to it, casting sidelong glances into its windows. Had he locked it? Blast! All he needed now was a theft!

He raced back, and once in range, pressed the button on his key fob, supporting himself against a lamppost, panting, his lungs aching, made raw by the frozen air. While he stood there, unable to move, he scanned his surroundings, pirouetting slowly on the spot for a three hundred and sixty degree view. There she was! She was standing by a bus stop on the other side of the street, only a couple of hundred yards away.

Forgetting all about his lungs, he shot off in pursuit, slipping on the smooth road surface and almost losing his footing in front of a car in his haste to get to her. Once he was close enough to grab her, he realised that he had made a mistake, turned on his heel and began the long trek back to the garage.

This was hopeless, suicidal. He must get on. She would be all right for now, would survive. Someone would look after her. Someone always did. First thing tomorrow, he would return with a plan, track her down properly, if she had not been returned before then. This had happened before, would not be the last time either, and he had business to attend to. Very important business indeed; and somehow, somehow, he would square it all with Lambie.

———

When the landlord called last orders the hum in the pub became louder, a few drinkers making their way through the crowd to the bar, others leaving their empties on the tables, bestowing beery kisses on each other and departing into the night, to be startled by the chill air. The girl sensed the movement around her, felt uneasy at the change and caught the boy's eyes. He, pleased that she seemed to have noticed him at last, got up and interrupted the stream of people going out to allow her to join the flow.

Once outside, he took her cold hand in his and began walking eastwards, in the direction of his home. A couple of hundred yards on, exhilarated by her company, he let go of her hand and playfully backed her against the tenement wall, caging her there with both his arms. Hesitantly, he placed his head on her breast as if to listen to her heart, astonished to feel it on his temple as it thumped against her ribcage. As he raised his head to kiss her, she poked him in the chest, dislodging his arm and ducking out of his unwanted embrace. Free, she began to run, her long legs as ungainly as a new-born fawn.

'Oh, for fuck's sake,' he said, looking round blearily for her, hurt and disappointed. Did she not want to kiss too? On a magical night like this, peaceful and still, heavenly, what could be nicer than the feel of warm flesh on warm flesh? She had only to say if she didn't like it.

———

At three-thirty in the morning, a householder in North Fort Street dialled 999 and asked for the police. She had been unable to sleep, had risen every hour or so to get a drink of water. Sipping it by her bathroom window, a figure had caught her attention. Someone, she said, was curled up in a doorway opposite, and the snow was falling on them, like it would on a wild beast.

'Homeless?' the call-handler asked.

'They must be.'

'Have you tried the Bethany Christian Trust or the Salvation Army or someone? That's a social services problem, not really a police problem . . . not an emergency.'

'It might be a child, for Christ's sake, it looks little more than a child.'

'You should have said that first, dear. We'll send someone round the now. What's the address?'

2

Before dawn that same day, a man lowered himself into a dinghy as it swung about at the stern of the Safety Boat. The deckhand above him hurled its painter down to him and, despite the howling of the wind, he heard the clicking noise made by the anchor chain as it was being pulled in by the winch. 'Are you not staying?' he bellowed, grabbing the oars and starting to pull. Lit up by the crewman's torch, he was still facing the larger vessel. Concentrating hard, he rowed the grey inflatable dinghy away from them, now exposed to the full fury of the weather himself. Straining against the cross-current, he lowered his head, putting his back into it, battling to cover the last few yards to his lonely destination. A wave caught his bow and, for an instant, he thought it would tip him over, upend him into the cold, grey water. Spray, thrown up by a mistimed oar-blade, lashed his face, dripping off the side of his ears and running down the inside of his collar.

'Nope,' the Captain's voice hollered back from the vessel, 'Andy's got to check the monitors on the Road Bridge.'

'How long will you be?' the man in the dinghy shouted, as loud as he could.

'Twenty minutes, half an hour at a pinch. The tide's already well on the turn. That'll give you time to check the scaffolding over . . .'

There could, the man thought, clambering up onto Beamer Rock, be few more inhospitable places in the world, at any time of the year, never mind in the middle of January, and in the pitch-dark. The whine of the Safety Boat's twin propellers as the skipper eased open the throttle, heading downriver towards the open ocean, underlined the fact that he was on his own. A blizzard was raging around the Forth, and as he switched on his torch to follow the disappearing craft, its beam illuminated a corridor of snowflakes, each one circling its way across the waves before disappearing into the turbulent waters. He breathed into his wet gloves and stamped his feet vigorously, trying to return feeling to them, so that he could get on with the job. Even tying up the dinghy would require a degree of dexterity. There was no time to waste. The generator powering the lighting rig must be fired up.

Once started, it released a throaty purr, more like a lion or a tiger than a machine, and hearing it lifted his spirits. The yellow light from the rig transformed everything, bathing the only two buildings on the rock in its rich glow, reminding him that shelter, even there, existed. Meticulously, he began to inspect the scaffolding around the base of the nearest one. The metal poles framing the red and white striped lighthouse seemed intact, secured by their ties; the wooden boards were still in place and the access ladder remained lashed to one end. Jetsam, in the form of a couple of milk cartons, had been deposited on the lowest platform and he tossed them back into the water, watching as one, then the other, was consumed by the waves. The clattering noise made by his tackety boots as he moved about was drowned out by the shrieking of the wind as it raced around the two bridges, searching for weaknesses and making any loose spars or struts rattle and zing with its passage. Finally, the job done, everything scrutinised and all slippery seaweed removed, he switched the generator off, instantly plunging his tiny kingdom into blackness again.

Keen to distract himself, knowing he still had time to kill, he turned his head towards the Fife coast and shone his torch on the north tower caisson. A couple of barges attached to it had cranes on board and his eyes alighted on the grab of one of them, suspended from its yellow, skeletal arm, hovering hundreds of feet above the vast steel structure of the bridge. Next, his beam picked out a tri-coloured German flag on one of the craft. It was writhing on its flag pole, faded and frayed, above the name-plate 'Gerhardt'. In the cutting wind, he shielded his eyes with his free hand, trying to make out the name on the other barge but it was no good.

Seconds later, he had to screw them up, the force of the flakes driving into them making his tear ducts pour with water. Pulling his white safety helmet down over his forehead, he covered his whole face briefly with his hands, the pain in his eyes temporarily unbearable. In his sight-less state, he was suddenly overcome by dizziness and all but lost his balance. Christ alive! When would that fuck-ing Safety Boat re-appear? Its lights, bobbing about close to the centre of the Road Bridge, did not seem to have moved an inch for at least the last ten minutes, and well over twenty minutes had already passed since his landing.

Determined to get back into the warmth the instant it arrived, he hunched himself against the force of the gale and started trudging towards the spot where he had tied up the dinghy, compelled every few seconds to turn his back to the blast. Slipping, thankfully, into the lee of the foghorn building, he swung his torch from side to side in time with his steps, sweeping the surface of the rock for the rusted ring and the blue rope tied to it.

Although his sight was still blurry, an unfamiliar bulky shape resting on the black dolerite surface caught his eye. His first thought was that it was a seal, and he was glad, grateful, that there was another living, breathing creature here with him in the godforsaken place. Sweeping along its length, his beam picked out a herring gull, its feathers rippling in the gale. The bird was perched on the thing, pecking at it.

Shielding his eyes with his hands, he edged closer, conscious that the thing must be dead, might even smell. Suddenly, he felt uneasy in its presence. In the bright light it looked solid, grey and fleshy, but its skin seemed to have come loose and was rucked up, corrugated around it.

At his approach, the bird opened its beak, let out a screech and flew off, banking against a wall of wind before disappearing up river and into the black. Gingerly, he went down on one knee to examine the thing more closely, stretching out to touch the head end, and on feeling it, instinctively whipping his hand back as if it had been burnt. Bile flooded his mouth. The pads of his fingers had not touched the wet seal fur they were anticipating, but skin, human skin, and smooth as silk.

Close up, bathed now in a pool of light, the thing remained recognisable, to one of its own species at least. By his feet lay the washed-up body of a woman – cold, wet and lifeless. Around her brow curled a strand of dark green seaweed, as if it had taken root there and was growing out of her skull. The involuntary squeak the man let out surprised himself, was the only external sign of his inner transformation from an adult into a frightened child. But here, on the sea-swept rock, there was no one to wake him up, put the lights on, comfort him and tell him that it was only a dream. His own eyes told him otherwise, staring as they were into the milky brown pair looking up at him from the dead face illuminated by his torch.

Desperate not to be alone with the body, he jumped up and started bellowing at the launch, waving his hands frantically, swinging his light at it like a wrecker's lantern. But every word that left his mouth was lost, obliterated by the roar of the waves and the shrieking of the wind. He felt no pity for the corpse, only panic and revulsion, a desperate desire to get away, to leave the thing before he saw its chest begin to expand with breath, its eyes begin to blink.

—

'Is that the on-call DI at St Leonard's Street?'

'Yes,' Alice replied, putting down her coffee cup, the millisecond of hesitation before she answered a testament to the unfamiliarity of her new title and the ungodly hour. Five a.m., and the caffeine was not doing its job.

'We've just received a report,' continued the man in the control centre, 'that someone dead – a female, apparently – has ended up on Beamer Rock. I'm to tell you that there'll be a launch waiting for you at South Queensferry, if you want it. It's been arranged by FCBC, the Consortium. They're the bridge-building people. One of them found it.'

'A launch? Beamer Rock? Where on earth is that?'

'In the middle of the Forth, some place near the Road Bridge. They said the central tower of the new crossing's to be constructed on it eventually. A workman was sent over to look at scaffolding on the rock, Heaven knows why, and he practically tripped over the corpse. They're keeping his boat there for the moment, in case she's washed away again. They want to know if we want it to stay with her until you get there.'

'Yes, keep it there. This woman, what's the story, was she washed up on the rock or left there by someone or what?'

'No idea. The only other information we've got is that the tide's coming in, so you'd better get your skates on. Correction, your flippers on. Apparently, it gets completely submerged at high tide.'

At that news, the detective inspector put the telephone down, snatched her coat from the back of her chair and called out for DC Cairns. Getting no answer, she went to look for her and, three minutes later, bumped into her as she was going down the station stairs and the constable was racing up them.

'The incident sheet says there's a body, somewhere washed up in the Forth!' the constable said breathlessly, a piece of paper in her outstretched hand.

'I know, Liz. Hurry, get your stuff. That's where we're going. I'll see you at the car.'

———

In the city, snow had continued falling throughout the night and, as usual, the capital was behind in its preparations, caught by the outlandish eventuality of a two-day blizzard in January. St Leonard's Street, already under a thick layer, was passable, but a delivery van impeded their progress up the slope of St Mary's Street, its wheels spinning ineffectually on the glistening surface as it endeavoured to regain its lost momentum and ended up straddling the road instead. Immobile, the driver ground its gears noisily for a few seconds before, admitting defeat, he signalled with a wave for them to squeeze round behind it.

'Arsehole, get yourself snow tyres! Pity we've no blue light, that'd put the fear of God into him,' DC Cairns exclaimed as they drove by, shaking her head at the seasonal ineptitude on display.

'You've got yours on, have you, oh wise virgin?'

'Virgin, indeed! Not as such. Wise as I am.'

'Did you phone the Duty Fiscal? Who's on call?' Alice asked, turning on the fan heater in an attempt to defrost the windscreen and herself.

'I tried that, by the way, it doesn't work. Derek Jardine. He said to give him a ring once we've got a better idea of the lie of the land. He's tied up, attending a hit and run at the moment in Liberton.'

'And the FME?'

'It's that tiny little irritable one. What's he called again?'

'Dr Harry McCrae.'

'Right, him. I told him to meet us at eight at Port Edgar.'

'You'll need to speak to him again. We're not leaving from Port Edgar. The Marine Unit Commander lives in Duns, and they'd take forever to get going. The Lammermuirs are probably knee-deep by now, anyway, if not the coast road. We're taking up the Consortium's offer of a launch.'

'So where are we leaving from? The top brass won't like it – all that expensive equipment rusting away, they won't like it one bit, they'll have no ammunition against the cuts,' the constable said, impatient to see properly, scraping the glass in front of her with a hand and dislodging a thin strip of ice.

'Needs must. He'd take an hour or more to get here from Duns, if he got through at all. The body would be long off to sea again by then. We haven't that long. Tell him to meet us at the Hawes Pier at, yes, say, eight o' clock – the one under the Rail Bridge, the one that the Inchcolm Ferry leaves from.'

'I'll let him know, then, about the new plan. This'll make a nice change from the usual, eh, Alice? A crime scene at sea, that's a first for me!' The young police-woman smiled at the thought and searched around the side of her seat for her seat-belt.

'For me, too, and if it's a murder, it'll likely be our last if they're all shunted off to these new Major Investigation Teams after the reorganisation. We'll be stuck with nothing but shoplifting, peeing up closes and runaway chihuahuas.'

'And we'll get to inspect, close up, the beginnings of the third Forth Bridge or whatever it's to be called, even if it will be a bit dark. There's a competition to name it.'

'So I've heard. "Salmond's Leap", that's supposedly the front runner along with the "It-should-have-been-a-tunnel-bridge", the green lobby's favourite,' Alice remarked, as they drew up beside a bus at the first set of lights on Davidson's Mains. It had one passenger in it, his head resting against the window.

'Some kid suggested Rusty's Pal. Actually, or accu-rately, it should be the fifth Forth Bridge. That would take into account the ones at Kincardine and Stirling as well as the two Queensferry ones.'

'Or, to continue with the powerful fish-politician theme, "Sturgeon's Passage". That got a lot of votes I believe.' A disturbing picture of the First Minister, pop-eyed and bubble-mouthed, swimming beside his little deputy, flitted, uninvited, into Alice's head.

'It'll be something dull, something safe . . . the Queens-ferry Bridge, the Queensferry Crossing. I ought to put money on something like that.'

Her boss nodded, now lost in thought, going through a checklist in her mind as the constable, untroubled by her silence, wittered on. Paper suits were in the case in the boot, gloves and bootees too. A photographer, Jim Scott, had been fixed up. He was coming straight from his house in Rosyth. With his ponderous manner, vast belly and elephantine legs, he would not have been her choice for this particular job. But beggars could not be choosers. And at least, with his help, the three of them should be able to move the body without calling out the coastguard or the lifeboat men, cutting out the delay and unnecessary contamination that their involvement might bring with it. Unorthodox as this approach might be, time and tide would wait for no man. No woman either, so normal procedures would have to take second place, whatever fuss was made later by DCI Bell or anyone else for that matter.

'Are you going to vote in September?' DC Cairns asked, breaking her boss's train of thought.

'Mmm.'

The roundabout at Barnton, usually clogged with cars in all four directions, was deserted, silent, still, awaiting the arrival of its daily visitors. Conscious of the privilege, they sped across it.

'And?'

'Same as most of the women in the country. Thanks to Dewar we've a fair amount of autonomy, and whatever happens, more is on its way. Blair went to school in Scotland, Brown's from Kirkcaldy. If John Smith hadn't died, he'd have led. Who's governing who? Salmond's just another maker of promises, another maker of mistakes. Look into his genealogy and he'll be a UK mongrel like the rest of us. I want fewer divisions, fewer boundaries, not more. Are you even old enough to vote?'

'Only just. At least they'd be our mistakes . . .'

'Shetland doesn't think they are "our". Nor does Orkney, nor do much of the Highlands. How local should we go?'

'Home rule for Leith, I say. And we'd be richer.'

'Away and sell your granny then, you patriot, if money's what it's all about. But best do it before the rush begins.'

'You care?'

'I care.'

The windscreen-wipers could not cope with the volume of snow now pouring from the heavens, so Alice speeded them up and began to accelerate up the brae beyond the Cramond Bridge, anticipating a straight run on the motorway ahead. But from the Kirkliston turn-off only the slow lane had been gritted. In the resultant bottleneck, they continued arguing, the pace of their journey dictated by a procession of others, all inching forward together at a speed sedate enough to make a hearse impatient. Their leader, an elderly white transit van, crawled onwards, its exhaust gassing them with an endless stream of noxious fumes.

'Like I said, we need a blue light,' DC Cairns repeated, as much to herself as anyone else. Cold, and desperate to get to their destination, her foot was flat on the ground, pressing an imaginary accelerator.

—

Fifteen minutes later they entered South Queensferry. Driving over the brow of the hill on Kirkliston Road, their eyes were immediately drawn to the long view of the estuary, its glistening waters cut in two by the sparkling, curved outline made by the lights on the Road Bridge. The pocket-sized royal burgh itself was at its picturesque winter best: snow lying in the interstices of the cobbles, capping the crow-stepped gables of the houses and coating the roof of the Black Castle, making it look like an illustration in an old-fashioned children's story book. Dawn still unbroken, no one was yet abroad on its narrow streets and the place was lit only by the ornamental lanterns dotted along the sea front. The sole sign of life they saw in the town centre was a tabby cat, walking purposefully along the length of the Ferry Tap Inn before dodging into the shadows in search of prey.

A huddle of FCBC men, all in hard hats and orange high-visibility jackets, had gathered by the Inchcolm Ferry ticket office. They were clustered together by the statue of a seal, chattering, their breaths steaming white from their mouths in the cold air. One of them saw the car. He pointed at the nearby turning and started jogging alongside the Escort as it took a left off the High Street. The others followed him, the sound of their boots getting louder as the road surface below their feet changed from tarmac to the blocks of rough-hewn stone from which the pier was constructed. In the distance, dwarfed by the gigantic outer cantilever of the Forth Rail Bridge, lay the Consortium's Safety Boat, the *Fiona S*. It was tied up at the far end of the Hawes Pier, rocking in the waves, its engine idling in readiness for the arrival of the police. Alongside it stood the corpulent figure of Jim Scott, cameras slung around his neck. He was looking anxiously in the direction of dry land and the Hawes Inn. Recognising the Inspector as she walked towards him, he waved a soup-plate-sized hand, saying morosely on her approach, 'I hate the water. Can you swim, Alice? I might need help.'

'Me? I'm a qualified junior life saver – although whether I'd manage without being dressed in my pyjamas, I'm not so sure,' she replied, throwing her case over the side of the yellow and black craft, then stepping on board and holding out a hand to receive, first, his rucksack of precious equipment, and then his leaden bulk. At the same time, a red life-jacket was thrust at each of them by a passing stranger, the stern rope around his free hand. The photographer, breathing noisily, picked his off the deck where it had fallen, turning it this way and that, examining the catches, trying to work out how it might fit his vast frame.

'This must be for a child,' he said, holding it against his fur-trimmed bulk, a look of dismay on his face. 'It'll never keep me up. Look at these pathetic, thin flotation bits – they're not even soft, air-filled. There must have been a leak. They're not safe.'

'They'll inflate,' the policewoman replied, passing a strap between her legs, 'when you hit the water. That's the whole point, so that they're not too bulky now.'

'When – don't you mean if? And there's a whistle! Fat lot of good that's going to do as I'm swept out to the open sea . . .'

'Just put it on, eh?'

No sooner had DC Cairns stepped on deck than she toppled forwards, hitting her elbow on a stanchion. With the last passenger on board, the Captain had ordered that they cast off and one of the deckhands had pushed off from the pier, making the boat lurch forwards in response. Another life-jacket was dropped unceremoniously by the same crew member on top of her crumpled form.

'Thanks a bundle,' she murmured sarcastically.

'Are you lot not supposed to be in a hurry? I'd get inside, eh? Otherwise, you'll miss the safety briefing,' he replied, unmoved, stepping around her and holding the cabin door open for the other two.

'I've had my accident already, or had you not noticed?' DC Cairns countered, righting herself, looking round to take in her surroundings. In the cabin, standing beside the Captain, was the only other member of the crew. He had kept himself busy chatting to his boss, watching idly while his colleague scurried about outside, casting off, pulling in the fenders, then coiling the loose ropes on the deck.

By the time all three passengers plus their equipment were installed safely inside, the vessel had already reached the centre of the firth, and begun to speed up. On hitting its near maximum of twenty-five knots, it started crashing through the waves, the hull slamming down in the troughs, then rising almost vertically and the engine coughing whenever the propellers left the water. Spray started to cascade over the bow, slapping against the glass of the windscreen, mixing with the falling snowflakes. The photographer, his face already pale, clung with both hands to the back of a blue, plastic seat, his feet set wide apart in a desperate attempt to steady himself.

'Are you not going to sit down?' Alice asked him, gesturing for him to take the seat beside her.

'If I move I'll be sick,' he said pitifully.

'We'll need,' Alice raised her voice, hoping to be heard above the roar of the engine, 'stills of everywhere – and video footage of everywhere.'

'Everywhere?' Scott retorted, looking doubtful, as if far too much was being demanded of him. Incongruously, for a sea voyage, he had chosen to wear a flat cap, and to emphasize his point he pulled the peak down over his forehead. Seeing him, a passing deckhand cheekily plucked it off his head and handed him a white safety helmet, murmuring, 'Rules is rules, you've got to obey the rules – on this site, any road. Hard hats on this site.'

'Video of everywhere?' Scott repeated, holding out a hand for the return of his hat.

'Everywhere,' she confirmed, then, seeing his fleshy shoulders droop, she added, 'it's only about ten metres by seven, Jim, and that's at low tide. It's not huge, OK? Now, we'll all need to tog up, ideally before we land.'

'Here? I'm not doing that now,' he protested, pressing his cameras to his breast with one hand as if they were his infant children. 'This thing's bucking like a wild west bronco.'

'We're going to a crime scene . . .'

'Will the suits be any use? Will they not just get soggy?' DC Cairns interjected, dragging a strand of wet hair out of her eyes. 'Then they'll tear.'

'Or turn to papier mâché, but too bad,' Alice replied, 'we'll have no time when we get there – possibly minutes only. At high tide, the whole rock's underwater.'

'Health and safety certainly wouldn't like it,' the photographer said darkly.

'Maybe,' Alice replied, 'but fortunately, they'll never know.'

'Unless we fall in . . .' Scott whispered.

'Dead men tell no tales,' she quipped, but his look of shock made her relent. 'Oh, all right, all right. But the second we come to a halt . . .'

Minutes later, the boat veered to the left of Mackintosh rock, the towers of the Road Bridge rising impossibly high above them, and Beamer itself came into view. The *Nicola S* lay immediately adjacent to the rocky outcrop. Seeing their destination illuminated by the lighting rig the skipper began to slow his launch down, anticipating tying up beside the other Safety Boat to allow his passengers to disembark into the dinghy. A foot or so from it, a deckhand threw a rope to one of the other crew who started pulling the vessels together by means of the bow and stern ropes. Fenders on both craft squeezed to bursting point, the skipper of the *Nicola S*, a former lobster fisherman, shouted out, 'Are we to stay then? The body's still on dry land . . . just. Can we go? Now you're here there's not much point in our hanging about, is there? I'd like to get Ewan home, into the warmth. He got an awful shock. Gav'll row you there. We've put the lights back on for you.'

'That's fine. On you go,' Alice shouted back.

Although unnaturally low in the water, the inflatable took their combined weight with the photographer sitting at the stern, acting as a counterbalance to the two women. Every time a wave washed over its sides, he grimaced, imagining the damage the salt water would wreak on his sensitive equipment. Once next to the rock, DC Cairns jumped on it, rope in hand, ready to hold the dinghy steady as they disembarked.

'You'll only have minutes,' their oarsman said, shaking his head at their ineptitude as the photographer lurched towards the stern, grabbing the man's shoulder to steady himself. Crunching barnacles as she did so, Alice stepped onto land, then walked forwards, zigzagging from one side of the black rock to the other, already scanning its surface for anything, any clue, before it was lost forever beneath the murky waters of the Forth.

On one of the low scaffolding boards, held between two piles of bricks from the partially dismantled lighthouse, lay a silt-covered green glass bottle. She picked it up in her gloved hand, making a mental note of where, precisely, it had been found, for the grid. If Jim did his job properly, there should be no problem. He would capture everything. But time was short, and when last seen, he was still behind the foghorn building, shooting the body from all possible angles, ensuring that its exact location could be pinned down on this featureless islet. Before he had even got round to removing a lens cover, precious minutes had been wasted by his protracted disembarkation, his togging up and the arranging of his equipment. A three-toed sloth would seem speedy beside him.

Her own scrutiny of the corpse, begun while he battled to stuff one of his corpulent limbs into a paper trouser leg, had revealed no obvious signs of injury to the woman. Her clothes seemed intact, although her tights were torn and she wore no shoes. Importantly, no smell of rotting flesh came from her, and no outward signs of putrefaction were visible. The word 'fresh', she thought, applied to a dead woman as opposed to a living, breathing one, had quite a different meaning, quite different connotations. No suggestion of flirtation there.

'Alice,' a voice shouted, and she turned to see the photographer signalling to her, his paper suit blown unflatteringly tight over the contours of his rounded, Buddha belly. DC Cairns was hunkered down beside the corpse, and as Alice approached she said something but her words were drowned out by the crashing of the waves.

'What did you say?' Alice bawled, turning momentarily away, attempting to protect herself from another gust.

'We'll lose her, if we're not quick,' the man yelled back. 'Since we've been here, the tide's moved up at least another six inches, the waves are getting bigger, look – one of her hands is back in the water . . .'

'You got her in situ – stills and video?' Her throat hurt with the effort of shouting.

The photographer's precious cap now back on, its peak protruding from under his paper hood, he nodded in an exaggerated fashion, then moved closer towards her. DC Cairns, her hands almost covering her face, followed behind him, protected by his bulk.

'I've already put my stuff in the boat,' he said.

'OK. That'll have to do, then. You take the head-end, Jim. We'll take a side each.' She bent down and gestured for the constable to do the same, 'On my count. And try not to touch her, lift her through her clothes if you possibly can.

'Should we not get Gav to help?'

'No. One, two, three . . .'

To their unspoken relief, pieces of the carcass did not drop off or fall to bits in their hands, as each had imagined might happen, and between them they managed to manoeuvre it successfully into the dinghy. There it rested, in an unnatural pose, legs propped upright against one of the wooden seats, shoeless feet pointing heavenwards. With all the exertion involved, sweat poured down the photographer's brow as he sat, leaning back in his seat to recover his breath, cap now in hand, his bald pink pate exposed to the falling snow. At that moment, a wave caught them broadside and he shouted 'Shit!' Two minutes later, a couple of pairs of gloved hands helped them unload their icy cargo onto the Safety Boat, easing it gently onto the floor of the cabin.

'OK?' the Captain shouted, 'everyone on board?'

'Aha,' Gav bawled back. 'Go canny though, or she'll roll about the deck like a ball.'

With the Captain's skilful hand on the throttle, the steady phut-phut of the diesel engine changed seamlessly, first, to a constant thrum and then to a full-blown roar as the craft's seven hundred horsepower engines started pounding through the waves, making a bee-line for the Hawes Pier. Just as the sun was peeping shyly over the horizon, they drew alongside it with their cold cargo, and wasted no time in unloading it.

No sooner was the body lying prostrate on the bare stone, than the first of the day's commuter trains rattled its way across the Railway Bridge, heading southwards towards Dalmeny, the Gyle, Haymarket and, finally, Waverley. The passengers within it, asleep, bleary-eyed or blinkered by their newspapers, were unaware that the speck visible hundreds of feet below them was the waterlogged corpse of a woman. One of them, reading the report in the *Evening News* on the homeward journey, realised what he had witnessed and felt a strange glow of pleasure at his involvement in the drama.

3

Dr McCrae, a slight, effete-looking little man with a permanently dripping nose, was hunched over the body. It had been moved to a cramped backroom in the lifeboat building, a tarpaulin spread underneath to protect it from further contamination. The dead woman lay on her back in a pool of seawater, sightless eyes open, arms stretched wide as if she had been newly removed from her crucifix. The Forensic Medical Examiner's inspection was almost complete, and with exquisite gentleness, he lifted the head off the canvas sheet and began to part the tangle of matted, dark hair at the back of the skull.

'That's more like it . . .' he muttered to himself, continuing with his task, easing more strands free and, finally, lifting his glasses and the thin gold chain attached to them and putting them on his nose. His face was now only inches away from the dead woman's skull. After less than a minute, he nodded as if he had found what he was looking for and took off his glasses, resting them on the top of his head, loops of chain now dangling below his ears like gypsy earrings.

'Anything?' Alice asked.

'Aha. She's got a large contusion over the back of her scalp. There are grazes, too, over the knuckles of both hands, the face, back of the hands . . . and a corker of a black eye. See?'

'Did she drown?'

'Think that would that follow, do you, Inspector? You'll have to wait until they've got her on the slab to answer that mystery. But the trauma to the head, the black eye – that'll certainly give everyone pause for thought.'

The doctor rose, carefully brushed the knees of his white paper suit clear of detritus, latched his briefcase and led the way out of the makeshift mortuary. As they hit the fresh air, snow was still falling around them, but now against a backdrop of dawn sky in which pinkish hues merged into a watery grey background. As if noticing the drifting flakes for the first time, the doctor held out his arms, child-sized palms upwards, allowing them to land on his gloved hands.

'Every single one unique,' he said, 'just like us . . .'

'The lucky ones among us may last that little bit longer. That injury to the back of her head – have we any clue as to the cause?' Alice asked.

'None whatsoever, at present. It could have come from a blow, damage sustained in the Forth, underwater rocks, a pier or something – a fall? Only the Good Lord knows. Once she's on the slab, as I said earlier, we'll maybe get a better idea.' He paused, glancing at the drops of melted snow on his right glove, sniffed, then added, 'Now, if there's nothing else, I'm off to the Inn for a café latte, a croissant and, possibly, a kipper. The witness is there.'

'What a good idea,' DC Cairns interjected. 'It's been a long night. I'll be having the porridge, followed by . . .'

Alice's phone went and she clamped it to her ear, a finger to her mouth to silence the constable.

'How did you get on?' the Fiscal asked. His voice sounded weary, hoarse, his question tailing off into a bronchitic cough.

'We got on fine. We've got the body back, it's on its way to the mortuary now and Dr McCrae's just given it the once-over.'

'Was there anything obvious on the rock, anything much to see there?'

'No. Jim Scott took shots of everything, yards of video footage too. Then we just had enough time to bundle her onto the boat before she was carried away in the rising tide.'

'What does Dr McCrae say?'

'Dr McCrae says,' she replied slowly, looking at the diminutive doctor quizzically and reading his moving, but silent, lips, 'suspicious – we're to treat it, for the moment, as suspicious.'

'Okey dokey,' the man replied, 'but I don't think I'll come out to South Queensferry for that, Alice. Not this a.m. After all, there's no scene, nothing more to be made of the body – nothing, really, for me to see or do just now. Have you spoken to the mortuary? With this nasty bug, I should be in my bed. You'll keep me informed, eh?'

Without waiting for her reply, and coughing noisily as if to impress his state of ill-health upon her, he terminated the call.

'Yes, suspicious, for now,' Dr McCrae said, starting to amble towards the public road, adding 'and that'll have been Derek Jardine, I'll be bound? The lazy good-for-nothing! Surprise me – tell me he is going to attend the scene?'

'He says there's no . . .'

'What is it this time, I wonder?' the doctor cut in, lips pursed tight. 'A cold, perhaps? A tummy bug? Never mind the fact that we can't exclude homicide yet. What the heck. I was saying that your witness is in the Inn, by the way. I saw him there when I was waiting for you to come back. The fellow that found her, he's near the bar.'

'Are the kippers good? I think I'll have a kipper,' DC Cairns mused, returning eagerly to the subject of her forthcoming breakfast and rubbing her hands together in anticipation.

'Loch Fyne,' the doctor replied, 'I checked.'

'No, not for the moment you won't, I'm afraid, Liz,' Alice cut in. 'Later, maybe. The woman was found near the bridge. We'll need to check that she wasn't a jumper.'

'A what?'

'Didn't you know? This place,' the doctor observed, wiping his nose with a red hankie, 'is Suicide Central. At least, it used to be.'

'We'll need to check that she didn't jump off the bridge. While we're here, get them to show you the CCTV footage. If she did, chances are they'll have got her on it. One other thing, Dr McCrae . . .'

'Yes?' the man was looking to his left and right, preparing to cross the road, but at the inspector's words he paused.

'Do you think she'd been in the water long?'

'It can only be an impression at this stage, mind. The mortuary boys will be able to tell you properly. But, no, not very long, not judging by the state of her fingers and her toes. I'd say a day, a couple of days at the very most? They've got wrinkles on them, but not that much. And there's no obvious sign of separation, sloughing – dermis from epidermis – when the skin comes off the flesh, you know, like a sock or something. Or, classically, like a serpent shedding its skin. I'd say a day, no more.'

Ewen Macdonell sat at a table by the open fire, his hands round an empty coffee mug. An oil-streaked orange waterproof hung from the back of the wooden chair and he was chewing gum, an old piece, unaware that his jaws were even moving. Between his fingers, he rolled the foil in which it had been wrapped to and fro, making it into a minute silver worm. He looked as reliable and straightforward as an Airedale terrier; his shaggy grey eyebrows overshadowing his eyes, making them appear more deeply recessed than they were. In the buzz and warmth of the hotel, in the brightness of its lights, the discovery of the body seemed a remote experience, one which might, almost, have happened to somebody else. He had, as he had recently texted his wife, 'got his head round things'. Consequently, when he spoke to the policewoman it was without emotion, in a matter-of-fact manner relating everything that he had seen.

'No,' he continued, 'I can't say for certain whether or not she was there when I first landed. The generator's too far away. Everything in that part's in shadows, the torchbeam's all you've got. She could have been there, I could have missed her. I wasn't looking.'

'But once the lighting was on?' Alice asked. Disconcertingly, although she was on dry land, sitting opposite him in another wooden chair, she felt as if she was still at sea, still in motion, having to balance herself against the rolling of the waves.

'I could easily have missed her first time round. I must have, if she was there,' he replied. He moved his chair further away from the fire and crossed his legs, trying to protect the inside of his calves from the blazing heat.

'How long were you on the rock?'

'I was there about half an hour, maybe a little longer. I was supposed to check the scaffolding before the team dismantling the lighthouse set to work. They were worried, with that last storm, you know, that it might have come loose, got damaged or something. It's a dangerous enough job already without that happening. The buggers collecting me were late . . .' He dropped his silver worm on the floor, caught her eye, then stooped to retrieve it.

'You don't think that in the time between your original landing and your return to the spot, the body could have been brought there somehow?'

'Other than by the tide? No one else came to call, if that's what you mean. It's a tiny place, you've seen that for yourselves. I'd have noticed another boat drawing up.'

'Did you touch her?'

'Only for a second, just her face. Just really to see what she was . . . if she was alive,' he replied, shuddering, remembering suddenly the feel of the cold, wet skin on his fingers. The dead flesh. Picturing her lifeless face, he could feel his composure crumbling. Unthinkingly, he raised the empty mug to his lips as if to take a sip.

'More coffee?' Alice asked.

'No, I'm awash,' he replied, lowering it again, his jaw working overtime on the gum, embarrassed that a stranger should witness his distress. 'Jesus . . .' he murmured, overcome again, losing the battle and covering his eyes with his hand.

'Are you all right?'

'Fine, I'm fine.'

He began rummaging in the side pocket of his coat, looking for another piece of gum, but his fingers found something else.

'I got this,' he said, offering an irregularly shaped badge to the policewoman. It was made of white plastic and looked broken. Only the central section and the clasp

35

behind it remained intact. On the fragment was printed 'O-O', and below that 'AN'.

'If you'd drop it in here,' she said, holding out a polythene bag and, once he had obeyed, sealing it up. 'I'll need to take your prints, a DNA swab, purely for eliminatory purposes.'

'No problem,' he replied, nodding his head but looking oddly anxious, immediately speculating on where precisely the swab was to be taken from.

'You found it on the rock?'

'Yes. It was just beside her, beside her right shoulder. A two-pound coin fell out of my pocket and when I bent to pick it up I saw that badge thing. It's light, I was worried that . . . I don't know, that it would be swept away, blown away or something. I thought you'd need to see it.'

'Did you find anything else?'

'No. And, to be honest, I didn't look, either. I got spooked . . . she's the first body, dead body, I've seen.'

'Right, well, thank you very much for all your help. I'm sorry you had to be the one to see her, find her.'

'How do you do it – how on earth do you do this job?' he asked, looking at the tall, dark-haired woman seated opposite him with genuine curiosity. Attractive as she was, she wore no ring. Despite everything, he had noticed that much. And she could not be much older than Ella, forty-five at a push, and here she was spending her days dealing with the stuff of his nightmares, most people's nightmares. He would go home, kiss his wife, maybe go on a long bike ride, ruffle the twins' soft hair and forget all about pale-faced corpses and icy flesh. Or try to.

'It's all I know, and . . . she was someone's child,' she replied, rising to go, surprising herself with her own answer.

'So, you have children?' he persisted. Their shared experience of the corpse, the cold and the wet meant, in his mind, that the barriers were down, that truths, as opposed to pleasantries, could be exchanged. For him, the paramount importance of the living, the loved, had been reinforced by his encounter with the dead and, for some reason, he wanted to hear her affirm that and agree with him. He wanted her to have the same comfort.

'No children of my own,' she said.

'Right,' he replied, finding himself oddly nonplussed by her answer.

Watching her as she left, he was reminded of a cat; a solitary, elegant creature that, through choice, walked alone. No doubt, he mused to himself, an effective hunter, too.

4

'Sweetheart, I told you this wasn't a good idea,' the man said, looking into his wife's tearful face and fumbling in his pocket in case, by any miracle, there was a hankie in it. If not, there would be a pack of Kleenex in the passenger's glove-box for sure.

'I'll be fine,' she replied, sounding defensive, her chin still trembling and tears from her blue eyes overflowing down her cheeks.

'This matters. I told you, we mustn't attract attention. People will wonder why you're weeping. They'll be curious. You know why, my love, light of my life,' he continued, putting an arm around her shoulder and giving her a quick squeeze. When she did not respond, staying stiffly upright in her seat, he put a hand on either side of her face and planted a kiss on her nose. It was not reciprocated.

'I still think the police . . .' she began.

'We've talked about that. Better without them, without those busybodies from Social Services too.'

She made no reply.

'You could always stay in the car?' he suggested.

'I'll be alright,' she repeated, her tone firmer, letting him know that her mind was made up, and that nothing he could say would change it. She looked away from him, out of her window, taking in their exact location for the first time. He had parked the car as close to the garage on North Junction Street as possible, without actually encroaching on the apron of the forecourt. He opened the door for her and she stood in silence beside him as he fed a couple of coins into the ticket machine, looking first westwards and then eastwards, overcome by the enormity – no, the impossibility – of their task. It was hopeless.

As she stood waiting, cars streamed by, the low winter sun reflected off their windscreens, the drivers inside invisible. Passing them on either side was a never-ending river of pedestrians, coursing along the pavements, heads down, blind to anything except their own concerns. There was something ruthless, inhuman, about it all. In their thousands, they were more like ants than people. Whatever happened, they would carry on, trampling on the fallen, fixated on their own business, oblivious to the pain of others.

The man looked at the watch on his wrist. 'We'll meet back here at, say, 12.30? That'll give us three and a half hours. Phone me, won't you, the minute you have any luck? Be careful, mind, you know what they're like.'

She nodded, her head down, her attention apparently solely on the street atlas in front of her. In fact, her eyes heavy with tears, she could see nothing. From somewhere deep within her a surge of anger rose and she said bitterly, 'This should not have happened. You should have kept an eye on her.'

'Sweetheart, it was an accident – I told you,' he answered, a note of hurt reproach in his voice. Ignoring it, she continued, 'You should have locked her in. That's what I do, that's what I always do. Then she's safe. I warned you the last time. I asked you to do it too. But, no, you couldn't be bothered – or didn't think, or didn't care! A second, that's all it would have taken. Less than a second.'

'I do care . . .'

'Not enough!'

'I forgot.'

'If you cared, really cared, you wouldn't have!'

'That's not fair, Lambie, not true,' he replied, and a faint warning tone now coloured his voice. Registering it, she fixed him in the eye, shook her head and headed off towards the turn-off to Prince Regent Street. As she walked, her back to him, she wiped away the remaining tears with his crumpled linen hankie.

For a second she halted, consciously gathering herself, looking down the street and noticing the huge, soot-covered neo-classical building at the end of it. Its tall steeple seemed unexpected, out of place, and offered her no comfort. It might be His house, but God had forsaken her; He had not looked after her child.

A thick-set woman closed her front gate and came towards her. She looked washed out, with pouches under her wary eyes. A hoover was tucked under one of her arms, its hose coiled around her neck. In her outstretched hand was its nozzle, held in front of and away from her, as if it was the head of a venomous snake.

'Excuse me,' Lambie said, deliberately stepping into the woman's path to block her way, accost her. 'Could I trouble you for one minute?'

'Not if it's another bloody survey,' the woman retorted hotly, looking at her as if she was an enemy, 'I'm not voting.'

'No I'm not doing a survey. I'm trying to find a missing person.'

'Are you the police, then?'

'No, but I'm helping them in their search for a missing girl. She's almost fourteen, but looks older, tall for her age and she's got cerebral palsy...'

'I've never seen her.'

'I've got a photo. She was here last night. Well, somewhere near here.'

'Like I said, I'm sorry but I've never seen her. I don't live round here and I wasn't here last night. I just came to help a friend this morning. I'm from Portobello, and this thing,' she said, nodding towards the hoover, 'weighs a ton.'

Having made her point, she lumbered off at speed, without a backward glance.

Lambie studied the other pedestrians coming her way, trying to decide who to approach. None of them caught her eye. A youth, weighed down by a rucksack, looked harmless enough and although it went against the grain, she forced herself towards him. But he ignored her and her query, making her feel invisible and powerless.

Before long, and after being subjected more than once to a barrage of guttural, alien consonants, she became even more reluctant to approach the strangers flowing past her. But it must be done. On Madeira Street she steeled herself to knock on a door, choosing a bottle-green one with a brass knocker in the shape of a dove. The householder, a tiny old lady with her hair scraped back into a tight bun, peeped out from behind her door chain. Down at her feet, her Jack Russell poked its sharp little muzzle through the opening and sniffed the fresh air greedily.

'Sorry to bother you,' Lambie began, 'but I'm trying to find a missing person. A young girl. She's only thirteen, nearly fourteen. She's got fair hair and she's tall for her age . . .'

'Well,' the old lady began, sounding puzzled, 'she's not in here, darling. I've not got her in here with me.'

'No,' Lambie continued, 'I'm sure you've not. But she was here, or somewhere round about here, last night. I just wondered if you'd seen her then?'

'A girl, you say, light-haired, tall, thirteen?'

'Yes, I've got a picture.'

'Lost, you say?' the old lady frowned, holding the photo at the end of her outstretched arm and peering at it. As she was doing so, her dog took its chance and attempted to wiggle its hard little body through the crack of the open door, whimpering when, in order to trap it, the old lady pulled the door more tightly closed on it with her free hand.

'Stop it, Millie! You're not getting out!'

'Yes, she's lost. It happened somewhere around here, yesterday evening.'

'At thirteen can she not talk, then? Use one of those mobile phones? Find her own way home or at least ask somebody? At fourteen, my dear, I believe they're going to be allowed to vote for independence!'

'She doesn't speak. Well, only to . . . a few people, those she knows really, really well, and she's got cerebral palsy, you see, so she's difficult to understand. She just makes noises, really.'

'Well, I've not seen her,' the old lady replied, handing back the photo and manoeuvring a stick-thin calf over the body of her pet in order to squeeze it back indoors. When she had succeeded, she smiled politely at the stranger and eased her front door shut again.

Waylaying others on Ferry Road, South Fort Street and North Fort Street brought no results. One lad, a green and white scarf tied round his neck, had even sworn at her. Feeling desolate, the woman decided to phone her husband.

'Any luck?' he asked.

'No. Where are you?'

She could hear the sound of the traffic in the background, cars passing him at speed.

'I'm on Dock Street heading towards . . .' he hesitated, consulting his *A to Z*, 'towards Commercial Street. Keep going, sweetheart. Someone, somewhere, must have seen her – they must have. She can't have disappeared into thin air.'

'I know,' the woman answered, sounding unconvinced, unable to say more, feeling tears pricking the back of her eyes and blinking rapidly in an attempt to stem their flow. What about Bad Men, what about them? But even mentioning them out loud seemed dangerous, as if naming them might annoy them, make them rise up and harm her child.

'Are you alright, Lambie?' he asked, knowing the answer. Maybe, as she had insisted, it was more efficient to split up; but, he decided, it was also too difficult, too much to expect of her. She was not coping. They would, from now on, and whatever she said, do it together, side by side. He could be back with her, his arm around her, in a tick, and by the time she realised what he was up to, it would be too late.

'Mmm,' she replied, wiping her cheeks with the heel of her hand and putting the phone back in her pocket. Feeling the cold, she turned up the collar of her navy blue coat, and began wandering along the last few yards of Portland Street, only to find herself back in Madeira Street once more. Thinking that she would try one last house farther down it, she continued northwards until she saw, ahead of her, a pub. It was called 'The Coach House' and was close to the junction with Ferry Road.

For about a minute, she watched people going in and coming out, too afraid to cross its threshold herself. Eventually, summoning an image of her daughter's face into her mind, she went in and began to work her way through the crowd towards the bar. The sole barman on duty was rushed off his feet. When, eventually, he looked inquiringly at her, she failed to speak. In a flash, he passed on to her neighbour, whirling round to pull his pint while she was still gathering her thoughts. The next time the barman's attention turned to her, she was ready for him and blurted out, 'I'm looking for a missing person. A young girl, nearly fourteen, fair-haired. I've a photo . . .'

'What d'you want to drink, doll?' he asked her, as if she had said nothing.

'I don't want a drink, thank you. I'm looking for a missing person.'

'You've said that already,' he interrupted her. 'I'm busy. You can see that for yourself. What do you want to drink?'

'Nothing.'

'Then I can't help you, I'm afraid,' he replied, signalling by a nod to the man behind her who, seizing his opportunity, edged to the front, a five-pound note ready rolled in his hand.

Defeated, she began to trudge back towards the door but, feeling she must give it everything she had, she tapped the tweed-covered shoulder of a sturdy man who was blocking her exit.

'I'm very sorry to bother you, but I'm looking for a missing person, a girl, almost fourteen, fair-haired. She's got cerebral palsy . . .'

He turned to answer her, taking a sip from his whisky glass and looking her up and down.

'Did you lot not pick her up, then?'

44

'Sorry?' she replied, not understanding his words.

'The lost girl, dear. I thought the police picked her up, that was what Hilary told me. The one who was sleeping in the doorway of number thirteen? I heard that Tricia rang 999 and that a bobby came from Gayfield to collect her. I didn't know she had cerebral palsy, though. You'd never have known.'

'No, I suppose you wouldn't,' she mumbled.

'Why are you asking? Aren't you from the police, then?' he inquired of her, taking another drink from his glass.

'No,' she replied, flustered, 'I'm from . . . a homeless charity. We had a call, you see. But if the police are dealing with it . . . with her, that'll be fine. I'll report that, and then we can close our file.'

Once outside the pub, she walked a few yards away before excitedly fishing her phone from her pocket.

'It's me. She's safe! The police in Gayfield picked her up. We could go and get her from them.'

'Thank God! That's wonderful news, sweetheart,' the man replied. 'Oh, thank you, God! Thank you! I'll meet you back at the car. It'll take me about ten minutes or so to get there. I'm on my way already.'

'OK. Then we'll go straight there and pick her up, eh?'

'Hold on, hold on, lovey,' he replied, sounding anxious. 'No, I'm not sure we can do that, quite. You know what'll happen, like the last time. Like I said. Remember? We don't want anyone trying to take her away, those Social Services types or anything. We don't want to get tangled up with them again. They don't understand the difficulties and everything. The police would be bound to involve them. Wouldn't they?'

'Maybe, but . . .'

'The important thing, sweetheart, is that she's safe. We know that now, eh? Now we know that, I'll be able to track her down myself, in a jiff, and bring her back home. Myself. Don't you worry, Lambie, not now that we know she's safe, eh? That's the only thing that matters, isn't it, my love? She's safe!'

———

'Do we have any notion who the drowned lady is, yet?' DCI Bell asked. She had turned sideways to her inspector, and was looking out of her office window onto Arthur's Seat and the parklands surrounding it. She appeared, Alice thought, distracted and out of sorts and was holding a postcard behind her back, twirling it round and round in her fingers. On her desk, poking out from a Co-op carrier bag was pack of sandwiches and a bottle of Diet Coke.

'I don't know at the moment. I've circulated her details throughout the force, including a photograph taken by Jim this morning inside the ticket office.'

'Have we got DNA, prints?' the woman demanded.

'The mortuary's going to see to that. I've got DC Cairns lined up to go once we get the warrant.'

'Mmm. We'll not get one, of course, not till we've got some clue as to who the hell she is. And I don't like them hanging around, not when they've been in the water like that. They go off quickly. Nor does Jardine, as I know to my cost. Any press involvement?' DCI Bell added, finally turning to face her subordinate.

'Not yet. I thought I'd give it another day. If she was killed, whoever did it doesn't know we're on the lookout yet. I'd rather keep it that way a little longer.'

'Of course, if this wondrous new all-Scotland regime was operational this floater wouldn't be troubling us at all, she'd be someone else's problem in all probability, not ours. Creamed off to the specialists, the lucky things. No descriptions in missing-person reports matching her? Nothing at all?'

'Nothing so far. But it's early, we've only just fished her out, got her back on dry land.'

'True. Now, look at this –' the DCI said, handing the postcard to Alice and adding, through gritted teeth, 'bloody Mauritius, if you can believe it!'

The picture on the card showed a beach, its white sand extending into infinity and turquoise waves lapping the shore. 'Wish You Were Here' had been crossed out hard, several times, with a red pen. Alice only got a fleeting view of the handwriting on the back but it looked vaguely familiar.

'I bought the ticket you know,' added DCI Bell hotly.

'To bloody Mauritius, you mean?'

'No, not to bloody Mauritius – where have you been? The lottery ticket that the bastard won with. I bought it for him!'

'It should've been me?'

'Well, it should. Thanks to me, Eric Manson and his missus will now be permanently swanning round the globe, golf-sticks uppermost, enjoying a sun-kissed early retirement – all thanks to me! And he's rubbing my nose in it. But no more,' she said, ripping the postcard into little pieces.

'We'll just have to hope he remembers his friends on his return, Ma'am. Otherwise on our retirement, like everyone else, we'll be eating our pets in our unheated hovels, and cleaning public lavatories daily for a few pence until we can collect our pensions at the age of a hundred and fifty-five.'

'Eric remember us? Fat chance of that, Alice. He'll be drinking himself senseless at Muirfield or . . . '

'Who paid for the ticket?'

'He did. But I chose it. I made that one in a million selection. Payment's a technicality, neither here nor there.' She let out a long sigh. 'Anything else I should know about our floating friend?'

'Yes. In a front pocket of her trousers, there was a fragment left of what appeared to be a Lothian Buses ticket. We also found, or rather the scaffolder who discovered her found, what seems to be a broken badge beside the body. Most of the printing on it has disappeared but it seems to say "O-O" and below that "AN". It may have been washed up independently of her, or fallen off her clothes. The pin's intact. I'm working on it now.'

'O-O? AN? What does it mean? Could it have fallen off anyone else, another workman or the one who found the body?' the DCI asked, dropping her multi-coloured confetti in the nearby wastepaper bin. Half of it fell on the floor but she did not pick it up.

'No, Ewen Macdonell didn't drop it, he found her and it, and no one else could have dropped it either. We were all suited and booted. Anyway, the rock's submerged every high tide, it'd be washed off. Either it came with her or on her.'

The office was quiet. Everyone was away, eating their lunch, jogging or cramming some hurried shopping into their already hectic schedules. Alice sat down in front of her computer, the badge in its polythene bag staring up at her. Thoughts of food were preoccupying her too, and picturing the DCI's sandwiches in their carrier, she had a sudden idea. It seemed a long shot, maybe even a waste of time, but it had to be tried. She found the website on her computer, then picked up the phone and dialled the contact number there. The Manchester headquarters of the Co-op directed her to their Scottish headquarters on Dalry Road, Edinburgh, a building she was familiar with and only minutes away from St Leonard's Street.

Once she realised who it was, the bored human being in the Human Resources department who took the call could not have been more eager to co-operate, to participate, to assist. Their employees were, she confirmed, usually supplied with a personal badge, one with the Co-op logo on it and the employee's name below. Yes, they did, indeed, hold photographic identification of their staff, assuming the employee had a passport. Otherwise, they would only have a copy birth certificate. But, she explained, apologetically, their business at HQ was usually with staff absences only of a week or more, at the point at which the absence might be, or might become, a disciplinary matter. Shorter absences were handled by the managers of the individual stores. The managers knew the shift patterns of their workers, which absences had been agreed, the difference between the genuinely ill and the shirkers, and dealt with the problem of day to day cover. Only persistent, unsanctioned absences were reported to them together with long-term sickness problems. Of course, she said, sounding thrilled to be personally involved in solving the mystery, an e-mail could be sent to all those managers to get a list of all recent, unexplained staff absences. She could do it on her head.

'I'll only need those relating to females . . .' Alice paused, recreating in her mind's eye the dead woman's face. 'Say, between 16 and 30.'

'No problem. For the whole of Scotland?'

'No, let's begin with Edinburgh and, if necessary, radiate outwards. Also Rosyth and Kincardine, Bo'ness and Grangemouth . . . any stores you've got near the shores of the Forth.'

'And for all our services?'

'Sorry?'

'We're not just food, anymore. Do you want the same information from our funeral care services, travel services, banking, insurance?'

'Mmm . . .' Alice hesitated, interrupted before she could respond by the woman's lively voice, unable to resist offering more advice: 'Given her sex, age and everything, our food stores are, by far, the most likely,' she volunteered.

'OK. Let's begin with the food stores. I'd like the e-mails directed here ASAP, but just from the food-store managers. We'll start with them. Tell them it's urgent, will you? We need all absences in the relevant category for a period of four to five days or less, but up to and including today.'

'Anything else?'

'Yes, ask them for a brief description of each woman, each absentee – hair colour as a minimum, please.'

'Forgive my cheek, you're the police and everything, not me. But, surely, they might have dyed it? Wouldn't colour of eyes be better?'

'Does anyone remember eyes? As long as the managers describe the hair colour when they last saw the individual, that'll do. Our lady was dark-haired. Gentlemen prefer blondes, they say. So, while countless brunettes become blondes, surely not many blondes go in the other direction, wouldn't you think?'

'No, you're wrong! I did, and, you know what, my IQ went right up. Which are you? No worries. I'll get onto it this very minute.'

—

Over the next four hours, responses from the branches flooded into the station. Females in the right age group had failed to show up, during the period in question, only within the capital, at the Nicolson Street, Pitt Street, Easter Road, Granton Road, Oxgangs Road and Portobello High Street branches of the Co-op. Photos of only six of them were held at the Manchester HQ, and copies of them were sent to St Leonard's Street. Of the ten named individuals, four were eliminated on the basis of their fair hair, one because she had already turned to grey. Only two of the remaining brunettes had the letters 'AN' in their names: Miranda Stimms and Jane Cook, and the latter, though hailing from Musselburgh, was dark-skinned, of Afro-Caribbean descent. Miranda Stimms was an employee in the Pitt Street store, in Edinburgh's South Side.

—

The manager of the Pitt Street store, a Mr Wilson, was busy with a customer when Alice approached him. Rocking forwards and back on his small feet like a music-hall policeman, he was trying to placate a woman who was determined to buy three products all containing Paracetamol from his shop. An anxious-looking assistant stood nearby, wringing her red hands, obviously defeated in the argument and having called on her superior for help.

'Sorry, but we don't make the rules,' the manager repeated in an avuncular fashion, a fixed smile on his face.

'I need the Calpol for the wee one,' his customer pleaded. 'He's teething. His cheeks are that red.'

From his buggy, the wee one held her hand. His nose was streaming, but he seemed untroubled by his condition, all his attention being focused on the confectionary display at the checkout.

'That's fine. But then you'll have to put back either the Lemsip or the tablets, I'm afraid,' the manager replied, holding out his hand for whichever one she returned.

'But they're for Bob. He's got the flu, he specially asked for them both, he needs them both, he's got a fever!'

'Sorry, Madam, but it'll have to be one or the other.' The man still held his hand out, periodically crooking his fingers to show that he did mean business.

'That's no good, that's what *she* already said,' the customer spat, glaring at the assistant. 'I'll just have to go to Boots, then, won't I?'

So saying, she let go of her wire basket, allowing it to clatter onto the ground, and flounced off empty-handed.

Exchanging a timid glance with her boss, the assistant bent to pick it up. A puddle of cream was spreading underneath and, the second she lifted it, a trail of droplets leaked from the split carton.

A man, his trolley swerving to the side, accosted her, inquiring peremptorily, 'Bananas? Where'd I find bananas?'

'First aisle on the right,' she answered, still on her knees, scarcely looking up.

'We'll need the mop, Suzy,' the manager said, adding as an afterthought, 'and the wet floor sign.' One problem solved, or at least as solved as it ever would be, he turned his attention to the next one, the policewoman.

'I've come about Miranda Stimms – we spoke on the phone,' she began, introducing herself.

'Oh, aye, Mandy,' he replied, 'our absentee. Better follow me to my office. It'll be quieter there.'

With the door closed in the windowless space, he gestured for her to take the seat opposite his desk. 'Office' seemed too grand a word for the room. It appeared to be as much of a storeroom as anything else; tins of dog food were piled high in one corner and cleaning materials, including a couple of long-haired mops in buckets, occupied the other. An unclean, vinegary smell pervaded the air.

'When did you last see her?' she began.

'It'll have been yesterday. She was supposed to be in today, but she's not turned up. She does three four-hour shifts a week. I phoned her, then I checked with Irene, her best pal, to see if she knew where she was, but she had no idea what was going on.'

'Has this happened with her before?'

'No. She's very reliable, very conscientious, actually. Mandy's not been with us long, only about six weeks but . . . this is quite out of character. If anything she was over-worried about things, over-anxious. Sometimes I told her to relax, lighten up. She seemed old for her years. What's she done?'

'She hasn't done anything. How old is she?'

'Twenty-one – that's what her application said, anyway. That's all I have to go on. She didn't have a passport and she was still looking for her birth certificate . . . she was supposed to hand it in.'

A young man barged through the door, a tray of poussins in his hands.

'Where am I to put the wee birds, Mr Wilson?' he asked, brandishing them in front of his boss.

'Knock next time, Raymond, please. Beside the chickens, in the chill cabinet.'

Once the youth had left, the manager explained, apologetically, 'He's learning disabled. New to the job, too.'

'Could you tell me what Miranda Stimms looks like?'

'Aye,' he nodded, 'she's a "babe", if you get the picture. She's dark-haired, a good figure. I thought of her like Catherine Zeta-Jones in the old days – you know, the Welsh girl that married Gordon Gecko or whatever he was called. An hourglass shape . . . a fox. He's one of those sex addicts, I heard. Done him no good, either.'

'I'm sorry to ask you, but could you look at this photograph,' Alice asked, handing him one of the shots taken by Jim Scott in the temporary mortuary.

'Jesus!' said Mr Wilson, sitting back in his chair, blinking rapidly, dropping the photograph on his desk.

'Is that her?' the policewoman asked.

'Yes. But she's not a fox any more. What happened to her?'

'That's what we're trying to find out.'

5

If he set about the exercise with military precision he would find her, he told himself. He must. Lambie, so weak, so loving, was depending upon him, and, this time, he would not let her down. He paced the length of his office, thinking as he walked, rehearsing in his head the logical sequence that would inevitably occur. His phone went, distracting him, and recognising the number, he switched it off. No problem. Salesmen, he told himself, persist or get sacked. Kevin, the Cute Cards Company's representative, would call again for sure. Not that he would be buying any more of their overpriced stationery in a hurry, not with Frankie Boyd setting up in competition to them. He'd offer a much better price, in all likelihood on far more amenable terms too.

'Boss?' A man's head, topped with a halo of red hair, appeared round his door.

'Yes.'

'We've got a big order to go to Berwick, they need it yesterday. Can I get a courier?'

'Yeah,' he said, immediately turning his back on the man to let him know that there would be no further chat, and waiting motionless until he heard the door close once more.

He sat down on the edge of his desk and lifted his cup of tea to his lips. The police had picked her up. So she was safe. But, in this day and age, she would not be kept in a cell or anything. No, they'd involve the Social Services, what with her being a child and everything. She was tall but still a child, anyone could see that, surely? What would they do with her – speechless, twitchy and, obviously, not normal? Lost in thought, he put down his cup untouched, and started to bite a fingernail, pulling at a ragged end. First of all, they would have to find a temporary home for her, and that would either be a children's home, if they still existed, or, more likely, a foster home. And school, they would be bound to think about a school because education was the law. But, if she couldn't, or wouldn't, speak, what then? They'd not put her in a normal secondary school, would they? They couldn't. That would be monstrous, did not bear thinking about. Imagining it, he began to sweat, could feel the moisture collecting on his brow.

No, they would opt, surely to goodness, for a special school. They'd be bound to. They'd be kinder there. Please, Lord, he prayed, help me find her, keep her safe, keep my child safe until I find her. Let me get to her first. Tears now pricking his eyes, he switched on his computer, intending to check out children's homes and special schools in Edinburgh.

'Boss?' the same man's head appeared round the door again.

'Not now, Jake!' he bellowed, embarrassed, turning his head away, angry that anyone should witness his weakness. Instantly, the door clicked shut and he returned his attention to the screen in front of him. Googling 'Special Schools in Edinburgh' brought up eleven possibilities, of which fewer than half appeared to cater for secondary school pupils. Four of them specialised in youngsters with communication difficulties, including those 'on the autistic spectrum', as their websites phrased it. They were based in Drumbrae, Abbeyhill, Liberton and Bruntsfield, respectively. Deciding to start with them, he wrote their addresses and details in his pocket notebook.

Faced with the results for 'Children's homes in Edinburgh', he sighed. There was such a multiplicity of choices and, feeling momentarily weighed down by the hopelessness of it all, he did not even bother to copy them down. He could hardly check them all out, watch all of them. It would take months, if it could be done at all, and Lambie would not stand for that. Last night she had taken too much whisky, two tumblers both well-nigh neat, and become argumentative, shrill and hectoring. Not like the woman he knew and had married. The woman he loved.

The phone went again and he snatched it up.

'Yes?' He sounded irate.

'It's just me,' she said, taken aback.

'Lambie . . .'

'You left so early.'

'I had to. I've got my work to do, I've got to keep things going.'

While talking to her, unseen by her, he rubbed his tired eyes with the tips of his fingers.

'What news, how are you getting on?'

'I'm getting on fine, my sweet. Did you speak to the school?'

'Yes.'

'What did you say?'

'Tonsillitis – that worked last time.'

The door opened and Jake began to come in.

'Get out!' the man shouted, then realising how it would sound down the phone, he immediately added, 'Not you, Lambie, I wasn't talking to you. Someone came in to my

57

office. It's busy here – it's a dispatch day. We've orders going all over the place.'

'But you have started looking – you are looking for her, too? I can't lose her. I've got to go to the meeting, but I couldn't bear to lose . . .'

The voice at the other end tailed away to nothing. Knowing the woman as he did, he could picture her in their kitchen, dissolving in her distress, her chin wobbling and tears starting to trickle down her cheeks. She would be biting her lip, trying and failing to stop herself from crying. Before too long she would start choking, unable to contain herself or breathe. Hysterical, enfeebled by her unhappiness.

'Lambie, my darling, it's alright,' he said, his voice firm and confident. 'Trust me. You know I *will* find her.'

———

Three-fifteen p.m. found him sitting in his Mazda 6 a couple of hundred yards from the low brick wall which enclosed the Cowan Lea Special School on Drum Brae Terrace. The school itself comprised an uninspired sixties building, flat-roofed and white-painted with a matching Portakabin tacked to one side. Around it was a small garden, the turf worn in parts, and dotted on the grass was the play equipment: a couple of swings, a roundabout and a slide. The only tree left on the site, a crooked Scots pine, had a circular tree-house round its trunk, a rope ladder dangling forlornly from its dark interior.

In the fifteen minutes or so that he had been parked, women had appeared from all four points of the compass and begun to congregate at the gates. Some of them were smoking, some chatting, others looking intently into the playground, ever watchful for the arrival of their own precious offspring. A solitary man, a small girl clutching his hand, joined the female crowd, getting nods of recognition from most of them. In her free hand, the little girl held the lead of a yapping Border terrier. As a white-faced teenager, pigeon-toed, bespectacled and with a strange bullet-shaped skull hurtled out of the gates towards it, the dog began pulling on the lead, rearing up on its back legs in its determination to greet its master. Eventually it broke loose, barrelling towards the boy, its lead dragging behind it.

No other child, he noticed, left the school unaccompanied; all the rest held the hand of schoolmate or a parent. Policy, no doubt; and that was, he determined there and then, how he would do it. If she was there, he would walk in, take her hand and lead her out. Knowing her, she would not protest or demur, or attempt to attract anyone's attention. And no foster mother would be half as sharp-eyed, half as vigilant, as him. She would be too busy gossiping and socialising with the other women in all probability to notice them leaving together, and she would not be expecting that. No, she would be looking only for a lone girl.

His phone went.

'Boss?'

'Aha,' he replied, never taking his eyes off the children in the playground.

'Dunfermline wants to know if we've enough stock for the next two weeks. Hughie's away and Davie's just left. What should I say?'

'Tell them that we're OK. We're OK. Right?'

He waited a second, then abruptly ended the call. Standing on her own he had spotted a tall, blonde girl. She had her back to him, her shoulders held unnaturally high, in a familiar way, and one arm moved every so often as if not fully under her control. He sat up, hunched over the wheel, willing her to turn round. Instinctively, he disengaged his seatbelt, opened the door, readying himself to move the minute he recognised her. His car keys were clutched in his hand, suddenly so tightly that it hurt, the metal digging into his palm. In his excitement he could hardly breathe. Let it be her. Let it be her. In less than a minute he would be beside her, hand in her hand, leading her back to the car. Then straight home to Lambie, with him triumphant and witnessing her joy.

'Turn round,' he ordered silently. 'For pity's sake turn around.'

As if they were connected, as if she had heard him and obeyed, the girl turned slowly in his direction. Seeing her, he closed his eyes. She was pregnant, her fringe had been dyed a shade of purple and she was massaging her awful, oversized belly in a circular motion with one of her hands.

'Oh, mercy!' he cried, his head slumping down, bowed down as if it was too heavy for his neck. Despair flooded over him, rendering him powerless, making him doubt everything, including himself. Head now in his hands, his features contorted in grief, his disappointment overpowered him, unmanned him.

A sharp knock on his window returned him to the present, and seeing an elderly woman looking in at him, her brows furrowed in concern, he wound it down.

'I just wondered if you were OK?' she asked, bending down slightly to get a better view of him.

'Fine . . . thank you very much,' he replied reassuringly, then, giving little thought to the lie, he elaborated, 'well, I've a headache but I've taken something, it's getting better.'

Satisfied, she smiled and set off down the street, pulling her shopping trolley behind her. As its rusted wheels rolled along the pavement they emitted a high-pitched shriek, tearing his already vulnerable nerves to shreds.

For another twenty minutes he remained sitting in his car, in the cold, now feeling stiff and uncomfortable, aware of an ache at the base of his spine. As his vigil came to an end, the stragglers departed. A thickset boy with a squint seemed unwilling to leave the playground, and had to be cajoled out of it by his mother. Shrugging her shoulders, she walked away from the gates, as if leaving him. A look of distress disfigured his large features, and he followed her, then stopped. She set off again, then halted, waiting for him to catch up. Using this method, the eccentric couple finally turned into Drum Brae Crescent and disappeared from view. Now, the playground was empty. Only a janitor and a teaching assistant remained near the school, talking, the assistant gesticulating at the litter near the front door as if ordering its removal.

He had failed. He drove back onto Drum Brae North, bringing his car to a halt by the line of bare poplars which mark the start of the descent onto the Queensferry Road. In his distress, the breathtaking view before him of the Forth and the blue hills of Fife left him cold, his eyes moving across it mechanically, blind to its beauty.

He punched her number in and waited, in vain, for her voice. After allowing himself a minute or two to collect himself, to ensure that his voice sounded strong, optimistic and confident, he pressed the redial button and began to speak into the answerphone. 'Lambie,' he said, 'it's me. She wasn't there. But don't you worry. She'll be at the next one, I know she will. We're getting closer all the time. Now, I'll need to work late tonight, in the office.

Be back nine, maybe. Or half-nine, ten at a pinch. But I love you. You know I love you. You and . . .' He stopped abruptly. Starting to say his daughter's name, his voice had begun to break.

'Bye, bye,' he ended, as brightly as he was able.

6

The dead woman had lived in Casselbank Street, a narrow, characterful thoroughfare at the bottom of Leith Walk, which was home to no less than three churches and a branch of the Cat Protection League. The League's terraced building sported a jaunty sign above its door, making it look more like a pub than a charitable institution. Opposite her tenement block was one of the churches, proclaiming itself on a hoarding in exuberant, purple loops as 'Destiny Church'. It had been constructed originally as a Turkish baths. With its pediments and lead-covered ogee domes, the building was eye-catching, looking both foreign and incongruously opulent in the small, unassuming Scots street.

A joiner, arranged by DC Cairns, was waiting in his van for the arrival of the policewomen, the engine still running. He had parked further up the road, opposite the columned and pilastered doorway of one of the few remaining Georgian houses in the location. Seeing the Scientific Support crew assembling outside the tenement, he threw away his cigarette and began to jog towards the group, keen to warm up. As each foot hit the ground, his work box swung uncomfortably against his thigh.

Seconds later, he and the rest of the party gained access to the woman's flat courtesy of a bell marked 'A. Anderson'. Waiting in the common stair they huddled together, talking in hushed tones as if in a church awaiting the entry of the minister. Alice went to speak to 'A. Anderson'. The owner of that name turned out to be a red-faced, middle-aged woman with a strange, fixed smile and few teeth. In her soft Highland accent she described her upstairs neighbour, and the rictus remained on her face when an image of the girl, cold and dead, was presented to her. Holding the photo about a foot from her presbyopic dark eyes, moving it forward and back in an attempt to see it clearly, she identified her neighbour in a matter of fact fashion, apparently untroubled by the death.

'Aha, that's her, but it's not like her. Not a good likeness. I've seen her a few times, not that I knew her. She's new. This is all like on the telly, eh?' she said, handing the image back.

'Thank you for your help.'

'No problem. You'd better watch out as she had a house cat,' she added by way of a parting shot, nodding to herself as she turned back towards her red front door and murmuring, 'as if there aren't enough of them round here. Yowling and screeching at all hours, like banshees. I'd drown them, kittens and all.'

Two minutes of the joiner's drill on the old, ill-designed mortise lock protecting the woman's flat was all it took, before it fell, shattered, onto the stone flags of the common landing. Once inside they set to work immediately, photographing and videoing all four of the shabby rooms, searching for any evidence which might establish conclusively that Miranda Stimms had been its occupant, and if she had met her end there. The forensic team, in their distinctive white garb, moved around the cramped space, performing figures of eight like reel-dancers, expertly avoiding each other as they attempted to gather DNA samples and fingerprints from all possible surfaces. A couple of them stood over the unmatched dirty crockery littering the kitchen table: two cups, a saucer and an egg-cup, droplets of bright yellow yolk staining its sides. The fridge had little in it bar a carton of milk, not yet sour, a half-tin of cat food and an opened slab of Red Leicester cheese. All, Alice noticed, picking them up in her gloves, reasonably fresh and bought from the Co-op. A cat-litter tray, unused, lay near the door. But of the cat itself there was no sign.

In the bedroom, away from the team, Alice peered into the only cupboard, a homemade hardboard construction which was missing one door. Inside was a solitary green coat hanging on a nail. The gloss-painted chest of drawers nearby, which still had the price ticket from Capability on it, contained more women's clothing. Every item was clean and neatly folded. On the bedside table were two photographs in cheap, plastic frames. One, badly out of focus, appeared to show Miranda Stimms at the seaside, laughing, her arm tight around the shoulder of a girl in a hat, receiving a kiss on the cheek from her. The other was of a young man. He looked shy and was self-consciously pointing a finger at the photographer as if trying to think of a wacky pose, or just something to do before the shutter closed.

The only item of any value within the flat was a massive flat screen television in the sitting room. Its matt-black, state-of-the-art design was in stark contrast to the thin nylon carpet and patched curtains with which the room was furnished. Accompanied by a DVD player, this prized possession squatted on a low stool, and the leads from both had tangled together like spaghetti, their plugs jammed into a socket which, in turn, hung loosely from the wall.

Moving into the bathroom, the policewoman sniffed the damp, fungal air. Black mould disfigured the walls and ceiling, and the avocado-coloured basin was cracked, a tap dripping incessantly into its stained interior. A tooth-mug, on top of a mirrored medicine-cabinet, contained two identical, crossed, pink toothbrushes. As she tried to open the cabinet, one of its doors swung off its hinge to reveal inside a couple of deodorants and a bottle of cheap shampoo. A black cat with white paws arrived from nowhere, leapt up onto the lip of the bath and began tightrope-walking its way towards her. Brushing himself against her, he looked up at her with his bright yellow eyes.

'I've got the post. One's addressed to Miranda Jane Stimms,' DC Cairns said as she entered, instinctively turning sideways, fastidious in her attempt to avoid touching the lavatory, 'and I think I might have found where the deceased's parents live.' In her hand was an empty envelope addressed to James Stimms, 'Fisher's Rest', Starbank Terrace, Edinburgh EH44 9MB, which she handed to the inspector.

'Finally,' Alice said, reading the address, 'we'll get her identified by a relative, and that'll be good enough to get us a warrant for the PM. And after all this bother,' she added, 'it had better be a sodding murder.'

'No sign of blood or guts in here or elsewhere.'

'Perhaps Felix here has been cleaning up . . .'

'You're joking?' DC Cairns said, looking at the beast in horror.

'Am I? I wonder if he'll be as well-fed with the Cat Protection League people,' Alice said, giving the creature a stroke, unable to stop herself smiling as the constable shuddered visibly at the thought.

The view to the north for the inhabitants of the terrace of red sandstone houses halfway along Starbank Road was not such as might be found throughout much of the capital, a short one, one of high harled tenements, symmetrical Georgian squares, cosy post-war bungalows, factories or even municipal sports facilities. Instead, the great grey expanse of the Forth stretched before them for mile upon mile, finally losing itself in the hills of Fife. Theirs was a simplified horizon, grand, and austere, one which spoke of Newhaven's fishing past. Not that in the absence of their sea view the locals could forget its history, living as they did in close proximity to places such as Fishmarket Square and Pier Place, with gulls instead of pigeons high above them and the salt-laden air reverberating with their raucous cries. That afternoon a gale was blowing, whipping up white horses and making the procession of clouds above scud past as if they were late for some grand occasion.

The woman who came to the door of Fisher's Rest to meet them looked worried, and none of her anxiety was relieved once they introduced themselves. She was slight, little more than a perfumed wraith, neatly dressed, with the gold buttons on her cashmere navy-blue cardigan fastened all the way up to her neck. Her profuse grey hair had been newly permed, but in a style last fashionable in the fifties. Navy slacks, with a single crease on each leg sharp enough to inflict a cut, terminated in tiny, flat, navy shoes. Around her narrow waist was an apron, a perfect bow tied at the back, and in one hand she held a canister of air freshener.

'Mrs Stimms?'

'Yes.'

'We're from the police. I'm DI Rice and this is my colleague, DC Cairns. Is your husband about?'

'James? No, he's away at the moment. On a job out near Livingston and he'll not be back until this evening. Do you want to speak to him?'

'Could we come in and speak to you?'

'Me? To me? Em . . .' She hesitated, fine lines furrowing her brow, 'Very well.'

The sitting-room that she showed them into looked as if they were the first human beings ever to enter it. Such a place in the sales showroom of a new housing estate would have some slight evidence of wear and tear, however minimal, but this displayed none. The beige cushions of the settee and matching armchairs were plumped up, the oatmeal carpet spotless and the ten folds in each of the cream curtains, both with a red piped tie placed exactly in the middle, were perfectly symmetrical. A ruler would have lain flat on the covers of the three piles of illustrated books on the coffee table, as if each volume had been chosen not for content but for its matching size in the array. In a cabinet, filling all five shelves, were cycling trophies. They alone provided some hint of the personalities responsible for such a temple of domesticity. And it was not just the lack of dirt, stains and creases on the pale-coloured furniture and elsewhere, the missing imprint of the living, which was remarkable, the very air itself felt dry, stagnant and unwelcoming.

'Have you a daughter, Miranda?' Alice began, taking a seat where she had been bidden. DC Cairns, also obeying instructions, sat in a nearby armchair. Alone, in the middle of the sofa and dwarfed by it, Mrs Stimms sat with her legs pressed tight against each other and folded to one side. Her hands, small and white, lay on her lap.

'Aha . . . yes, I have, aha,' she replied, nodding. Her complexion was unhealthily pale, and her large dark eyes flitted, covertly and frequently, between the inspector's face and the floor.

'When did you last see Miranda?'

'Em . . . a good wee while ago. Months, maybe, at least two months? Two and a half? She doesn't live here now, not with us. Not for a while since. She's moved out – on her own, flown the nest. She lives her own life now, she's a grown up, an adult . . . Grown up as a "Gay" as people say nowadays, in fact, you see. So she has her own life now.'

'Does she have a partner?'

'I wouldn't know. I don't know anything about that side of her life. It's not my business, is it?'

The woman picked up the nearest cushion, put it over her lap, and automatically, almost as if it was a pet, began to pat it, smooth its creaseless silk surface.

'When did you, or your husband, last speak to her on the phone?'

'Me? Months ago. We're not that close any more. My husband . . . oh, I don't know, you'd have to ask him.'

'But her name is Miranda Jane Stimms – that is your daughter's name?'

'Oh, yes. That's her name. Yes. Why are you here? Is she in trouble of some sort? Is she alright? Has she been in an accident or something?'

'I'm sorry to be the bearer of bad news, but I'm afraid we think she may be dead.'

'What are you talking about?'

'We found what we're all but certain is her body, and we need your help . . . to identify her. It's little more than a formality at this stage, really.'

The woman blinked hard, as if it might help her to comprehend the news.

'Dead? Don't be ridiculous, she can't be. I told you, she's in Edinburgh. She's living in Edinburgh, in a flat. How could she be dead?'

'I'm very sorry, but we're almost certain that it's her. Her body. We've been to her flat in Casselbank Street in Leith, and we've spoken to her employer. He identified her. A neighbour did as well.'

'No . . . no. It'll not be her. It'll be someone else – some other young girl. Not Miranda. I don't know her address – but this'll be a case of mistaken identity.'

'Could I ask you to look at a photo of the dead girl, Mrs Stimms? We have a photo of the dead girl.'

The woman nodded, and bent down to retrieve her spectacles from the dark blue handbag which was lying at her feet.

'Is this your daughter?' Alice asked, stretching towards her and handing over the photograph. For over a minute, blinking abnormally frequently once more, but remaining speechless, Mrs Stimms studied it before, with a long sigh, she offered it back to its owner.

'Is that your daughter, Miranda?'

'Yes,' she said. Behind the spectacles, tears were brimming in her eyes, and her grip on the cushion had tightened, squeezing it out of shape and whitening her knuckles. 'What happened to her face . . . who gave her a black eye?'

'We don't know yet. I'm sorry to ask, but could you come to the mortuary to identify her body for us? DC Cairns here will come with you, she'll take you there, and bring you straight back. We could contact your husband for you, if that would help, so you could go together?'

'What happened to her?' Mrs Stimms enquired in a thin voice.

'I'm afraid we don't know yet. That's what we're investigating.'

'Where did you find her?' She was looking directly into the policewoman's eyes, a strange pleading expression on her face. She was defeated, all hope gone.

'In the sea, the Forth – washed up near South Queensferry. I'm sorry to ask, but could you come?'

'But she could swim!'

'Could she?'

'Like a fish. She loved the water, loved the seaside.' Both her hands now covered her face, her bony shoulders heaving with a series of dry sobs. When Alice came and sat next to her, intending to comfort her, the woman edged along the sofa as if to escape the possibility of human touch.

'Do you need me to come right now?' she asked, her face still hidden.

'Yes. If at all possible.'

A minute passed, the silence in the room broken only by the ticking of a grandfather clock which sounded to both policewomen abnormally loud, insistent and intrusive. Mrs Stimms remained motionless. Eventually, she stood up and drifted towards the window, gazing out at her view of the sea as if her visitors were no longer there.

'Mrs Stimms . . .' Alice began. The woman did not respond.

'Mrs Stimms.'

'I'll come,' she replied, turning round to face them. 'I want to see her – and this'll be my last chance, won't it? You know, I missed her when she was away, every day, every *single* day. You do, don't you, anyone would . . .

miss their child, I mean. However old they are . . . They are always your child, aren't they? Always part of you. You never stop worrying about them. Whatever happens, whatever anyone says, whatever they've done, they're always yours. My husband's away, off on business. I'll go and get my coat. Don't worry, officers, I'll manage on my own, I'm sure I will.'

‘Hello,’ Dr Cash said coldly, her voice leaving her caller in no doubt that the interruption was not appreciated. Hands-free sets, the pathologist had long ago concluded, were instruments of the devil, extending the working day unnaturally and wrecking, all too often, one of her few pleasures in life: catching ‘The Archers’ on the car radio on the drive home from the mortuary. And here, on Sir Harry Lauder Road, she was only minutes away from her own house, her own supper. Two post-mortems and a couple of lectures to the third years had taken their toll, not to mention the interviews for a new technician.

‘You'll get my written report in a couple of weeks as usual, Inspector,’ she added, unasked, recognising the voice and knowing exactly what the call would be about.

‘I know,’ Alice replied, ‘DC Cairns passed on the message. But I'd like to ask you a few questions now, nonetheless.’

‘It's late. I gave DC Cairns a verbal report . . .’

‘Yes, I know, but I'd still like to talk to you.’

Tired, but certain from past experience that her will was not the one that would prevail, the pathologist was already removing the barley sugar from her mouth, and, finding nowhere to store it other than on the dashboard, she tutted to herself at the thought of the sticky mess that she would have to clear up after supper. A second later, her fingers stuck to the volume dial on the radio as she extinguished Ruth Archer's nasal whine.

'Bugger!' she murmured.

'I only need your principal findings, Helen. Just an outline, simply so that we know whether we're dealing with a murder or not. The cause of death, you know . . .'

'Did that gabby youngster not pass them on to you, then?'

'I've not spoken to her yet. I'd like to hear them from you.'

'Fine, fine, fine,' said the doctor irritably, then beginning to intone as if speaking into her Dictaphone:

'She had an occipital fracture, stellar, radiating from the point of impact on her skull with a coup contusion on her brain, at the back, and a pronounced contra coup over the brain surface. There was shearing of the brain surface, at the front, over the orbital plates, plus an orbital blowout contra coup fracture resulting in a black eye . . .'

'All caused by what? A blow to the head?'

'Unlikely to be a blow – much more likely by a fall backwards. She had abrasions over both cheekbones, the points of both elbows and grazes to the back of her hands and all of her knuckles.'

'What's likely to have caused them?'

'One moment, safety first, I need to concentrate to get through this roundabout onto Portobello Road.' She hesitated for a few seconds, before resuming: 'Right. In a fall, if she went backwards, say, she'd put out her arms to save herself, catch her elbows, then her knuckles – hit them on the ground.'

'She didn't drown, then.'

'No, she didn't. She had features consistent with immersion but not drowning. Her lungs were normal, normal size, normal weight. No signs of air trapping, no froth in the trachea or the bronchi.'

'So, she was dead before she hit the water, so to speak.'

'I think so, yes. It would also explain why she didn't get out, assuming she could swim or whatever. I think the grazing on her face and the back of her hands may have occurred while she was drifting about in shallow water. It's all a bit of a mixture, hard to tell.'

'She could swim. The mother told us that. Before, when Dr McCrae saw her in South Queensferry, he reckoned she hadn't been in the water very long. Nothing today's made you think otherwise about that, has it?'

'Not a thing. I think he was spot on. The washerwoman wrinkles and thickening weren't that extensive, just her fingers and toes. And she had minor gooseflesh only. There must have been air trapping in her clothes to keep her near the surface.'

'So, how long d'you think she'd been in it?'

'My best estimate . . . twenty-four hours, possibly less than twenty-four hours.'

'What? I didn't hear what you said.'

'I'm losing my voice . . . up to twenty-four hours.'

'And the head injury – when would that have been sustained?'

'Judging from the look of it, of everything, not long before she went in the water. I don't think she'd been lying about the place beforehand for long, if that's what you mean. There is lividity on her now but that's from her spell with us, in the mortuary. In the water she's moving, being moved, rolled about. There was some but not much when she was seen earlier. I checked with Dr McCrae and the photos to be sure.'

'So, we're still looking for a murderer.'

'Yes, more likely than not. After all, someone probably put her in the water. Now, if you don't mind, I'm exhausted. 'Front Row' will be on soon, and I intend to hear the interview with Hilary Mantel.'

'Was there anything else?'

'Yes. I don't know how significant it is to you, but she was pregnant. That's it.'

'How far gone?'

'Not far.'

'What does that mean?'

'Oh, for Heaven's sake . . . I can't remember, offhand. Not far, like I said. Ten, twelve . . . not more than fourteen weeks. It'll all be in the report. You said you only needed an outline . . .'

'Had she been drinking? Maybe she fell in, overbalanced?'

'God knows. I certainly intend to start doing so, if you'd just let me off the phone. I'll give you an alcohol-level tomorrow. Now, my working day is over, Inspector, even if yours is not. That's me at my own front door.'

7

Four hours later, in her own flat in Broughton Place, Alice Rice pulled the curtains and put on a CD of Pergolesi's 'Stabat Mater'. She knew every note of it, could anticipate the very moment when the soloists would draw breath and, despite such familiarity, was still moved by it. Eleven had not yet struck, so there was time for a couple of her favourite tracks, a glass or two of wine and a quick bath. All three in combination, if the speakers in the bathroom decided to behave.

Sitting in an armchair and uncorking the bottle, she realised that her choice of music had been unthinkingly apposite, and was suddenly impatient for the alcohol to do its job, help blur her memories of the day, numb her feelings. The momentary expression of agony that she had seen on Mrs Stimms' face seemed to have imprinted itself on her mind. Each time such news had to be broken the reaction of the bereaved was subtly different, but it was always heart-rending, whether they wailed, sobbed, became silent, angry or whatever. And the task was getting no easier. Bringing about – no, announcing, then witnessing, the collapse of other people's worlds drained the soul. Drained her soul. And what was there to replenish it? Quill, her dog, as if in sympathy with her, came and sat beside her, allowing her to cradle his head between her hands and finger his soft ears, before, tired of the attention, he wandered off in search of his favourite toy.

Over the past year, since Ian's death, she had slowly become accustomed once more to living alone. In fact, to her own surprise and, to some extent, shame, she had almost begun to enjoy it. Quill, though effectively shared with a neighbour, helped of course. Thanks to him, one warm, living, exacting life was usually present, needed her, and demanded that attention be lavished upon it. And that was a small price to pay, she had long ago decided, for unconditional love, together with an unwavering contentment in her presence. Once or twice, in idle moments, she had attempted to analyse the attractions of the solitary state, pin down as precisely as she was able what it was about it that she now enjoyed. It was not the total selfishness it allowed, even positively engendered, although that was undeniably part of it. Nor was it the simple maintenance of order, although that had its charms, too. It was, she had finally decided, the quiet; the lack of any need to speak to, or listen to, or react in any way to the presence of another. Only her love for Ian, and his for her, had outweighed that benefit. Her love for him and his particularities, peculiarities even.

Her mother, usually intuitive to an almost supernatural extent, too often gave in to the need to warn her about this perceived weakness, explaining that it might grow, make her unfit for life with another, make her 'spinsterish', in a word. Originally, the very sound of that archaic adjective, undoubtedly pejorative in her mother's mouth, had annoyed her. Later, she had consciously 'reclaimed' it. Because she was one, as properly defined, and now unapologetically so. The unmarried, partnerless state required independence, self-sufficiency, and self-reliance, and they were good qualities, sterling qualities. If others considered that, in a woman's case, they carried with them a connotation of coldness, unnaturalness and self-ishness, so be it. If they considered the absence of the need, the desire, to nurture others, unwomanly and unattractive, let them. She had no such need, no such desire, at least not in the abstract. For her it was always directed at a concrete reality, at the person who had evoked it in the first place. Others existed, programmed differently, who searched – wanting, needing, to care for the world or some imaginary creature in it. But not her, not any longer.

Her friends, she knew, were mystified, if not exasperated, by the withdrawal that they perceived in her. Some, kindly intentioned, sought to 'save her from herself' as one of them had unwisely put it in her hearing. Introductions had been arranged and engineered. Meetings had happened, apparently spontaneously, but with one or other of the concerned friends, coincidentally, always around. Once, provoked beyond endurance by a particularly clod-hopping and manipulative attempt she had snapped, exclaiming that she was quite capable of finding a man herself if she wanted. This had been taken as proof positive of her loneliness by the more soft-headed amongst the soft-hearted matchmakers. A few let her be, and it was their company she sought.

Once immersed in the warm water, her cordless house phone and her glass of white wine by the bath, her mind, involuntarily, drifted off, returning to the anguished countenance of Mrs Stimms, tears glistening on the woman's cheeks. Determined to banish the image, she turned the music off and dialled 1571. A calm female voice informed her that she had two messages. The first, though ostensibly dull and dry in content, brought a smile to her lips. It was her solicitor informing her that missives had now been concluded and that everything was on course for the date of entry for the end of next week. Assuming the bank transaction went through, the cottage in Kinrossshire would then be hers, together with its pond and three acres of ground. At this news, she picked up her wine glass and took a long drink. That glorious prospect would sustain her throughout this investigation and beyond, made her feel wide awake here and now, alive, and, suddenly, delighted to be so.

The second call dampened slightly her newly lifted spirits, although it had been prompted by a phone call she had made herself a couple of weeks earlier. A hesitant male voice said, 'Alice? This is Father Vincent – from Kinross, Ian's friend. You got in touch, suggesting a meeting one evening next week? How about Friday or Saturday? I'm free both nights from seven o' clock onwards. You could come here for a drink, if that suits you. Otherwise we could go to the Kirklands Hotel, the Green or somewhere? Let me know what suits you – and I do hope this is your phone!'

She lay back and took another sip. Contacting the man had seemed a good idea at the time, but already she was having doubts. While it was true that she knew nobody in the Kinross-shire area, was he a good place to start? A Catholic priest about whom she knew next to nothing, except that he was a bit of a wine buff, loved his cat and should, Ian had always said, never be underestimated. What, she wondered, if anything, did he know about her? But it was too late, she decided, to worry about such things. Tomorrow would be another early start. And already her mind was turning to what must be said at the morning meeting, what new lines of enquiry they should begin to follow, and who should do what.

'So, that's what we've got so far? Nothing else new?' Alice continued, looking round her squad the next morning. Her eyes caught those of Elaine Bell. The DCI was by the door at the back of the room, leaning against the wall, having slipped in after everyone else as the briefing was coming to close. The others were unaware of her presence.

'I've got the results from the phone check,' DC Cairns said in a thick voice, another spoonful of cereal hovering at her mouth. 'Most of them were to her work, oddly enough. The phone was cheap, fairly new, and she didn't have a single app. Stone-age! The very last call she made was to a Hamish Evans. That number came up few times. I've tracked his address down to Raeburn Place in Stockbridge. Will I check him out?'

'Yes, well done,' Alice replied, looking round at the five others present, inviting their contributions, then adding, 'I'll come with you.'

'The force systems, including the intelligence check that we ran on the flat, produced nothing. No hits. None of the neighbours, including Miss Anderson, heard or saw anything either. Two are away. One's probably not back for a couple of days, and the other's been away somewhere in France for over a week, not due to return until the beginning of next week or so.'

The speaker was DS Ranald Sharpe, a small, bandy-legged Renfrewshire man seconded from Gayfield Square, who had, Alice knew, applied for the post she had secured. On sight they had disliked each other, and the difference in their respective accents further alienated them from each other. Sharpe identified hers with his view of Edinburgh and its faults: middle-classness, ostensible respectability, a missing heart. She equated his with her perception of Glasgow's worst traits: loudness, an aggressive couthiness and shallow, emotional lability.

'Anything on the CCTV?' she asked him.

'Nothing useful has shown up so far, not for the period we're working on.'

'Speak to the Forth Ports Authority, would you? They're based near Rosyth, Port of Rosyth, near the Consortium's headquarters. Or maybe the Leith harbour master? Thinking about it, he might be a better bet, he might be the man for the job. See if any of them can help at all in pinpointing where she was put in the water. After all, we know where she ended up and, roughly, how long she was in there for. Dr McCrae estimated twenty-four hours at the very most, Helen Cash agreed. See what, if anything, they can give us, eh?'

'Right. Boss.'

From his mouth, to her ears at least, the epithet had a mocking ring.

'I spoke to Farrar from the *Evening News*,' DC Trish Rennie chipped in, a half-eaten apple in her hand. 'Gave him a few titbits, like you said. They're going to do a wee piece, and they'll include the usual stuff about "anyone with any information. Blah, blah".'

'Good. Pick up any post from her flat, OK, and get the rest intercepted and sent straight here, please. Check the flat, though, for the first few days – sometimes there's a bit of a delay with the system. At the same time you could see if that neighbour, holidaying in France, is back.'

'Don't bother about that today. She's not,' DS Sharpe said, arms crossed. 'I got her house number from Mrs Anderson, rang it this morning and there was no answer.'

'Nothing to be lost in checking it again anyway, Trish,' Alice replied, rising from the desk she had been sitting on, signalling that they should all be on their way, make a start. The annoying little git, countermanding her orders like that.

'One other thing,' DS Sharpe said, also getting to his feet and finding himself, to his surprise, looking up at her, 'I've got the fingerprint results. Apart from the deceased they found the prints of three other individuals. Unfortunately, none of them are on the database.'

'That was quick,' Alice said, taken aback, 'I thought we'd have a couple more days to wait, at least. How on earth did you swing that?'

'I've got friends,' he said, winking at her, 'in high places an' all.'

'And the DNA results?'

'Not that high . . .'

The cleaner, a pale weasel of a man, answered the door at the flat in Raeburn Place, Stockbridge. Instantly, Adele's rich tones floated out of the open door, filling the common stair. Reluctantly, he led the two policewomen into the hall, past his scuffed trainers on the doormat, and then, a little sheepishly, told them to wait while he went to turn the television off. The warm atmosphere inside was scented by a trio of sweet, throat-catching scents: floor-polish, unwashed feet and the fumes given off by an overheated hoover shortly before the motor fails.

'I wasn't watching it or anything,' he remarked, unnecessarily, on his return.

'We're looking for Mr Evans, Hamish Evans,' Alice said.

'Aren't we all!' he replied, looking discontented, 'Join the club! As usual, he's not left my money out for me. He remembers without fail to buy the cleaning stuff, but my money? Forget it!'

'When did you last see him?'

'I don't see him. Well, hardly ever. He leaves notes for me, telling me what to do, like. Lists. Didn't even bother to do that this time. And the place is a tip today. Drawers out, stuff all over the bedroom floor. I'm not supposed to tidy, just to clean. The boy needs someone here every day to pick things up, do his washing up. But I only come once a week and he leaves it all for me. The kitchen's not been touched, all his supper things, all his breakfast things left for me to deal with. He's an animal. He's a mink.'

'Is it unusually messy?'

'No – why?'

'So when did you last see him?'

'Sometime last month. He came back while I was still here.'

'Is something burning?' DC Cairns said, sniffing the air loudly.

'Shit!' the man exclaimed, turning on the spot and racing into the galley kitchen. He returned less than a minute later, a crumpled dishcloth over one thin shoulder.

'My breakfast sausage roll,' he said by way of explanation. 'Cinders.'

'Where does Mr Evans work?' Alice asked.

'At a solicitor's office in Howe Street – McPhees, I think it's called.'

He giggled, and when they did not join in, he added weakly, 'McPhees, get it! They're lawyers! I only just thought of that. He's not a solicitor or anything, he just helps out in the property shop, shows folk round, that kind of thing. He's not qualified.'

On the wall opposite them was a photograph of a young man, tanned and smiling, with a pair of skis over his shoulder.

'Is that him?' Alice asked.

'Hamish?'

'Yes.'

'Aye.'

'Can we borrow it?'

'Help yourselves, you're the police, aren't youse?'

Noticing a thin stream of water working its way along the floor of the narrow hallway, DC Cairns tapped him on the shoulder and pointed to it.

'Oh God, that's all I need, that's the bath overflowing now!' he shouted, dashing towards the bathroom.

'Jesus!' he said, breathless on his return. 'I just had the tap on, cleaning it and everything. I didn't realise the plug was still in. You'll have to go, the pair of you, I can't do everything myself when you're around. I've a job to do.'

He raised his left foot, inspecting the sole through a hole in his grey sock and muttering crossly, 'Now I've got a skelf off the floorboards . . .'

'One final thing,' Alice said. 'Did he have a girlfriend?'

'Him?'

'Yes,' she said patiently, 'him.'

'Maybe, must have. I found a pair of panties recently and they weren't his. Far too small for that. Scanty, if you know what I mean.'

'Could you describe her?' DC Cairns asked, pushing her gold-rimmed spectacles up the bridge of her nose.

'Aye. A size 10. I never seen her, just her panties.'

The conversation between the police inspector and the manager of the property shop, a Mr Penny, was short and to the point. Hamish Evans had not turned up for work that week, although he had been expected from Tuesday onwards. Prior to that he had been in London for a week, seeing a sick relative, and the firm had sanctioned that absence. They had left phone messages for him three times, but had received no response. Looking affronted at the question, Mr Penny told them that he had no idea whether the lad had a girlfriend or not. He suggested that they speak instead to Lorna, the 'wee girl' in the front office. She, a trim, petite figure with a black bob and long, highly manicured nails, blushed continuously as she spoke, confiding that he did have a girlfriend, a new one. One called Mandy.

—

'It's him,' DC Cairns said gleefully as soon as they were both back in the car. 'It all makes sense, give or take. He'd have time to get back from London, have a lover's tiff – maybe they even had the tiff on the phone.'

'Don't you think that's a bit premature?' Alice answered, checking her mirror before joining the traffic, and signalling to turn left onto George Street.

'Well, he is missing, isn't he? Why else would he go missing? He seems respectable, has a cleaner, works in a property shop, he's not exactly a vagrant. And why didn't he report her as missing? She was missing, after all, she didn't turn up for work.'

'Maybe he didn't know, maybe they weren't due to meet. This was a new relationship. Maybe they hadn't arranged anything until the weekend or something.'

'But she wouldn't be answering her phone either.

They'd be bound to be phoning each other, surely! Texting, Facebooking or whatever. Tweeting even. He'd leave messages. No, he's done a bunk . . .'

'But she'd no apps, no computer, remember? Maybe they'd had a row?'

'Exactly!'

As Alice tried to remember what new, young love was like, the excitable constable continued talking, arguing with herself as well as her superior, picturing the whole thing and concluding, satisfied, 'It's always their nearest and dearest, isn't it? That's the rule.'

'You get out here. Find out,' Alice said, turning the car into the pound at St Leonard's Street, coming to a halt but keeping the engine running 'whether he caught a flight back from London. Get the time of all the evening flights. We know they spoke on Monday night. Speak to our people at Edinburgh Airport, get them to check BA, easyJet, Flybe, Virgin . . . whoever they are, all the airlines who run flights between London and Edinburgh, the whole lot. Better check the trains too, he might have used them for all we know. Oh, and check if he had a car, and if he did, find it. Make sure everyone's on the lookout for it.'

'Where are you going?' the constable asked, keeping a hand on the open door, awaiting an answer.

'Me? I'm off to see Irene and find out a bit more about our deceased, Miranda – Mandy Stimms. I've got no picture of her, of her character, what she was like, what to expect. At the moment, all we have is a dead, twenty-one-year-old, pregnant lesbian with a boyfriend, who worked in a Co-op shop and liked red Leicester cheese. Oh, and who probably wore size 10 underwear and had a cat.'

'Seventeen. She was actually seventeen.'

'What makes you think that? That's not what the manager said. He told us that she was twenty-one.'

'Yes, but her mother says that she's seventeen and she ought to know. The girl probably lied about her age because of the minimum wage thing. Who can blame her? They get a pittance, it's like slave labour . . .'

'That's possible. He said that she hadn't handed in her birth certificate, maybe that was why she didn't.'

'Who is Irene?'

'Her best friend in the Co-op, the one the manager mentioned.'

———

To the inspector's surprise Irene was not a fellow teenager, someone with whom Miranda Stimms could laugh and giggle, go clubbing and compare notes about boyfriends, Instagram, Primark and TK Maxx. Instead, she could have been the girl's granny, or possibly even her great-granny. She had a benign, matriarchal aura about her, and radiated a quiet but unmistakable authority. In appearance, she resembled an elderly chimpanzee, with small, deep-set brown eyes, an oddly pronounced upper jaw with a faint black moustache and a receding chin. Due to her pigeon-toes, she waddled when she walked, elbowing herself from side to side as if setting out on a long trek.

'I knew you were coming,' she said, on meeting Alice, 'Mr Wilson told me about Mandy. He says we're to use his office. I'm to take my lunch break in there.'

Once she was settled in her seat, her meal of an egg roll and a flask of soup in front of her, she looked at the policewoman as if to let her know that the interview could now start.

'Could you tell me a bit about Miranda, what she was like, and so on?'

'I could,' she said, taking her time, removing the aluminium foil from around her roll. 'A great lassie, I thought. She was a real worker, unlike some of them they take on, she never stopped. When she first came and we were unloading bakery goods together, I had to tell her to slow down. "Slow down, hen!" I says, "for pity's sake!" You have to take your time, you see, otherwise you'll not manage the whole shift, you'll get tired out too soon. Others'll get sacked, an' all. I got her the job in the first place.' She paused.

'How did you meet her?'

'Em . . .' she hesitated, thinking, 'at the bus stop. The bus was late, we got talking. I was going to my work, told her they were looking for staff. She jumped at it. Now, let me get a bite, eh?'

After she had swallowed a couple of mouthfuls and dabbed the ends of her lips carefully with a paper hankie, she nodded, signalling her readiness to continue.

'Did she make other friends in the shop, among the younger ones?'

'Not really. She was funny that way. It's hard to describe. I never met anyone like her, like her in that way, before. I think a lot of the young ones scared her.' She took another bite. Flour from the roll cascaded onto the surface of the desk, then was efficiently wiped up by her with another hankie.

'Did they bully her or something?'

'No, I don't think so. It's just she wasn't like them. Sometimes I don't think she understood what they were on about. You know about the TV programmes and suchlike. That Facebook, YouTube, computer dating, that texting they all do all the time, chat-rooms or whatever they're called. I don't have a clue myself, half the time.'

'Was she slow – I mean, mentally slow?'

'No. She learnt everything in the job easily, really quickly. You only had to tell her once where things were supposed to go, where to put things. She picked up the till, just like that. Mr Wilson thought she was the bee's knees.'

'Old-fashioned, then?'

'Yes,' she said, starting to unscrew the stopper of her flask, 'that's what Jocky, my man, said when she came for her tea. He said she was more like us, you understand – out of touch, past it, you might say.'

'Did she have a boyfriend?' Alice asked. Unconsciously, her eyes were now fixed on the woman's tomato soup as it steamed in the plastic cup of the flask.

'You want some, hen?' she asked. 'I could see if I can get another cup. There'll be some where we have our tea-break.'

'No, but thanks. I'll get my lunch later, back at the station.'

'Be sure you do, then. A boyfriend? Yes, she did. She was that excited, told me all about him, couldn't stop herself from talking about him. Fell for him, like that . . . like a duck to water. I seen him, once, just the once, nice-looking laddie and all, well-dressed. She loved him to bits. Besotted, she was.'

'What was his name?'

'I cannae mind,' she replied, then, smiling, obviously pleased at her recall, she corrected herself, 'Aye, I can. Sammy. No, silly, silly me – Hamish – that was it. A plain name, Scottish. That's it. I thought at the time, a good old-fashioned name, just like my man's. Sammy was the first one. But Hamish took her off Sammy.'

'Sorry, who was Sammy? What's his full name?'

'Sam Inglis. Just after she started at the shop he was after her. He's a big, fat fellow. I don't like him. He's after them all, all the young ones, the lassies, every time a new one comes. I reckon he's only got one thing on his mind. He's always making jokes, filthy ones, but they don't make me laugh. Miranda wasn't like that – she was . . . proper. Yes, that's how I'd describe her, proper. He didn't like it when she threw him over, but he had it coming. Hamish was much more her style.'

'Finally, and it's an odd question to ask, I appreciate, but . . . as far as you know, she wasn't a lesbian?'

'A what?'

'A lesbian?'

'Och, away with you!' the woman said, startled at the very suggestion. 'I've just been telling you about her boyfriend, about Hamish, have I not? Whatever gave you that idea? She was proper, old-fashioned, I told you. Not like that, not at all.'

He sat outside the house in his Mazda, unwilling, despite the cold, to go in. Huge raindrops hammered on the roof, pouring down the windscreen in a never-ending flood and blurring the headlights of the oncoming cars. A light was still on in the kitchen and through the rivulets he could just make out a figure, seated, slumped forward against the window. It must be her. His eyes felt hot and gritty, an ache behind them somewhere deep inside his brain, and he rubbed them in the vain hope that it would ease. He ought, he knew, to go in and try and comfort her, but he

could not face it. He no longer had the energy. The inef-
fable weight, the blackness of her despair would pull him
under too, disorientate him, drown him, and he had to
be strong. He had to be strong enough for both of them,
Lambie and him, strong enough for everyone. Otherwise
they would never get back up, up to the surface, back into
the light and the air.

She would have got the message by now, but there had
not been space enough on the answering machine to say
what he needed to say, what she needed to hear. Why
hadn't she been at home? Where on earth had she been?
Panicking as always at the very sound of the strange
recorded voice, he had had to gabble away like a madman,
'Lambie, it's me. She wasn't there, not at that school. The
Ardtean one, from my list. But don't you worry about a
thing, I've another to try tomorrow, OK? Now I've got to
go. I'm off to Aberdeen for a meeting. See you tonight,
late, maybe very late; I've got to see a few of our people
on the way down, one in Brechin, one in Kelty . . .'

That had been it, all that there was room for. But
he knew what its effect would have been, that amongst
all the tears and snuffles, there would be wailing, then
body-racking, soul-tearing sobbing. And more. Like the
last time. And the time before that. But, by the look of
her, she had had a support this time, one offering sweet,
silent succour, one with many names in both English and
Gaelic. In his absence that was the one, the only one,
which could take his place.

As he opened the kitchen door, she did not stir. Her
head was down, resting on the table top. Seeing her there,
mouth open, face distorted, flattened against the wood,
he had a sudden terrible thought. She'd done it, this
time she'd actually done it. She had killed herself. But

as he ran towards her, crying out her name in his terror, he caught sight of the half-empty whisky bottle by her head and felt, first relief, and then waves of hot, scalding shame. Because, seeing the Famous Grouse label he had been pleased for a second, knowing it would have done the trick, done the job for him. Gently, taking care not to wake her, he fetched the rug from the chest, placed it over her and then, exhausted after fourteen hours on the move, went up the steep stairs to his bed. She was past comforting by him.

8

Hamish Evans' father, Christopher, was the sole partner in a legal firm specialising in criminal defence work, with an office in Stafford Street. A brass plate on the door read 'McBryde and Evans' and blue and white legal-aid stickers adorned every window. No McBryde had ever been involved in any capacity in the business, but Mr Evans had added the name, his Granny's surname, as he believed it had a streetwise ring to it, and that it made the firm sound older and more established. It gave a bit of Scots back-up to the Welsh, too, no bad thing in these times. His secretary, or slave (as, unknown to him, she introduced herself) was off at a dental appointment that morning. When Alice and DC Cairns reached the man's premises, he was already late for court, had his black gown over one arm of his close-fitting, shiny grey suit and was searching in a filing cabinet.

'I'm in a rush, my taxi's outside, waiting for me,' he said plaintively, head down, elbow deep in the drawer, pulling out each identical blue file, sighing, then dropping it back in the cabinet.

'We'll be as quick as we can,' Alice said. They were going to have their talk.

'Fire away,' he replied, pulling a couple of files out, double-checking the names and murmuring to himself, 'Thompson, Adam . . . Thompson, Colin . . . we've too many of those sodding Thompsons!'

'When did you last see or speak to your son, Hamish?'

'Eh . . .' he said, eyes glued on the contents of another blue file, sweat now shining on his brow. 'Eh . . . we spoke a couple of days ago.'

The phone rang but he ignored it, waiting for the reassuring click of the machine cutting in. Tutting loudly to emphasize the inconvenience of their demands, he put the file back and began rifling through the rest, pulling a few out and dropping them on the floor in his frustration, to make his point. His head, like a child's, was disproportionately large for his little body.

'Was it when he was still in London?'

'Why are you asking all of this, Inspector? He's alright, isn't he?'

For a second he stopped his feverish activity and, file in hand, looked up, giving them his full attention.

'As far as we know he is. We're simply trying to trace him,' Alice said.

'Why? He's not in trouble, is he?' the distrustful, raisin eyes embedded in his red face suddenly narrowed, as if he was now on duty, protecting a client.

'Because . . . he may have information that would be helpful to us.'

'I get it. He's witnessed something, eh? You just need his help?'

'Yes, we do need his help.' She smiled at him.

'OK. It's my job, eh? My line of work. It makes you suspicious – no, makes me suspicious – whatever. You lot are always suspicious, eh? He was in the airport, actually. He was killing time at Heathrow, otherwise he'd not have phoned. His mother's always asking him to call but . . . well, he's a young man, got better things to do with his time than call his mother. All he could think about was seeing his girlfriend, Miranda. He seemed agitated about her.'

'Do you know if he caught the flight?'

'No. But he will have, he was in the airport, had work the next day. He's bound to have. Why on earth wouldn't he have? You see, like me, he loves his work. He's earning a bomb, too, compared to most of his school pals. Half of them can only find work as hod-carriers or waitresses.'

'Why was he agitated about Miranda?'

'No idea. I did ask but . . . he wasn't for telling. Just clammed up. I expect that they'd fallen out over something, not yet made it up. He was certainly cross about something. You'll need to ask him.'

As he was speaking, he was busily leafing through another of the blue files, licking his finger every so often for maximum speed. The sound of a horn hooting a couple of times made him look up again momentarily, hissing 'Shit!' through his teeth as he did so.

'He didn't show up at his work,' DC Cairns said, 'we checked it out yesterday.'

'That's my taxi. Maybe he's not well or something.'

'Maybe. He wasn't at home though,' Alice said.

'He's a young man! Staying with a friend? Being looked after by a friend? Perhaps, God forbid, taking a sickie?' Evans replied, closing the file and tucking it under his arm. Below his raffish, pencil-thin moustache, a relieved smile was taking shape. It transformed his features, making it almost impossible not to like him. Members of the jury often fell under its spell, particularly the older female ones. Addressing them, in full flight, he resembled a diminutive Italian tenor striding about the stage, gesticulating excitedly, quite carried away by his own performance. The beauty of his voice, whatever gruel-thin defence he was peddling, guaranteed him a good hearing. Listening to it, one of them had once remarked, was like having warm chocolate poured in your ear.

'He's not answering his phone,' Alice persevered.

'Switched off? Broken? Run out of money? Lost it? Look, I don't know. I'm sorry not to be more help, I really am . . . but I'm rushing. You can see I'm rushing. I'm supposed to be seeing a client for a plea,' he looked at his watch, '. . . ten minutes ago. You lot know what it's like, what appearing in court's like. He's a big boy, my son, I don't worry about him any more. Now, forgive me, ladies, but I must be off!'

As they were walking across the road to their car, Christopher Evans' black cab sped past them on its way to the Sheriff Court in Chambers Street. Catching sight of them, he waved cheerily.

'Why didn't you mention Miranda Stimms' death to him?' DC Cairns asked. She jinked suddenly off the pavement to avoid a woman pushing an old man in a wheelchair, the lead of a poodle attached to it stretched taut, ready to trip up the unwary.

'Because,' Alice paused, 'because . . . oh, I don't know. It's been in the papers by now. I didn't feel I had to tell him. He might not even have known her, personally, I mean. Hamish Evans is only a suspect. And that's as much as anything else because we can't find him. And, I suppose, because he was her boyfriend. We need to eliminate him as a suspect. To do that we need Evans Senior's full co-operation. It's always a fine balance, what to say, what not to say. I didn't want him immediately phoning the boy, tipping him off. Not if he did it.'

At informal meetings held in St John's House, Ailsa Whyte had decreed that biscuits were allowed, and chocolate ones at that. Cake, however, would be a step too far. Before the others had even arrived in the designated meeting room of the social work department, she had helped herself to one, a 'Rocky', and she was considering whether to have seconds, this time in the form of a triangle of shortbread. Her social work colleague, Eileen Polson, wandered in, looking red-nosed and even more glaikit than usual, Ailsa thought. With the beginnings of a cold, from her appearance, or something worse, flu or pneumonia even. She was carrying the tray with the teapot, hot water and coffee flask on it, and seemed to be struggling under the weight. These skinny types had no reserves, Mrs Whyte decided, no proper immunity, and when they were infected, as she plainly was, they dwindled away to nothing, took weeks to recover. And why in the name of the little green man did they come to work in such a state, jam-packed with viruses? Did they imagine that they were irreplaceable or something? The selfishness of it took your breath away.

'Are you alright?' Ailsa asked, in a concerned tone, smiling kindly at her colleague, and hoping that she would not take a seat anywhere close by.

'Soldiering on,' Ms Polson replied, through her blocked sinuses, setting down her burden with a clunk and opting for the chair beside Doug Brunton, the bearded police sergeant from Gayfield. He took one look at her and then shuffled his chair sideways, as if to afford her extra room. Frank Tyler, the school psychologist, glanced up at her, settling on little more than a wave of his pen by way of greeting. Unbeknown to her, it was no longer a pen but a baton gripped between his long fingers, his mind busy elsewhere, conducting the introduction to 'Zadok the Priest'.

'Well, let's get going,' Ailsa Whyte said, looking round the table at the five seated there, deliberately including and involving them before continuing. 'We're here, as you all know, to discuss Susie's progress, since she was found in Madeira Street four days ago. Susie's given name is currently unknown to us as she does not speak, for whatever reason. Now, has anyone got anything to share?'

A seemingly endless thirty seconds passed without anybody volunteering a comment. A look of pained disappointment now crossed Mrs Whyte's features as she exercised her right as chair to extract contributions from the others.

'Frank,' she said brightly, gazing at him as if he might have something momentous to impart, 'why don't you kick off for us. You've met Susie, haven't you? What's your thinking at this moment in time?' With his cloud of auburn hair and long, aquiline nose, he had the looks, she had long ago decided, of a pre-Raphaelite angel.

'Well,' he began, laying down his pen and dragging himself away from the, as yet incomplete, organ solo playing in his mind, 'I have seen her, yes, but only for five minutes, to see if we'd be a suitable school for her. I'll need to do a proper assessment. At the moment, I don't know what's wrong with her. Plainly, she has communication issues, but I'm sure she understands a certain amount. Karen, our speech therapist, has been seeing her and she's quite optimistic, all in all. I'll need to draw up a Co-ordinated Support Plan if she's staying with us, unless you're going to see to that, Laura?'

'Laura?' Mrs Whyte interjected unnecessarily, swatting an impertinent fly away from her mouth.

'No problem, I'll attend to that,' the head teacher replied, raising her eyes for a second from her tablet and watching, entranced, as the fly redoubled its efforts to land on the senior social worker's lips.

'Hold on, hold on,' Ailsa Whyte said, shaking her head. 'Are we not getting ahead of ourselves? We don't even know where she's from yet. Can we open a support plan?'

'Right enough, Ailsa, good thinking. No, we can't. Anyway, she probably has one somewhere already. So, other than fixing up the assessment, I'm not sure there's anything else much I can add at this juncture, to be honest,' the man said. And as if his contribution was complete, he tucked his pen into the breast pocket of his plaid shirt.

'Any developments in trying to find out who she is?' Mrs Whyte demanded, ignoring his silent, but eloquent withdrawal, her arms now flailing around her face in her attempt to ward off the bluebottle.

'No. I've e-mailed all the schools to see if they have any absentees matching her description, but half of them haven't got back to me yet. If that doesn't work I'm going to try the private schools.'

'Fine. Good. Excellent,' Mrs Whyte replied, at last managing to squash her tormentor with a corner of her file, and favouring the psychologist with one of her rare smiles. 'That leads us nicely back to you, Laura . . .'

'Susie, as I believe we've all agreed to call her,' the head teacher began, glancing round at the group as if seeking their assent again, 'is settling in quite nicely. She's not said anything yet, or used any of Karen's boards or anything, but we're quite happy with her progress, all things considered. As we don't know her age we've put her in, at present, with the S 4's, but that may be subject to review. At the moment we're concentrating on one-to-one work. We've only had one episode of challenging behaviour when she pushed somebody against a wall. She didn't hurt them, but she might have done. We have only one issue with her – she won't eat. We've tried everything we can but, to be honest, we've failed.'

'OK, thank you for that, Laura. Now, Jane?' Ailsa Whyte said, nodding at the woman next to her, an emergency foster parent, to coax her into speaking. Eventually, in the ensuing silence, she had to repeat her invitation to speak: 'Jane?'

In response to the forceful prompt, Jane Caterall, a large woman with both arms crossed over her massive bosom, looked up and began to talk in a low, gravelly rumble. 'It's early days, obviously, but she's getting on alright with us at home. Knows her way about, she'll sit with Bill 'n' me and watch the TV and that. Loves the TV, particularly the cartoons. She's sleeping fine, too fine, almost. It takes a deal to get her up in the morning. But she'll not eat. We've tried everything, vegetarian, pizzas, I've even made soups, but she'll take almost nothing. She cries a lot. I'm worried about her.'

'Have you got her to say anything, to communicate with either of you in any meaningful way?' Ailsa Whyte asked, watching out of the side of her eye as her sickly subordinate picked up a piece of shortbread with her germ-covered fingers, then replaced it. She made a mental note to steer clear of the shortbread. In fact, it should be in the bin with the lot, the second the meeting was over.

'No. I mean she'll point and that, if she wants something. Or, sometimes, just sometimes, mind, she'll grunt, sort of moan. I don't know if she can speak. Her understanding seems OK, that's not really a problem. I let her play on the computer after tea sometimes, to cheer her up, she likes that fine. Games and everything, she'd play them all night. Loves her games. TV, too, she watches everything with a big smile on her face.'

'Sergeant Brunton, any progress at your end of things?'

The policeman stopped doodling toadstools on his papers. Taking his time, he returned the sheets to their proper sequence. When finally he spoke, everyone was listening hard, expecting him to have something significant to contribute.

'No,'fraid not. There have been no missing person reports, which I would not have believed. I suppose her parents may not speak English or something, but you'd think, wouldn't you, that someone would be looking for her – for a child. You'd expect someone to get in touch. The descriptions we've given out in the press and so on haven't worked. Nor have the door-to-doors which we carried out. No one's come about the posters either. Honestly, you'd think that she'd fallen off the moon.'

'Very good,' Mrs Whyte said, adding, 'you'll let us know if there are any developments?'

'Of course,' he replied huffily, annoyed that she thought he needed to be asked.

'Laura,' she said, pausing theatrically to allow Ms Polson to sneeze, 'I should have asked, are we at the stage of speaking to the school doctor? About Susie's eating, I mean?'

'To be honest, I did think about it. She's such a skinny wee thing, there's nothing of her . . . she's all wrists and legs. I'm worried about anorexia. She'll get weak Maybe she should go to one of the specialist units?'

'Is she drinking?'

'She is, yes.'

'I'll think about it,' Mrs Whyte said, collecting the tea cups and letting everyone know that the meeting was over, 'but we must be careful. She's bound to be unhappy, confused, depressed even. She'll likely be missing her home, her parents, her siblings. Her refusal may stem from all the changes she's undergone. Possibly, by refusing to eat she's regaining control over the situation – in her own mind, to her own satisfaction. If we refer her elsewhere, say, to a specialist unit in another region, it may compound the problem, lengthen it. It would be worse yet, if she had to go to another school as well.'

'I'll speak to Dr Leven at the school, see what he says. His input should keep us right, eh?' Ms Polson murmured, rising from her chair and dabbing her nose with a damp paper hankie.

'I need to put down a marker,' Jane Caterall said, sounding anxious, but truculent. 'I'm worried, really worried about her. Bill 'n' me have no experience of this; I've had no training for this. It'll all need to be properly minuted, my concerns and everything.'

'Leave it with me, Janey,' Ailsa Whyte replied, her hand on the woman's shoulder. 'And don't you concern yourself – if a move has to be made, we'll make it. You'll only have her for a couple more days, max, until we find a more permanent placement. Anyway, if need be, to my certain knowledge there's an excellent specialist unit in Aberdeen, but, in the meanwhile, let's give it just a few more days, eh. Hopefully she'll settle down and start eating.'

'See if she'll eat if you leave her on her own,' Frank Tyler chipped in. 'Maybe it's people watching her she doesn't like – that's not unknown.'

'Bill 'n' me aren't "people",' Jane Caterall replied, affronted.

'No?' he answered, baffled by her response.

'Or, better still, Sergeant Brunton will finally find her parents, and discover for us what's been going on,' Mrs Whyte said smoothly, determined to defuse the situation, avoid any unnecessary misunderstandings.

'Her parents,' the policeman replied, unsmiling, 'may not be fit to look after her. From the way things look, that's what I'm guessing. After all, where the hell are they, if you'll excuse my French? Unfit parents, that's what I'm expecting here.'

The shabbiness of the dead girl's flat was even more apparent in the absence of the photographers, fingerprint officers and the other members of the forensic team carrying out their duties, chattering, bustling about and crowding its cold confines. Empty, all its inadequacies were revealed. Every single thing inside it had been skimped on, from the patched, stained curtains and carpets, to the ill-fitting kitchen units, ply-board doors and the mismatched plates. The very floors sloped and there was not a right angle in the place. Old cables, beaded with clots of dried paint, ran down every wall and seemed to have mated, producing yet more lumpy, paint-encrusted cables. In an earlier, more romantic age, the flat might have been described as a garret and the poverty of its pretty inhabitant would either have been overlooked or have enhanced her appeal. Now, it reeked of damp, deprivation and mice, and any charm it had ever possessed had died with its last tenant.

'I'll get the photo,' Alice said as they entered, key still in hand, 'you check the post.'

'Nothing here by the flap,' DC Cairns replied, glancing at the doormat. 'Anyway, I thought Trish was going to do that,' she added, looking about the dismal little place, preoccupied by the fate of the black and white cat. Having briefly pictured it licking its blood-spattered nose, the creature held a grim fascination for her.

'Others will have been in and out. They might have put it anywhere. I did ask Trish, but she probably won't have been here yet today. So there's nothing to be lost, we can always phone her and put her off. If she's already taken it, that's not a problem. The intercepts don't work immediately or like clockwork once they've begun. So just check, eh?'

'Jawohl,' the girl replied, setting off for the kitchen.

The photographs, when Alice held them side by side, were, clearly, of the same young man. The one in the girl's flat was more recent, more flattering than the image of the skier, so recently taken off his own wall; but they both were portraits of Hamish Evans. If she was in luck, she thought, his prints might even be on it.

'This is all there is,' Elizabeth Cairns said, returning to the hall and handing over a brown envelope with a window to her boss. 'It was the only one, someone must have picked it up and put it on the top of the TV.'

Through the window of the envelope could be seen a couple of names, 'A Tennant' and 'N Mills'. Inside was a letter headed 'Survivors Sanctuary, Windsor Gardens, Musselburgh', and dated three days earlier. It read as follows:

Dear Miranda,

I was sorry that you were unable to attend your appointment on Tuesday at 3 PM with me. As you know we discussed a course of twelve sessions. Unless you let me know otherwise, I'll assume that you are going to come to the next one which has been fixed for the same time on the next Tuesday of this month. Look forward to seeing you then.

Yours faithfully
Aileen Tennant.

'Did that moggy go to the Cat's Protection League or did the girl's mother take it, or what?' DC Cairns asked, reminded of it once more on spotting deep claw marks on the outside of the kitchen door.

'Neither,' Alice replied, stuffing the letter back into its envelope and putting it into her pocket.

'Neither?' the constable said, 'Christ! It wasn't put down, was it? What happened to it?'

Before Alice had a chance to reply, there was a knock on the front door and she pulled it open. Standing on the landing was a short, portly man with watery, grey-green eyes, holding a copy of the Yellow Pages in one of his plump white hands. His profuse hair looked unnaturally dark against his pale, dry skin and his sparse eyebrows and eyelashes suggested it might not have grown from his scalp but have come, ready styled, through the post, probably in a cardboard box together with adhesive and fitting instructions.

'Mandy?' he said in a warm tone, looking pleased to see her and holding the phone directory out for her to take.

'No, I'm sorry, she doesn't live here any more,' Alice replied. Her colleague peered over her shoulder, keen to get a glimpse of the caller, particularly as he did not seem to recognise the person he had, apparently, come to see.

'Where's she gone? She never told me she was leaving,' the man said, crestfallen, letting the directory drop against his side with an audible thump. His eyes rolled around erratically as if to emphasise his surprise.

'How do you know her?' Alice asked.

'Because I'm your landlord, dearie. I live in number five. The lease has months to run. I never thought she'd do this to me. Do a runner, and she's not paid this month's rent yet, just the first month. And you're not allowed – I never said you could get the tenancy. So you can sling your hook or I'll get my solicitors onto you. Right? Got that? You can't just take over like that, you've got to get my permission, which,' he added, wrinkling his pink nose in distaste, 'you'll not get. Not now, not with Mandy gone.'

'I'm not sure who you're mistaking me for, sir, but I'm Detective Inspector Rice from St Leonard's Street Police Station.'

'Bloody hell! What's Mandy done?' he exclaimed, stepping back, both eyes now swivelling rapidly from side to side.

'She's done nothing. I'm afraid she's dead.'

'Dead? Murdered? That baggage will have done it, then, and then buggered off,' he murmured to himself, chewing his lips and flapping the phone directory against his thigh. 'That other one. She'll have done it.'

'Who?'

'Her. Her,' he said impatiently, 'the one who moved in with her. The one I thought you was. The lesbian lady, you know. I didn't say anything at the time, I didn't know how long she'd be staying. The lease don't prohibit boyfriends, so I couldn't have got her out at the best of times. Tenants' rights and that. It's swung too far the wrong way with the Nats. It all made the hairs on my neck stand up.'

'How do you know she was . . . was a lesbian lady?'
DC Cairns interjected. Hearing a different voice, his eyes
widened and, for a fleeting moment, shifted onto her
before the irises rolled upwards once again, all but disappearing behind his eyelids.

'Where the hell did you pop up from?' he demanded,
sounding surprised.

'I'm DC Cairns, sir. I'm with the inspector.'

'Any bloody more of you?' he said, shaking his head
as if in disbelief at the numbers appearing from nowhere.

'No,' Alice replied, 'just the two of us. Forgive me for
asking, Mr . . .?

'Mr Dowdall. I own this property.'

'Mr Dowdall, but have you a problem with your eye-
sight?'

'Aha,' he replied, his eyes flitting across DC Cairns'
face. 'I'm registered blind. Can make out light alright,
outlines at a pinch, if I'm close enough but, nowadays,
not much more. I'm due to get an op at the eye place but
my GP says not to hold out too much hope. I know my
way around here though in the dark. I was born here.'

'Going back to Mandy, how do you know about her
lesbian friend?'

'I've not met her, but there's only one bed in the flat.
Used to be my mum's, actually. It stands to reason. The
old girl upstairs seen them too, holding hands and that,
canoodling. She's never away from her window – likes to
see who pops into the church opposite. Sinners, she says.
She told me all about it, about the argument and everything. There was a man in the stair, shouting and bawling.
Margaret said she could hardly hear her programme at
times, had to turn the sound down.'

'When was that? What was it about?'

'What? The argument? I can't remember when. Margaret told me on the phone about it, maybe a week ago or less. I've been away since last Saturday, I've a caravan near Eyemouth that I go to when I can, with a friend, like. We like going for walks, but I had to come back, it was that cold. I only got back earlier this morning. She needed to speak to me about a common repair notice-like thing. A council letter. I never heard them arguing myself. I wasn't here.'

'Where's Margaret now?'

'Away. She's got a son in Port Seton, Cockenzie or wherever, somewhere near the harbour, and she's away on her holidays with him.'

'Do you know his name?' Alice asked.

'William Stobbs . . . Stobbs, like her. He'll be the same as her, won't he?'

'Could you give us a description of the girl, the lesbian lady?' DC Cairns inquired. The sound of footsteps on the stone stair could be heard and DC Trish Rennie appeared on their landing, huffing and puffing, hauling her considerable bulk upwards by the bannister. Seeing them, she said, breathlessly, 'Can anyone come to the party then? I thought I was supposed to be here this morning, checking the post, not you, Boss. It's a long way up for nothing.'

'Who's that?' Mr Dowdall asked, looking in the direction of the voice.

'No one,' DC Cairns said coolly. 'No one to trouble you, at least. It's just a colleague of ours. Late, as usual. So, what did she look like – the girl, the one you were telling us about, do you know her name?'

'D'you not listen to me, dearie? I'm blind, *blind*. I couldn't describe you, her or her. Mandy, I could describe.

She let me feel her face once. She was pretty, I felt that. Such a nice wee thing, even if she was a lesbian like Margaret says. But the other one, I never even met her. Try Margaret, she'll be able to help youse if anyone can.'

'Do you know what she was called, the lesbian?'

'No,' he replied, then he smiled and corrected himself, 'I do, of course, I do. Her name was Anna. I'm sure I heard Mandy call her that. Don't ask me for a surname, though. That I cannot tell you.'

⸻

Once they were back inside the flat, DC Cairns said, 'So, what happened then?'

Trish Rennie, red in the face after her exertion, snapped back, 'How do you mean, what happened then? I got here, didn't I? No one told me there was a race to collect the post!'

'No, Trish, sorry, I didn't mean that. I was talking to Alice about . . .'

'Sssh!' the inspector said, gesticulating at the phone held to her ear, turning her back and determined to finish giving the instructions she had started to issue.

'Find out where a William Stobbs lives, could you? It's somewhere in Port Seton or Cockenzie. Phone me back, eh? Trish is going to bring back another photo of Evans, get it copied and handed out. We must find him. It seems there was an argument here on the night she probably died. I'll get more about it, with luck, from Stobbs' mother who is staying with him. Presumably, prints are being taken from the framed photo too, to see if they match any of those found in the girl's flat? Get copies made of the other photo, too. The one of the deceased and the girl in the hat. OK? Bye.'

Seeing her opportunity, the young constable tried again. 'What happened?'

'I don't know, we don't have enough information yet. Maybe there was an argument, maybe the vanishing "lesbian lady" was involved, maybe the boyfriend. We can only guess at the moment, we'll . . .'

'No, no,' the constable butted in impatiently. 'I'm not talking about the bloody deceased. I mean about the cat, what happened to the cat?'

'Oh well, that one's easy. No one wanted him, claimed him, so . . .'

She hesitated briefly and, aghast, the girl finished her sentence for her: 'He was put down!'

'No, no – I took him home with me.'

'Tiddles?'

'Was that his name? I call him Hannibal. It fits him rather better, I think. Not that he was a cannibal or anything . . . Now I'm off to speak to Aileen Tennant in Windsor Gardens. I need you to check that no one else has returned to the block since the first door-to-doors – that there's no one else who might have seen or heard anything and who we might have missed first time round.'

9

'The Survivors Sanctuary' was on the east side of a square of Georgian terraced houses, and separated by the old A1 road from the Musselburgh Race Course, the Ash Lagoons and the sea. All of the houses in Windsor Gardens, other than the Sanctuary and a nursing home two doors along had the sort of well-tended exterior usually associated with affluence, security and comfortable living. Smugness, some might say. The gloss paint of their front doors was chip-free, trellises had been provided for each clematis and rose to climb and their names, painted in gilded letters on the door lights, obviated the need for any vulgar enumeration. The nursing home, with its extended ramps and unsightly handrails, was a final residence for the aged and well-heeled of East Lothian. So, with a view to the future, it was tolerated.

The Sanctuary, however, was considered by its neighbours to let the square down. It would pass for a hostel. Posters were stuck inside its slightly grimy front windows, a flattened cigarette packet lay on its cracked doorstep among piles of dog ends, and a large dark-green stain disfigured its frontage. This eyesore was the result of a permanently overflowing gutter. Funding for the Sanctuary, after the cuts, no longer ran to routine maintenance. Opposite, in the centre of the square, was a small, enclosed garden which had been planted with trees and a few flowering shrubs.

Since the City Bypass had been opened property prices in Windsor Gardens had rocketed. It had become an exceptionally tranquil place, a backwater, isolated from the hustle and bustle of the town for most of the year. On race days alone its peace was shattered. The hubbub they created transformed the square, to the chagrin of residents and visitors alike. Jaguars, Range Rovers and Saabs revved on the nearby Linkfield Road, nose to tail, queuing to enter the grandstand, their numbers augmented by horse-lorries, horse-boxes and coaches, the pavements on either side of the road overflowing with streams of chattering, enthusiastic pedestrians. Later the pounding of hoofs and the roar of the crowd would further enliven the noisy mix, until finally, in the late afternoon, the meeting would come to an end. Then the punters would depart, tired and hoarse, their wallets lightened, some going to console themselves with an ice cream from Luca's Café in the High Street, some in search of more alcohol. All that would be left would be litter, blowing like tumbleweed about the place for days.

Aileen Tennant, a plain woman in her mid-forties with thin, mousy hair, was employed as a counsellor by the charity which owned and ran the Survivors' Sanctuary. That afternoon she was exhausted. Her last hour had been spent empathising and communing, almost exclusively in silence, with Allan, one of her regular clients. He invariably wore black and was, she intuited, mourning his lost innocence. When she had mentioned this to Janice, the secretary, she had opined that he was probably just a Goth.

As the minutes of the session had ticked by, she had had to remind herself, several times, that the pace of the meeting must be dictated not by her or her needs, but by him and his needs. Months earlier, the lad had confided in her the cause of his distress, but since then, at their five subsequent sessions, he had uttered hardly another word. All of the sympathetic noises, remarks and inquiries that his counsellor had made that afternoon had been greeted with either silence or, at best, a flash of his shy and unhappy smile. Today, quarter of an hour into their allocated time, Allan had shaken his head, clicked his tongue and said, 'Women, eh?'

The last time he had made this precise, solitary and momentous remark, she had seized her chance and immediately inquired if he would prefer to speak to a male colleague. It could easily be arranged, she had assured him. No offence would be taken by her. But he had declined, shaking his head at the suggestion and, reluctantly, she had accepted his decision. There was no point in repeating the offer now.

And all her subsequent gentle prompting had produced nothing more until, having racked her brain for inspiration, anything to help her client to open up, air the issues which so obviously preoccupied him and paralysed him, she said, 'Is your mother . . .'

His response was immediate and silenced her once again.

'I have no mother!'

The emotion so briefly displayed died down as quickly as it had flared up, and he shifted his wooden chair away from her, scoring the lino in the process. Motionless once more, he emitted one of his long, hopeless sighs.

A vase of white lilies stood on her desk, brought by her from home to shield the cat from their deadly pollen, and, deliberately, she inhaled their strong, musky scent, hoping that it would have a soothing effect on her. 'Touchy' was the word that trespassed into her thoughts. No, no. Vulnerable, damaged.

It was odd, she reflected, that sitting still, moving not a muscle, simply trying to emanate sympathy and understanding, could be quite so wearing, so tiring. Listening, proper, active listening, even to nothing, required intense concentration, drained the last drop of life-energy. Mid-session, forgetting herself for a moment, she had jotted down a list of things to do for Duncan's birthday party. There were not enough hours in the day, what with that, organising the builders, finding a home for Granny and helping Hannah with her Healthy Eating project. When Allan had caught her writing (could he read upside down?), she had smiled, closed her notebook, and tried to return her full attention to him and his issues. Thankfully, there was only ten minutes to go, only ten minutes to coffee time. And a Jaffa Cake, possibly, if there were any left. Perhaps, she wondered, counselling was, after all, not for her? How could she beam off safe, soothing, relaxing vibes if her mind was constantly elsewhere, on her next break, or planning her post-work work? That thought recurred when Allan rose from his seat and said, warmly, and with more animation that she had ever seen from him before, 'Great. See you next week, then, Aileen.'

From his tone, they might have been regulars at the same pub, arranging another convivial drinking session. Baffled, she nodded her assent.

As he left, Janice on the desk rang to say that a police-woman wanted to speak to her. This news both rattled and perplexed her. She was in sore need of a break, not to mention the coffee and Jaffa Cakes.

'Now? You're joking. Why?' she asked, feeling unreasonably put upon by the world and its unceasing demands.

'Now,' Janice replied, before adding, to protect herself, 'that's what Mr Tranter says. You've an emergency appointment coming next but they've not arrived yet. She was your client, the woman they want to speak to you about. I'm to bring in her notes to you now.'

Once the policewoman had introduced herself, her request for information about Miranda Stimms caused the counsellor further perplexity. She could feel herself becoming hot and bothered, her hunched posture betraying her inner turmoil. No secrets, she had determined, would leave her lips. Usually, if there were questions to be asked, she asked them. Usually she was in control, even if she did not dictate the pace.

'I'm afraid, Inspector Rice,' she replied, disconcerted, her brow furrowed, 'that I cannot disclose anything about Ms Stimms. All our clients are assured of confidentiality. It's to do with trust, trust is central to the relationship between counsellor and client. No one would tell us anything if they could not be sure that what they said would not leave this room.'

'I appreciate that, but Miranda Stimms is no longer your client since, as I explained, unfortunately, she's dead.' Alice said. Her firm tone should have made it clear that she would get the information she had come for.

'Still . . . I'm still not sure. The bond must not be broken. Trust is the cornerstone of everything we do,' Aileen Tennant reiterated, her face reddening as she tried to tread water, wondering what her duty might be in these unexpected circumstances. The handbook, inadequate document that it was, would not cover it. None of her clients had, as far as she was aware, died before. A dreadful thought suddenly struck her.

'Was it suicide?' she demanded.

115

'No.'

'Thank God!' she murmured, sighing out loud with relief. A client's suicide was, obviously and as everyone said, *not* the hallmark of failed counselling, but it must be hard in the deep, dark depths of the night not to view it as such.

'No, it was murder. That's why I need your help.'

'I see,' Mrs Tennant replied, feeling almost faint at the news, unreal, conscious as she looked at the policewoman that by giving such help she might be dragged into her life, a life lived faster, a life incalculably more dangerous than her own. This inspector person inhabited a world where things, bad things, not only happened, but had to be dealt with by her. She picked up the pieces with her own hands, got them dirty. Got them cut and bleeding, quite possibly. This woman did not just listen and then go home.

'Was she referred by her GP here? How did you come to see her?'

'No. I asked her that, how she came to us. She told me she picked up a leaflet, one of ours, in a doctor's surgery. She went in to make an appointment but never actually had any contact with the GP, any GP, she said. People do that sometimes – it's easier for them. That's why we leave our leaflets in these sorts of places.'

'Why did she come and see you?'

'She's only been once. She needed help, someone to talk to, someone to listen to her . . . to be a witness, you could say.'

'To be a witness to what?'

'To her story . . .'

'What story?'

'To affirm her survival.'

'What ordeal *exactly* had she survived?' the police-woman asked, failing to conceal the irritation she felt in the face of the counsellor's evasive replies.

'As I recall, she was experiencing . . . difficulties, relationship difficulties . . . sexual difficulties within her relationship. Nightmares, she had them too. She had anger issues as well.'

'Why?'

'Because of the damage . . .'

'What damage?'

'The damage to her psyche – to herself.'

'I note that your clinic specialises in cases of child abuse, helping the victims get on with their lives – focusing on the fact that they have survived their ordeal.'

'Yes.'

'Was that her problem? Sexual abuse? Had someone abused her sexually when she was a child?'

The woman hesitated, before committing herself and answering, 'Yes. It was. If you need to know more I'd have to consult my notes.'

'On you go,' Alice said, sitting back in her chair and looking properly around the room for the first time. Apart from posters giving the address of various genito-urinary clinics within the capital, nothing decorated the green-painted walls except for a child's drawing of a snowman and a snow-woman, their gloved hands linked as if they were about to dance. No clinics required for them, she mused. Breathing in, she smelt the heavy scent of the lilies, and wondered if they had been chosen for their perfume, specially selected to obliterate any underlying human notes arising from repressed emotions, panic or anxieties felt by the countless clients seen within those four walls.

Less than a minute later the woman closed the file in front of her and, brows still furrowed, said, 'What else do you want to know?'

'Anything and everything. Please.'

'There really isn't much. She'd only come here once.'

'Whatever you have will be fine,' the policewoman said, trying to sound reassuring, encouraging. Surely the need for such information was obvious?

'We'd other sessions planned. She didn't say much at our first meeting . . . and I have to go with that, accept that, allow her to move on when she's comfortable with that.'

'I understand.'

'All I can tell you from our meeting is that she was abused, sexually, from about the age of fourteen onwards. From puberty. Hence her sexual difficulties, her low self-esteem, anger and so on.'

'Do you know who was responsible?' Alice asked. At that moment, her phone rang and, gesturing an apology, she answered it, hearing DC Cairns' voice at the other end. The constable's words tumbled out in her enthusiasm. 'I've got an address for William Stobbs, and his mother, Margaret Stobbs, is at home there just now and will be for the rest of the afternoon. She's due to get a hairdo, at home. The son's away at his work.'

'Well done, text it to me and I'll meet you there in, say, half an hour?'

Putting down her mobile, she looked expectantly at Aileen Tennant, eager to get an answer to her last question. But the woman's attention appeared to have drifted, seemed focused on something outside in the square. She had, in fact, taken in every word of the phone call, and was pleased to know that her ordeal was all but over.

'Do you know who was responsible?' Alice repeated.

'For what?' Mrs Tennant asked, managing to sound startled, as if her reverie had been disturbed.

'For the sexual abuse of Miranda Stimms.'

'No. I never ask,' she replied, slightly condescendingly. 'If my client wants to tell me I listen and react accordingly – but I never ask. They'll tell me if they want to. Some do, some don't. It's not necessary for healing to take place. Could have been a family friend, a teacher, a parent, the family doctor, a brother . . . They tell me sometimes.'

'Child abuse is a crime. Did you have any suspicions, from anything she said?'

'It's not my place . . . as a counsellor – to have "suspicions", I mean. Who the abuser was matters to me only because it matters to my client. Because it matters to them, sometimes they tell me. That's really all I can say...'

'You'd tell us if anyone came to mind?'

'Of course – but I can't tell unless I know.'

Two worlds, Aileen Tennant sensed, were colliding within her office. In hers, the counselling world, the victim was genuinely of paramount importance, all that really mattered. The perpetrator of the abuse had, at best, a walk-on part and then only if he, or she, was invited. But to the policewoman and her kind, once a crime had been committed, the victim became a means to an end. Everything might be done in their name, but what counted, really counted, was catching and prosecuting the criminal. Miranda Stimms as Miranda Stimms no longer counted.

'Did you know that she had a boyfriend?'

'Yes,' she hesitated for a second, returning her thoughts to the particular, to her own client, 'I did. I assumed he was the catalyst, part of the reason, certainly, that she decided to come here – the sexual difficulties, fears and

119

so on, I assumed that was with him. Hamish, I have noted he was called. Someone, him presumably, wouldn't understand. Not that she'd said anything to anyone, but she didn't want to lose him, or whoever it was. She was afraid of that, I know that much. She was, as she put it, "trying to sort herself out".'

'Did she tell you that she was pregnant?'

Looking alarmed, the woman shook her head. 'Maybe . . . maybe that's what he wouldn't understand. Maybe she thought she'd lose him?'

'Because of the baby?'

'It would make sense, wouldn't it?'

'What about a girlfriend?'

'Girl friends?'

'A girlfriend – did she mention a girlfriend? It appears she may have been in a lesbian relationship, too.'

'She didn't tell me that. She could have been, I suppose. I can't say one way or the other. It's not uncommon in her situation. Sometimes victims of abuse are confused about their sexuality but, in her case . . . well, I have no way of knowing. Why do you ask?'

'She never mentioned anyone called Anna to you?'

'No. Why do you ask?'

'What sort of person was she?' Alice persisted, ignoring the woman's questions. Catching Aileen Tennant's exasperated sigh, she added, 'I know, you only saw her once . . .'

'From memory . . . I was impressed by her. Anyone would be. A survivor. That's how I'd describe her. She was, genuinely, trying to sort herself out, and she was very, very young. Seventeen, I see I've noted down. Not many come to us that young.'

A survivor. An odd choice of words for a dead girl, Alice thought.

William Stobbs' flat in Cockenzie faced the harbour which, like many on the east coast of Scotland, became a sad sight when the tide went out, reduced to a field of stinking, grey-brown mud within crumbling, guano-streaked stone walls. Its air of quiet desolation was reinforced by the presence of a wrecked fishing boat, barnacle-encrusted and with a gaping wound in its side, propped up against the sea wall; a reminder of a more prosperous past. Fifty years earlier, the quay there had been alive with a cacophony of sounds: the thuds made by heavy fish-boxes landing on stone, the shouts of the men as they hosed down the decks, and the cries of the gulls as they swooped around the vessels, desperate to catch any discarded entrails in their beaks before they sank into the oily, black water. However, in one respect at least, Cockenzie Harbour, along with the rest of the sleepy village attached to it, was unique. They were all dwarfed, miniaturised, by the gigantic geometry, largely rectangles and squares, of the power station that stood, incongruously, a little distance from the end of the Hawthorn Bank road. This monumental, sculptural presence on the skyline, with its cloud-stroking twin chimneys, skewed perspectives for miles around and made the whole of Cockenzie look like a toy town.

Watching from her own car as the inspector parked her Escort opposite Dickson's, the fish merchant's shop, DC Cairns got out and crossed the road to meet her.

'How did you get on?' she asked.

'Alright. But, if anything, the waters are further muddied. She was sexually abused as a child, as an adolescent. That's why she went to the Sanctuary, for counselling.'

'Who by?'

They had begun walking towards the two-storey white-painted building in which William Stobbs had his flat.

'I don't know. Counselling by a Mrs Aileen Tennant – abuse by a person, or persons, currently unknown. The woman treating her never found out who was responsible for it, so for the present we've drawn a blank. How did you get on, hassling the lab?' Alice asked, her finger poised over the doorbell.

'The same prints from the photo, Hamish Evans' prints, presumably, are all over her flat. Just as you might expect. He took a flight from Heathrow back to Edinburgh, arriving at about ten-thirty. He was definitely back in the city on the night that she died, but we've still not found him or his vehicle, and everybody's looking. And I mean everybody. He must, I reckon, have gone into hiding.'

'Like Anna,' Alice replied, 'and her prints must be all over the place too, if they were living together there. If so, that's two of the three sets identified.'

'One other thing . . .'

'Yes?'

'There was a message from Dr Cash, apologising for the delay. The alcohol level showed she'd had a couple of glasses of wine, something like that, shortly before she died. Pregnancy or no pregnancy. I wonder if she even knew she was expecting? At seventeen, you might not.'

―

Inside the warmth of the flat, an eighty-five-year-old lady was bending over her eighty-seven-year-old sister, attempting to roll a curler through her thin white locks. Margaret Stobbs, the elder of the two, resembled a bulldog, being squat with powerful shoulders and a couple of pointed incisors in her bottom jaw, visible due to her massive underbite. Her sister, Jessie, cursed with similar, though slightly less pronounced, features, had never rid herself of the unfortunate maiden name they had both been born with: Bottom.

'How's that feel, Maggs?' Jessie asked, peering through her pebble thick glasses at the large mirror to see her sister's response to her ministrations.

'A wee bit over-tight, Jessie,' the answer came back, accompanied by a delayed grimace of pain as she tried to raise and lower her eyebrows, feeling the skin of her forehead tighten and loosen with each movement. The half-smoked cigarette in the corner of her mouth waggled up and down as she did so.

'I'll try again, give it a wee tweak,' Jessie said, pulling out the grip, unrolling the hank of hair and gathering up another one. In passing, she adjusted the pink towel over her sister's beefy shoulders, retying it under her ample chins, while skilfully avoiding falling over the two crossed walking sticks which rested on her sister's lap.

'I'm going out for my tea, officer, so I need my hair done,' Margaret Stobbs said. 'It's a Golden Wedding celebration – old, old friends of mine in the village. But you just ask away. Take no notice of Jessie. She's not going, not been invited although they know her too. Do you want any tea or coffee? She'll get it for you, won't you, Jessie? She knows where everything's kept in my son's house, in my William's house.'

'Mmm,' replied Jessie, lips pursed, not bothering to hide her annoyance at being asked.

'I understand, Mrs Stobbs,' Alice began, 'that recently you overheard an argument on the stair of your flat in Casselbank Street. Is that right?'

'Did you, Margaret? You never told me!' Jessie said, her previous grievance replaced by this one.

'I don't have to tell you everything, dear! You've got your own life, haven't you? I did, yes, officer. A man was bawling the place down – shouting away. He sounded furious.'

'When did you hear it, the argument?' Alice asked.

'Oh, I don't know. Monday night? Aye, it was the night before I came here. When did I come here, Jessie?'

'Tuesday morning,' her sister replied, concentrating on unfankling the next curler, which had somehow caught its spikes in the neck-fastening of Margaret's Alarmaid.

'Careful!' the old woman hissed, aware of a sudden strangulation.

'What time was it when you heard the argument?' DC Cairns interjected.

'Late. It must have been late, I'd been asleep in my chair . . . after nine, ten, eleven. Something like that. He was mad, shouting at the top of his voice, screaming at . . . Well, it was more of a wee nap, I'd just had . . .'

'Who was the man shouting at?' DC Cairns interrupted, leaning forward, her curiosity getting the better of her manners.

'That's what I'm trying to tell you, lass. At Mandy or . . .' she paused for dramatic effect, 'her Fancy Woman.' Having dropped her bombshell, she raised her eyebrows impishly, knowing that her sister would be electrified by her words. As if to underline their importance she removed her cigarette, holding it between her forefinger and her middle finger in a rather louche fashion.

'Mandy! That Mandy! You never told me that either, that she had a fancy woman!' Jessie said, now openly peevish, placing a roller on the crown of her sister's head and tugging none too gently at another lock of hair.

'Jessie!' Margaret moaned.

'Sorry, dear, I'm a bit out of practice.'

'The argument in the stair,' Alice prompted, 'what was it about, Mrs Stobbs?'

'You're more than a bit out of practice. That hurt, Jessie! Be careful! Well, the man, he was shouting, saying that she'd no right, no right at all – that the girl should not be with her, that she had no business having her there – that – I think he called her, or one of them, an unnatural cow or something like that, too.'

The roar of a hairdryer starting up drowned out the rest of her words.

'Turn it off, Jessie, for pity's sake, turn it off! I'm trying to speak here. The police have come here, all the way out here, specially, to speak to me,' Margaret shouted, determined to be heard, whatever the cost. Jessie, giving her sister's reflection a malevolent glare, grudgingly obeyed and laid the dryer down.

'So, what did Miranda say?' DC Cairns chipped in, once more unable to contain herself.

'She said,' came the slightly hoarse reply, 'that she loved Anna. That Anna was her life, that she was not giving her up, that he should go and never come back. She said, actually, that he was a monster . . .'

'A monster!' Jessie repeated, hands now on her hips, enthralled by the description.

'Do you know her surname?' Alice asked.

'Stimms.'

'Anna's surname,' Alice clarified.

The woman shook her head, watching herself intently in the mirror as she did so and then answered, 'I heard her called Anna. I heard her name being called once or twice in the stair.'

'How often is the stair cleaned?' Alice asked.

Eyes narrowing, flummoxed at this unexpected question, Mrs Stobbs said, 'Cleaned? Never! The woman from number three was supposed to arrange it and I've seen once, mind, just the once, a Polish girl with a mop on the steps. It's filthy. I'm ashamed if I have guests. If I was younger, if my legs worked, I'd do it myself. But nobody cares nowadays, do they?'

'Did you see the man – do you have any idea who he is?' Alice asked.

'Nope, I never seen him,' Margaret replied, gazing at her own reflection and patting the curlers on her head with one hand, adding, 'he'd be her boyfriend, I expect.' Having dropped that further morsel, she carefully reinserted her cigarette into the side of her mouth. There it rested secure, wedged between her lips and one prominent fang.

'Her boyfriend!' her sister said in shocked tones, 'For pity's sake! Did she have a boyfriend as well as a fancy woman? She was AC/BC?'

'She did. She was,' her sister replied smugly, forcing a jet of smoke through her lips as if to underline the fact.

'How did you know that the girl . . . whoever she was, living with Mandy, was her "fancy woman"?' Alice asked. 'Perhaps, she was just a lodger, a friend, something like that?'

'Sure you'd not like a tea or a coffee, officers? Jessie would happily get it for you,' Margaret said, mischievously, willing them to take up the offer. Jessie would be desperate to hear this snippet.

Jessie signalled her happiness to do so by glaring at her sister.

'No? Sure? Jessie would be delighted, really. No? OK. I knew because I seen them together, holding hands, arm-in-arm in the road. Would you hold hands with your lodger? Anyway, Ronnie Dowdall told me, there's only the one bed in the flat. They must have shared it. Would you share your bed with a friend? I wouldn't, I can tell you. I wouldn't share with her, with Jessie. I know what they were. Modern. You could tell, just looking at them, what they were up to. One day they kissed in the street. In public. They'd no shame.'

'I'd not share with you either,' Miss Bottom said trenchantly, lower jaw jutting even further out in her defiance.

'Did you see the man?' Alice inquired.

'No, I was in my flat.'

'Did you not try and see him after the row? Did you not think to look out of your window then?' Jessie demanded, unimpressed by her sister's culpable lack of curiosity, her lack of diligence.

'No. I would have done but I had a call.'

'A telephone call? Who'd call you? You didn't have to answer it!'

'I did. Eh . . . eh . . . my pal – Nan, my old pal, said she'd give me a call on her return from Florida, and it was her. I couldn't have put her off, could I? Anyway, I know what her boyfriend looked like.'

'You could have put her off!' Jessie replied hotly, quite carried away by the mystery of it all.

'I,' Margaret answered coldly, blowing her smoke directly into her sister's face, 'have friends, Jessie, real friends. Real friends make demands.'

'Margaret!'

'We could get the time of the call, Nan's call – that would give us a better clue as to the time of the argument,' Alice said, turning towards DC Cairns.

'No – no,' Margaret Stobbs cut in quickly, 'it wasn't a

call . . . not then, thinking about it again. No, it was a call of nature. I had to answer a call of nature. Nan called the day before.'

'Nan being your real – or is it your *imaginary* friend?' Jessie inquired, a look of triumph on her face.

'Can you give us a description of the girl, Mrs Stobbs?' Alice intervened, halting their endless sparring for the moment.

'Aha, she was a white "Caucasian" as they say on the TV,' the woman continued confidently. 'What else do you want to know?'

'Hair colour?' DC Cairns volunteered.

'She'd a hat on. A woolly one, you know, with a bobble on the top.'

'Did you see her face?' Alice inquired.

'Not really, not from my upstairs window, looking down on her. I don't get out much nowadays, with my legs. Those stairs will be the death of me. And it's been that cold, she was always wrapped up to the nines. Hats, gloves, scarves. My carers, Gloria and Theresa, do all my shopping for me.'

'What about her height, can you help us with that?' Alice tried again.

'I'd only a bird's eye view, remember. All I can tell you is that Mandy was smaller than her, quite a bit smaller than her.'

'You're not much help!' Jessie said dismissively. 'Did you never bump into her inside, on the stair or anything? You don't know what the man looked like . . .'

'I told you, it was her boyfriend!'

'How d'you know that? Do you know what he looks like, then? How do you know it was him? What does he look like, then, tell us that!'

'I've not seen him that night, Jessie. But it was him alright, I could tell from the words . . . anyone who'd ever been married could tell.'

'Hopeless,' Jessie said dismissively, 'quite hopeless. You don't know what the man looked like, what the girl-friend looked like. And maybe she done it – in a love triangle or something. There might be an identity parade or something and a lot of use you're going to be. They've got to catch this Mandy girl's murderer. There are a lot of white people, a lot of white women, in Edinburgh and that's all it amounts to! Your so-called help –'

'So, Jessie, dear,' Margaret replied, her eyes flashing with fury, 'what exactly are you suggesting? Should I, per-haps, just make it all up? Just to please these two ladies so that they can go away with something? A love triangle! What would you know of a love triangle . . . of love for that matter?'

By way of reply, her sister sniffed and said, 'I watch the TV like everyone else. If you're to get to your tea, I'll need to start drying your hair now.' So saying, she let rip with the hairdryer, holding it like a gun at maximum heat, its nozzle only inches from Margaret Stobbs' pink skull.

Taking the photo of Miranda and the girl in the hat from its brown envelope, the inspector held it in front of the older woman.

'Is that the girlfriend?' she asked loudly, determined to make herself heard above the din of the hairdryer.

Instantly, Margaret Stobbs stuck a thumb up from under her towel and cast an exultant smile at her sister.

The stress of it all was getting to him, he knew. Nowadays, from the moment he woke up, he seemed to be in pain, whether in his head or his tummy or, unexpectedly, across his shoulders. At work they had noticed the change in him. Steve had remarked how pale he looked and Rhona at reception had said the same, and kept offering him tea or coffee at all hours. He reached inside the glove compartment of his car, pulled out a can of boiled sweets, a packet of spare tissues, finally extracting a roll of leaflets held together by a rubber band. But, despite further rummaging, he found no headache pills. As long as it did not start thumping he would manage, he told himself. At least this time he was early.

Knowing he had over twenty minutes to kill, he started reading his newspaper, but after scanning the front page he gave up. Nothing was going in; he could not have repeated a word he had read. Never mind. Soon the women would start assembling by the gates, relaxed in each other's company, some with buggies, some carrying their shopping, a few loners patrolling the periphery, acting like another species, aliens, apparently disdainful of their own sex. What were they playing at? Did they not like motherhood? Perhaps they were nannies, or paid carers of some sort. Disability was nothing if not democratic, after all. Among those damaged boys and girls there might well be a lord or lady to be. With that thought in mind, he turned his attention to the school itself.

Nothing seemed to be happening inside. Lights were on in a few of the rooms but otherwise it appeared to be almost dormant. It was, he noticed, a beautiful building with its cut stone exterior, pillars and long, symmetrical windows. Georgian, probably, not the usual purpose-built monstrosity considered good enough by nameless officials for those with 'Special Needs'. Such children, apparently, had no ordinary, never mind special, need for good architecture. But his child did, she liked Edinburgh Castle, smiled every time she saw it.

Why, he wondered, glancing at his watch, were the mothers not beginning to make an appearance? In case it was fast, he turned on the radio and caught a time check. Ten to three, as both the clock in the car and his watch confirmed. Had something gone wrong? At the very thought, the pain in his head became more intense, throbbing over one eye and making him close it in an attempt to block out the light, ease the pain. His phone went and he picked it up, hardly able to speak, knowing who it was.

'Is she there?' Lambie demanded. Nowadays, she was utterly single-minded, viewing him as no more than a conduit to her daughter, uninterested in anything but news of her. If she was next to him, and could see him now, bleeding from multiple wounds, her question would be the same. She had a cold, unnatural, unwomanly streak about her sometimes. Couldn't she tell from his voice, if nothing else, that he was poorly? Early mornings and late nights, work, work, work, never mind the stress of a missing child, must take their toll. He was not made of iron.

'No,' he said unhelpfully, forcing her to reveal herself and ask for more.

'Why not?'

'Because it's too early, it's not yet three. They're not out.'

'Have you seen her though, is she there?'

'No, I told you. It's too early. Now, love, I have to go, really, otherwise I might miss her again.'

He got out of his car and wandered over towards the sole woman standing at the wrought-iron gates. Hands in his pockets, he stood beside her, ignoring her, all his

131

attention fixed on the playground. Surely to goodness something must happen soon. Maybe the bell would go and then they would all start flooding out, like birds released from a cage.

'Are they not coming?' the woman said to him in a strong Glaswegian accent. Turning to face her, he saw a stunning Marilyn Monroe lookalike with white blonde locks, blue-powdered eyelids and a mouth to die for. Her tiny waist was pulled in by the belt of her red mac, but perched on her strapless stilettos, she was a good three inches taller than him. Before he had opened his mouth to answer her, she exclaimed, 'Fuck!'

'What's the matter?' he asked, watching as she shook her head from side to side, her glorious curls tumbling over her face and perfuming the air around them.

'Fuck! Fuck! Fuck!'

'What is it?' he repeated, moving closer to her.

'Today's Friday, isn't it? It's a half bloody day. Micky must have collected her, taken her home. I came straight from my work, dozy bitch that I am.'

'Half-day?' he said weakly, its significance just beginning to filter into his pain-befuddled brain.

'You forget an' all?' she said, smiling sweetly at him like the screen goddess she resembled. 'Bet your wife won't have! How could I bloody forget, eh?' she mused. 'Too much on my plate, that's how. They'll wonder what I'm up to at my work, disappearing like that – asking nobody or anything.'

———

Back inside his car, he dialled home. His headache was worse, splitting his skull in two and making him overheat, sweat now running down his body.

'Lambie,' he said, his head bent forwards, resting on the wheel, his eyes closed.

'You haven't got her, have you?' her voice sounded stern, like a schoolteacher reprimanding a pupil, cold as ice.

'No, I haven't,' he replied, adopting a defiant attitude, leaving it at that, incomplete.

'Why?'

'She wasn't there.'

Instantly her tone changed and the panic that he knew she tried to suppress bubbled up to the surface, audible in her unnatural, high-pitched tone, in her garbled words.

'Why? Why wasn't she there? Where is she then . . . is she not at that school then? I thought you were sure, I thought she was there. How do we know she's safe? Maybe she's got lost again, wandered away from them. That's what she does, isn't it? Where is she, why has . . .'

'Lambie, Lambie,' he broke in, softening at her first display of weakness, desperate to reassure her. 'It's alright. Truly, it is alright. She is alright. I couldn't pick her up because today's a half-day, I didn't know that. So I turned up too late, but don't worry yourself, I'll pick her up tomorrow. If she's there, I'll get her tomorrow for sure.'

'No . . .' she said, sobbing, hardly able to catch her breath.

'I will,' he said, comforting her, making it sound as if nothing could now go wrong. Horrified by his own cruelty.

'No,' she repeated, 'you won't. You won't be able to. Tomorrow's Saturday, there'll be no school on a Satur-day. We'll have to wait two more days. I'm not sure I can bear it, darling. I've had enough. It's been so long. I'm going . . . let's go, both of us, let's just go to the police.'

'Lambie – my love,' he said slowly, playing for time, trying to work out the best way to handle her. 'We could do that, of course. If that's what you want I'll go along with it, that's what we'll do. *But* . . . I really don't think it would be a good idea. This way, we'll get her back on Monday, I'm confident of that, I'd bet my life on that. If we go to the police now you know what'll happen. The social services people won't let her go, not just like that. They have no idea, remember, how difficult it is to keep her safe. Someone will be sent round, like the last time, to decide if we're "fit" or not. Some do-gooder who knows nothing about her, or about us. What if they decide that we're not? What then? It took weeks last time, and the time before that, remember, when she was little. This is the third time this has happened. Maybe we won't get another chance. Have you thought about that?'

'No,' she replied, 'all I want is her back.'

'Well, do. That's all I want too,' he said, pressing his advantage home. 'Haven't I done everything I said I'd do? Tracked her down, found her? I'll get her back, and once she's home we'll never lose her again. I'll lock my car door, just like you said, that's the only weakness in our system. Everything else we'd figured out, hadn't we?'

'Monday, then, you're sure about Monday?'

'I'm sure,' he said, relieved beyond words by her compliance, 'You can rely on me, Lambie. You know you can. When have I ever let you down?'

'Never . . . well, almost never,' she answered, genuine warmth seeping into her tone as she considered the truth of this. 'You've almost never let me down. Twenty years – for twenty years, you've looked after me.'

This was balm for his soul. With her behind him, he could conquer anything, achieve everything. All was not lost, and putting his mobile in his pocket he smiled to himself, felt like a different man. His headache was no more than an inconvenience, one that would go soon. And on Monday, for sure, he would get her. His whole world depended upon it.

10

On Saturday morning at nine o'clock most of the inhabitants of Casselbank Street were either in their beds, dead to the world, or awake, sitting up in crumpled night attire, rubbing their sleep-filled eyes and beginning to wonder whether to be virtuous and consume muesli, yoghurt or fruit for breakfast, or, since it was the weekend, to risk clogging their arteries and enjoy a cooked breakfast instead. From the enticing smell in the murdered girl's tenement, the majority there had opted to die young.

All of Miranda Stimms' neighbours had agreed to remain indoors, within their own four walls, for half an hour whilst the forensic team examined their common stair. Consequently, before most of them had begun to cut into their rashers of back bacon, it was giving up its secrets to a band of technicians in white overalls. As instructed by the inspector, the team paid particular attention to the stone landing outside Miranda Stimms' empty flat, the one below it and the set of six stone stairs connecting the two.

While fried bread was still being consumed in the surrounding flats, their painstaking scrutiny revealed traces of blood, individual hairs and what appeared to be a sliver of sheared skin on the outer edge of the fifth step; with more blood on the landing nearest to it. Two more steps in the flight leading from it to the ground floor, in turn, yielded up a couple more bloodstains, the magic of the luminol spray making the invisible visible. Despite all their wizardry, nothing was found on the third flight of stairs or the top floor landing reached by it.

Each time an operative called Alice over excitedly to look at their finds, she praised and encouraged them, listening to their banter as they chattered and joked amongst themselves; relaxed now, sure of their skills and pleased with a job well done. But she could not share their simple happiness, felt oddly ambivalent, each new find increasing her own self-doubt. True, this time her decision had been vindicated, her suspicions confirmed, but should she not have ordered this inspection when the flat was originally subjected to forensic attention? Why had she limited the original scope of the search to the girl's flat, ignoring the rest of the building? Fool! Luck alone, in the form of an absent or slovenly cleaner, had prevented these crucial clues from being lost. After all, bleach produces the same chemiluminescence as blood.

And they were crucial clues, case-changing clues, leaving no room for anyone to suggest that the fatal head wound had been acquired in the sea or elsewhere. Evidently the killer, or killers, had transported an adult human corpse down the remaining six stairs, out of the communal front door and spirited it away into the night. A normal funeral cortege merited six men as pall bearers and they often broke sweat. If only one person had carried the body then, surely, it must be a man? But if Hamish Evans was that man, where was Anna at the time, and why had she not done something, called the police or screamed the place down? Maybe she had been involved too, but from the information gleaned from the dead girl's landlord and her neighbour, Margaret Stobbs, it seemed an improbable, an unholy, alliance. Why would two rivals for Miranda Stimms' love cooperate on her death?

In her office in St Leonard's Street, Elaine Bell was striding up and down in her stocking feet, partly because she was impatient to know the results of the search, and partly because she had read that constant movement, fidgeting even, was the secret to effortless weight-loss. Of late, undressing had become an ordeal, a distressing exposure of red weals where her bra and skirt waistband had cut in; mirrors had to be avoided and today even her shoes seemed tight. The offending pair lay together, in disgrace, under her chair.

'You'll need to talk to everyone else on the stair again, find out if they knew about the girlfriend, heard the dingdong with the boyfriend,' she said, marching past Alice and then turning smartly by the door like a guardsman and passing her again.

'I know – Trish and Liz are there now, plus some uniforms. I understand that one resident is still on holiday in France, camping in the wilds, incommunicado, but we should be able to speak to the rest of them.'

'Surely to God one of them will have seen something, heard something, now we can jog their memories just a little bit. Mrs Stobbs can't have been the only one. And why,' the chief inspector demanded, continuing her patrol, the thudding of her feet a rhythmic background to their talk, 'the hell didn't you check the whole building on day one?'

'Because . . .' Alice replied, at a loss for words, her mind racing in search of an acceptable response. Her boss's ceaseless activity did not help her to concentrate.

Fortunately for Alice, Elaine Bell failed to follow up her own question, her swinging arms and marching feet distracting her as well as her inspector. Instead, she remarked as if it was a logical progression, 'I gather you've tracked down a missing person report about Hamish Evans now, one from a squash partner. That's all well and good, but why have there been none for this Anna character? She's disappeared without trace too, hasn't she? Did she not have a job, a friend in the world? Parents? Do we know what she looks like yet?'

'Yes, we've a horribly blurry photo of her with the deceased. Unfortunately she's wearing a hat in it, but Margaret Stobbs confirmed that it was her. It's being circulated everywhere. That's almost all we've got, though. With luck someone in the building may produce something else, some other snippet about her this morning. Maybe she's currently going to her job, phoning her parents, staying with a friend. As I said, we know so little about her.'

'What about the body? Have we any idea yet where it was dropped off?' Elaine Bell asked, suddenly feeling a little woozy. She settled her buttocks gratefully on the edge of her desk. Perhaps a slice of Ryvita in the morning provided insufficient fuel for brain *and* body?

'No, not really. Ranald Sharpe's been looking into that. He was in touch with the Forth Ports Authority but they said to talk to the Leith Harbour Master. So far, he's not been able to help much, as he says there are too many variables to give any meaningful answer – tides, weather, clothing, even the deceased's physical state.'

'Yet another bloody blank then! What about DNA? Are we making any headway there?'

'No, not yet. The lab's slower than ever. We've buttered them up, twisted arms, begged, all to no avail. There's a long queue, what with the hiatus resulting from the reorganisation, but we are, supposedly, moving up to the front. It's only been four days, remember.'

'Alice,' the DCI said, now raising and lowering her arms like a bird flapping its wings, 'a murderer is still on the loose. This is your first case as an inspector. Let's get a result, eh? Four whole days! Time is ticking past. If you've any ambition to join the Leith Major Investigation team you'd better get this one under your belt, and ideally PDQ. There will be immense competition, I imagine. Incidentally, your predecessor, now in Kerala, supping, I'll be bound, with maharajas and maharanis, sends his "salutations". I got another of his cheeky postcards today. That's somewhere I would like to go. On your way out, send in Ranald, he wants to talk to me about something.'

'Planning to fly there yourself, are you, Ma'am?' Alice said, marvelling at her boss's eccentricities, sidestepping to avoid a collision with the DS as he barged into the detective chief inspector's room.

At Tyninghame beach that same morning the sun was not shining. Clouds scudded across the slate-coloured sky, pursued by a wind which seemed to have taken possession of the world, making free with the sea, raising huge waves and, as they crashed forwards, blowing their crests off, unbalancing any birds foolish enough to be on the wing, and whistling through the leaves of the grey-green buckthorn bushes. Behind a large concrete cube, a man, wearing three coats and a striped scarf, crouched. He was determined to succeed in lighting his penultimate match, and shielding the wavering flame from the wind. The cube was a relic from the last war, designed to protect the homeland from a German invasion by sea. On the barbecue tray in front of him sprawled a row of pallid sausages, naked and sand-specked, looking like sunbathing tourists who had recently arrived at their resort. Ten or more spent matches littered the ground by the tray. As soon as he struck the new one, the wind carelessly extinguished it. He tossed it over his shoulder, picked up his tin of Tennent's lager, took a swig, held it in the pouches of his cheeks, and looked out slowly across the bay. There was no point in getting cross.

In the foreground, his children were playing amongst the labyrinth of scattered rocks, dodging to and fro, engaged in some kind of chase. His dog, Ivan, a black and white collie, raced after them, barking wildly, ecstatic at being included in their game. Their buckets, he noticed, lay abandoned further up the shore. He must not forget them, as they, assuredly, would. Sarah would not forgive him.

The town of Dunbar was visible, though over four miles away, reminding him that if all else failed they could retreat there, find a café and have their lunch inside, in the warmth. It would not be the same, though. And, please God, it would not rain, and he would manage to light the barbecue. He pulled his legs up to his chest, hugged his coats about him, and sighed contentedly. William, when he was an old, old man would remember this birthday, remember this winter picnic, remember his old dad. And Ivan would be part of that memory, too, with luck, though he would long since have turned to dust. Kath, thankfully, seemed to have forgotten about the cold, darting all over the place in pursuit of her older brother. All that running must have warmed her up nicely. A buttered roll with a couple of sausages in it would be the perfect tonic, the perfect lunch.

Remembering suddenly how long barbecues take to heat up, he got onto his knees on the sand, opened one side of his coat over the tin tray as a windbreak, struck the last match and prayed. Eureka! It caught, and he stayed motionless, tending the tiny flame, despite his fear that his coat might catch fire too, until one end of the mesh began to glow. Certain, now, that everything would be fine, he looked out again at his children, congratulating himself on the whole adventure.

Three-quarters of an hour later they appeared, huddled themselves by the barbecue, sniffing the air and looking hungrily at the blackened sausages. Ivan, wet and bedraggled, sat down beside them.

'They ready?' Kath asked, bending down to inspect the sausages. At that moment a blister of hot fat burst, splashing her right hand and making her leap away.

'You alright, darling?' her father asked.

Mouth turned down, but nodding, she inspected her hand; then, as if suddenly appreciating the danger, she pulled the dog away from the spitting sausages.

Spearing a charred one with a stick, the man placed it in a buttered roll and handed it to the birthday boy.

'No ketchup?' the child said, tossing paper cups, a tin, napkins and packets of crisps out of the nearby carrier bag, before alighting with glee on the sought-after bottle. Patiently, before the wind dispersed them, the man gathered the items up and restored them to the bag.

Kath, giggling at the thought, tore a bit off her buttered roll and threw it for the dog to catch. Instantly, Ivan leapt off the ground, jaws agape, twisting in mid-air in his desperation to secure the morsel. For the next few minutes nothing was said, the man watching his children as they ate, pleased that he had not allowed the weather, or Sarah, to put him off his plan. He might not see them often, but he knew what they liked.

After he had, ceremoniously, handed each of them a slice of the chocolate cake that he had made with his own hands, he said, 'Well, William, want your present?'

Cheeks too full to speak, the boy nodded repeatedly, holding out his hands. Kath, chewing busily, edged closer on her knees, determined not to be left out of the celebration. On the boy's outstretched hands the man placed an envelope. Looking a little crestfallen, William said, 'Is it money then, Dad?'

'Open it.'

'Yes, go on, William. Open it. I want to see what you've got,' Kath said, bending towards him, her head at his shoulder and her long hair blowing across his face. With unexpected precision the boy tore through the flap and extracted the contents of the envelope.

'Keeper for a day,' he read; then he repeated the phrase excitedly as its meaning sank in. '*Keeper for a day* – at Edinburgh Zoo! In the Reptile House! Unbelievable, that's unbelievable! Dad, thanks, that's great! I've always wanted that, since I was little.'

After lunch the pair sped off, shrimp nets in their hands, skipping across the sand towards a promontory of rocks which reached northwards and terminated opposite the end of the headland. A little further out, line after line of breakers were being formed, the rows of foam-streaked parallel lines warning those in the know of the presence of a reef.

The picnic took only minutes to clear up. Tethering the rubbish bag with a fallen branch to stop the wind from snatching it, the man started walking towards the specks that were his children, his eyes cast down, gathering flat skipping stones as he went for them to skim across the water. He had Ivan by his side, the dog having stayed by him as he cleared up, desperate to catch any leftovers. As he got closer to the children, amusing himself by jumping from one sandstone boulder to the next and feeling oddly exhilarated, he could make out their excited chatter. Their discarded nets lay criss-crossed by a tiny rock pool.

'It's a goat!' the boy said, pointing with his finger towards the reef.

'No,' his sister replied, 'it's not. It's a hippo – a hippo or, possibly, a badger. A great big, bald one.'

'Don't be silly,' William said, looking disdainfully at her. 'Hippos and badgers don't float.'

'Goats don't float,' she replied, equally authoritatively.

The dog had rushed ahead and was now dancing around the children like a dervish, overjoyed to see them, relieved that the pack was now reunited. Catching its paws as it jumped up on him, the boy started dancing with it. His father, breathing hard, came up to them and was immediately asked to adjudicate their quarrel.

'What d'you think, Dad? It's a goat, isn't it?' the boy said, raising his voice to be heard above the noise of the wind and waves.

'No. It's a huge badger. I can see its claws,' his sister cut in, flicking her hair out of her eyes and flexing her fingers in and out as if they were claws.

At first the man could see nothing, but as he gazed at the incoming waves his eyes made out an object, something rolling with them, but incapable of keeping up with them or with their rhythm, something always left behind. The wind stinging his eyes, he put a hand to his brow like a sea captain of old, and stared hard at the thing. It was solid, pink in parts and surprisingly large.

Unable and unwilling to adjudicate between their

competing claims, he took out the skimming stones he had gathered and offered them mutely to them.

'The waves are too big,' the boy said, looking at them and then back at his father.

'OK,' the man said, 'we'll play a game, see who can hit the sea creature first.'

'It's not a sea creature,' Kath replied firmly.

'OK,' he relented, 'we'll hit the sea creature, badger or goat.'

He himself took aim at the thing and missed, the stone falling a good two metres short. The boy, moving forward to make sure that he was standing exactly where his father had stood for his shot, flung his stone and let out a loud whoop as he did so. Once more, the stone disappeared into the water, far short of the target. Kath, now occupying the throwing zone, raised her thin arm and flung her stone. It flew over her head backwards, bouncing off the rocks, the noise it made attracting Ivan's attention. Instantly, he set off to retrieve it, returning in seconds with it in his mouth.

'Your turn, Dad,' the boy said, solemnly. This time, the man thought, he might have a chance. The thing, still revolving in the waves, was undoubtedly closer. Looking hard at it, fixing its precise location in his head, he fired the stone at it, also mistiming the release and watching, powerless, as it rose upwards. Once again he failed to hit the thing but, as he focused on it, a slow realisation dawned. It was not a goat, a sea creature or badger. It was a human being, floating, with the back of its head and buttocks above the water. Kath, stone in hand, was already readying herself for another throw.

'Stop, darling, now!' he said, sufficiently gruffly for her to turn and stare at him, afraid she had done something wrong. Seeing her serious little face, he could not think what to say. The picnic would be ruined. William and Kath would remember this day for all the wrong reasons, possibly have nightmares from now on simply thinking about it. Sarah would blame him, however blameless he was, maybe even use it as a pretext to stop him seeing them. Somehow it would all be his fault: for having taken them there, for having arranged a picnic in the middle of winter, for having been born. That thought galvanised him into action.

'Hot chocolate time! The first one to reach the car gets to choose what film we're going to see. Ready, steady, *go!*'

Forgetting about the stone-throwing competition they both ran off, the dog barking in their wake, forgetting their nets and everything else. He picked up the nets and stowed them under his arm, looking at the corpse as he did so, watching it bob about, now only five metres or so from his feet. Although he did not say anything out loud, he felt like cursing it. This strange, waxy, horrible thing, drifting towards him, had almost ruined the day. William and Kath would remember a carefree Saturday, see in their minds' eyes the waves, remember the burnt taste of the gritty sausages, hear Ivan's joyous barking as he raced into the sea. But not him. For him, William's tenth birthday would be The Day I Found the Dead Body. Everything else would drift into the background, obscured, obliterated by the horror of it all.

Fishing about in the pocket of his coat, he brought out his mobile phone. Was this an emergency? Did one dial 999? Whoever was washing ashore was dead after all, and no amount of blue lights or sirens would alter that. In some ways, there really was all the time in the world.

II

As soon as the postie left, Dr Harry McCrae went into his kitchen and ripped open the wrapping of the small parcel that she had delivered. He knew what was supposed to be inside, and, in some ways, had been looking forward to its arrival. His already late lunch could wait. From the cardboard box he removed a small, white rubberised face mask and the spacer that went with it. Shu-shu, his companion, watched him. Little did she know, the man thought to himself, as he looked into the cat's unblinking eyes, that its contents concerned her.

At last everything was ready. He had the treats, the inhaler and, finally, the mask and spacer. The YouTube video of 'Fritz the Brave' was still fresh in his mind. Now was the time. As if to stiffen his sinews for the task ahead, the cat began to cough, stretching her neck forward, her sides heaving as she gasped for breath, trying to draw it through her constricted airways. 'Blessed asthma!' he said to himself, fitting the inhaler into the spacer, ready for action.

First she must have a few treats, then, please God, she would associate the dosing with food, with a pleasant experience. Had the treats been made of dried goldfish, she could not have gobbled them up faster from the saucer. She ate each one, whole and at speed, expressing her delight by purring loudly and rubbing her flanks against his calves. While she was gazing up at him, licking her lips, possibly trying to hypnotise him into giving her more, he grabbed her, sat her on his knee and jammed the mask over her short muzzle. At first, no doubt shocked by the novelty of the experience, she did not move. But the second he squeezed the inhaler, making it hiss like a snake as it released its metered dose, she began wriggling, scrabbling her back legs on his thigh, digging her claws in. Knowing she must take at least five breaths, he tightened his grip, speaking gently to her, trying to calm her and reassure her.

At that moment his phone went. Still grappling with his squirming, frightened pet he ignored it, but it was difficult for him to do so. He was on-call, and conscientious. Making sure she took a couple more breaths, he held her steady and then, the second he released her, threw down a whole handful of treats. She fell on them as if starved. Fortunately the phone was still ringing and, nerves jangling, he answered it.

'Yes, it's me, Dr McCrae. OK . . . a body in the water at Belhaven Bay, off the coast at Tyninghame? I'll be there. I'll get my things and leave in ten minutes. It'll take me, say, an hour and a bit.'

It could have been worse, he thought, packing away the cat inhaler ready for the next time. Shu-shu had, hallelujah, had her first dose; and Dunbar harbour was a pleasant enough place to spend a Saturday afternoon, even if the only sightseeing he would be doing was of an expanse of dead flesh. Somewhere there, or at North Berwick, he might even pick up a fresh lobster. Shu-shu, now sitting a safe distance away from him, turned her head in his direction, a reproachful expression on her face.

'You'd like a morsel of lobster claw, my darling, wouldn't you?' he crooned at her. He got no answer and, in the silence, sniffed, his cat-allergy worsened by their recent proximity. 'It's for your own good, my sweet,' he said, rising and hoping to resume cordial relations with a stroke, but finding only thin air as she dodged his hand. Implacable, holding her lightly banded tail upright as a mast, she strode through the kitchen door, without giving him as much as a backwards glance.

—

By the time Dr McCrae arrived, the corpse had been moved from the lifeboat to a disused shed nearby. A young constable stood guard at the door. Inside, the body had been laid out on a polythene sheet over the bare wooden floorboards for his inspection. Cobwebs draped across the only window, thick as a lace curtain, beaded with the desiccated remains of bluebottles. Waiting a couple of yards away was an ambulance with its engine running, the driver leaning against the bonnet, spellbound, watching the clouds racing across the grey sky.

The forensic medical examiner dropped his bag down on the only table, raising a cloud of dust and immediately holding his breath, unwilling to inhale anything. Already he had been hit by the overwhelming stench of creosote in the place. Hell's bells! In minutes he would have a headache to add to his congestion after sneezing his way along the A1. He'd suffer an asthma attack himself, to put the tin lid on it.

Thinking that the sooner he started the sooner he would finish, he squatted down beside the body, his paper suit crackling as he did so. Bending over the boy's face, its youthfulness struck him immediately, that and its loveliness. Caravaggio alone might have done such a face justice. His gaze travelled downwards to the bloated, gas-distended torso. That aspect of the boy's anatomy would perhaps be portrayed elsewhere, in textbooks seen only by students of forensic pathology. In their gruesome pages he would be accorded a figure number, not a name, and God help his parents if they ever stumbled across the plate.

Something, a crab perhaps, had nibbled away the edge of an earlobe. Continuing unconsciously in work mode, he registered the minuscule abrasions on the side of the boy's face, and his hands with their thick washerwoman wrinkles. A rock, or maybe the barnacles on it, had cut into the loose skin on one palm, most likely as he drifted about in the shallows, scraping along the seabed. But it was not the slight, superficial striations on the skin that drew his eye, or kept his attention. When the body was turned over, to the left of the boy's spine, opposite his heart, five large incisions were revealed. He had not died of drowning. Not with those white cuts. Days at sea, with water caressing every inch of his skin, cleaning him, leaching the blood from the wounds, might well account for their appearance. No, this was not rock damage, pier damage or even propeller damage. Dr McCrae bent further over the body, examining each wound minutely. The edges were the same in every case: clean and regular. Sharp force wounds. In all probability they were made by the same implement, a knife of some sort.

While the doctor continued his inspection, recording the precise extent and location of every injury, checking as far as possible beneath the victim's clothes and hair for any other concealed damage, examining his airways, the young constable outside, guarding the door of the shed, was making a phone call. As he did so he was exposed to the full force of the wind as it howled through the gaps in the red sandstone cliffs, buffeting the harbour walls and making the open sea beyond them boil. While he waited to speak to Chief Inspector Bell, the constable studied the horizon, tracking a squall as it made its way landwards, rippling and darkening the water as it moved across it, disfiguring it as a frown disfigures a face. Rain began to fall on the harbour, blowing horizontally, driving into his eyes and making his acne sting. Cold, and increasingly impatient to break his news, he fidgeted, fingering the coins in his jacket pocket and playing with the zip. Today, he knew, was his lucky day. Already he had rehearsed what he would say. He wanted to sound articulate and confident. Credit was on offer, and he intended to be the one to get it.

'Chief Inspector Bell?'

'Yes.'

Unable to hear her answer due to the background noise, he said, 'Sorry. What did you say?'

'Yes. It is Chief Inspector Bell,' she confirmed, enunciating extra clearly.

'This is PC Alan Learmonth,' he gabbled, flustered by the tone of vague annoyance he detected in her reply. 'It was . . . I just wanted to let you know we've got your man. He's dead. Dr McCrae is with him now.'

'I can't hear you.'

He repeated what he had said, turning in towards the shed, trying to cut down the noise of the wind.

'What man?' came the irritable reply.

'Hamish Evans? The one you're looking for in relation to the Stimms murder case. I recognised him from the posters, the circulars. He's the body the coastguard took out of Belhaven Bay.'

'Fine. And Dr McCrae's with him now, you say?'

151

'Yes.'

'Right. Thank you. Goodbye.'

It was, he thought, a most unsatisfactory exchange. The chief inspector would probably not even remember his name, maybe had not even heard it with all that racket going on. And worse yet, it was not clear that she had taken on board the fact that he had been the one to recognise the body, that it wasn't the police surgeon or anyone else. None of the glory would go to him, and his chances of joining the CID had not improved one bit.

On their return from the mortuary, Mr and Mrs Evans had, immediately and independently, gone to the drinks cupboard and got out a bottle. In the car on the journey home to the Dean Village they had sat side by side, scarcely exchanging a word, too shocked by what they had seen to formulate a sentence, never mind comfort one another. Feeling disorientated, adrift in an unfamiliar world, Christopher Evans sat cradling his tumbler of Highland Park between his hands. He stared out of the window onto the Water of Leith below as if the sight of the river was holding his attention, but his focus was elsewhere.

On the sofa, directly behind him, sat his wife. Her eyes were closed, and though present physically, she was absent in both mind and spirit. The enormity of her loss was incomprehensible to her, her brain no longer obeyed her orders, wandering off, uninstructed, retrieving memories of Hamish's third birthday, then settling on yesterday's shopping or darting in search of a great aunt's name. But always, always, like a butterfly around a flowering buddleia, it was circling about Hamish, coming back to settle on him, reminding her that he was dead, laid out in a fridge in the Cowgate, the beautiful white skin of his chest as mottled as a toad's, his face bloodless and looking as soft as soap.

Gazing at him, changed as he was, she had known in her heart, as much as her head, that it was him. Something in him had reached out to her and spoken to her. Twenty-four years ago, they had been linked; linked literally, viscerally, and even now, in death, some shadow of that bond remained.

Often, when he was small, subject to the usual illnesses, she had been frightened for his very existence. Once she had seen her only child, she had tied her life to his. No little boy of hers would wander alone in the valley of death, so, as she had told him, wherever he went she would go. She had meant it then and he was still, would always be, her son, her little boy. Nothing could change that. She would not break her word and desert him now. How, she wondered, had she not known of his death? Surely, something should, would, have told her. Why had the sun not failed to rise, the moon not turned red, the earth not ceased turning on its axis? How could she not have known? With him dead, how had her own heart continued to beat, blood flow in her veins?

'You alright, Eve?' her husband asked.

'I'm OK,' she replied, 'You?'

'I'm OK too.'

Between them, as neither could tell the truth, words had lost their meaning. But language was not required, because their eyes did not lie. Looking only for a millisecond into his, she had seen that he had shattered into a thousand pieces.

'What time are they due?' she asked.

'Any time now,' he replied, moving away from the window, standing in the middle of the room, paralysed, unsure where to go next. That inspector and her sidekick were likely to arrive in minutes, but there was no point in going to the door until they arrived. So he remained where he was, standing motionless in no man's land, until a knock at the door resolved his quandary.

Normally, in their marriage, Christopher Evans spoke for the couple. After all, he made his living by his tongue, came alive at the sound of his own voice, and usually could not get enough of it. His rich, brown tones, which conveyed integrity, solidity and reliability, convinced jurors that his clients must be cut from the same cloth. Someone who sounded like that would, surely, not be able to defend a guilty person? His wife, by way of contrast, lived largely in her own head, and rarely felt the need to burden others with her thoughts or views. But, confronted by Alice, and as if they had reached an unspoken accord, Helena Evans took on the role of their spokesperson.

'Neither of us had seen him since he went to London,' she replied, answering that question, as she had its predecessors, carefully and truthfully. Already, with the strain of the day's events, she was hoarse.

'Have either of you spoken on the phone to him since then?'

The man nodded his head and the woman said no.

'Like I told you before,' he clarified, 'I spoke to him when he was in the airport, on his way home.'

'Did he often go to London?' Alice asked.

'About once every two months,' Mrs Evans said, not looking up, running her forefinger around the edge of her wine glass.

'If he took his car to the airport, where did he usually park?'

Seeing his wife's blank look, the man said, 'One or other of the long stays. He always took his car.'

'Do either of you know if he intended to visit his girlfriend immediately on his return?'

They exchanged glances again, and then Mr Evans chipped in, 'When I spoke to him in the airport, he was a bit bothered about her – agitated. It wouldn't surprise me a bit if he went straight to see her. She was plainly on his mind.'

'When visiting her, have you any idea where he usually parked?'

They both shook their heads.

'Were you aware of the cause of his agitation, had there been any falling out between them?'

'A falling out between Hamish and Mandy? You mean a row? No. Why? He never said anything to me about a row. Did he say anything to you, Chris, about a row?' the woman, clearly perplexed, asked her husband.

'Nothing to me,' he replied, taking a long, deep drink from his tumbler, and then feeling the need to clarify his earlier remarks, adding, 'On the phone, I tried to speak to him, find out what was wrong, but he didn't want to talk about it. I thought it was just a misunderstanding. I know he was angry about something. He wanted to see her, speak to her.'

'Did you know Mandy, had you seen much of her?'

'No,' the woman replied, feeling suddenly exhausted, 'it doesn't work that way with Hamish. He was always a bit shy about these things. It's always been the same, ever since he first started going out with girls. To begin with you just hear a name, a new name – it'll start bobbing

155

up in conversations. Then, eventually, he'll bring the girl home for tea. We'd only met her twice – well, I'd met her twice. Chris hadn't, had you, dear? He was off the first time. You were doing something, weren't you, dear, but I can't for the life of me think what . . .'

'Golf, at Gullane,' he said morosely.

'That's right. You were playing golf with Derry, a friend of ours. Have you told her . . . Miranda, about Hamish, I mean?' the woman asked, looking anxiously at Alice.

'No, I haven't. She's dead.'

'Mandy?' the woman replied, incredulously. 'How d'you mean? How can she be dead? Did she drown too then . . . with Hamish or something? Did you know that, Chris? That she's dead, too? '

'No, I didn't,' the man said, looking hard at Alice, the bits of the jigsaw beginning to fall into place. Carefully, he placed his glass on the wing of his armchair as if it had been a distraction. Suddenly, he was completely sober.

'Did you know she was dead when you called at my office, asking questions about Hamish's whereabouts, Inspector?' he asked.

'When did she call at your office?' the woman cut in.

'A couple of days ago, I called a couple of days ago,' Alice replied. 'Yes, I knew Mandy was dead then – but not Hamish, I didn't know about him. Mandy was taken out of the Forth last Tuesday morning.'

'Are their deaths connected?' Mr Evans asked, then he added, as if it was an afterthought, 'with Mandy, was it murder? Is murder suspected?'

Alice nodded her head.

'He was a suspect?' he asked.

'What are you going on about, dear? Hamish, a suspect? Hamish is dead!' his wife exclaimed.

'With Hamish . . . murder is suspected too, I daresay,' Evans remarked, picking up his glass but taking nothing from it.

'Really! What are you talking about, Chris?' his wife demanded angrily. 'That's not what the constable said, that's not what they said there . . . it could have been an accident, couldn't it? Murder! Hamish murdered! He's dead, that's enough, isn't it? Why should it be murder? You've been dealing with criminals too long, dear.'

'I don't know,' Alice replied. 'We won't know for sure until after the post mortem. But, I should tell you, our forensic examiner's initial impression was murder. It's certainly the assumption that we're proceeding on at the moment. The pathologists will confirm one way or another.'

'I'm sorry, officer,' Mrs Evans said, tears now streaming down her face, 'I'll have to go. I'm not feeling well. Chris, will you manage?'

He nodded his head, touching her hand lightly with his own as she passed by his chair on her way to the door.

'What was Mandy like?' Alice asked, once she had left. 'I asked you if he was a suspect, but you didn't answer me.'

'I'm sorry. He . . . we needed to eliminate him as a suspect. She was dead, he had gone missing. Inevitably, we thought about him. What was Mandy like?'

The man sighed before answering, 'Mandy, Mandy. Why are we talking about Mandy? Hamish, my son, my only child, is dead. Hamish is my concern.'

'I know. And I'm very sorry about it all, but I do need to know. Their deaths may well be related. In finding out about her, we're finding out about him – about, in all probability, their killer.'

Before continuing he paused, looking across at the policewoman, searching her face as if checking her sincerity, and then continued. 'OK. Like Eve said, I only met her once, so remember that. She was nice, I liked her actually. She was a bit Olde Worlde, if you know what I mean. Mandy was unlike any of his other girlfriends, they were glamorous, with-it, in comparison. She was . . . well, like Julie Andrews if you get my drift. It was almost as if she was foreign. Thinking about it, now, it's hard to explain. Timid, as timid as a wee mouse. But I could see what he saw in her. She was pretty, very pretty – defenceless in a way. I don't know . . . all I can say is she wasn't like the others, wasn't much like anyone I've ever met. It was almost as if she was, or had been, stuck in a time warp. As if she was stuck in the fifties, or something.'

'And you knew nothing of any row?'

'Nothing – nothing of what it might have been about. If they had had a row.'

'Did Hamish ever mention anyone called Anna, a friend of Mandy's, who may have been living with her?'

'No.'

'Did you know that she was pregnant?'

'Who? This Anna girl?'

'No, Mandy.'

'Mandy! You're joking!'

'No.'

'Mandy? I have to admit, I'm surprised, amazed, in fact. She didn't seem like that type. I wonder if Hamish knew. I can't believe he did. She must, I suppose, have been stringing him along. I wouldn't have thought that of her. She wasn't that type at all. And God knows I've met them. Meet them often enough in my job. Are you absolutely sure about that?'

158

'Sure. Could it not have been Hamish's baby?'

'No, it could not. Hamish was infertile. We . . . he had no MMR. Eve couldn't stand the idea of the jabs. He got it when he was eleven, mumps, very badly. He was hospitalised, it was so serious. Of course he recovered, but we were told he was infertile, would always be infertile. He said he didn't care, he didn't want children and said that if he changed his mind he'd adopt. If Mandy was pregnant, whoever it was by, it wasn't by Hamish. Maybe that was what the row was about, maybe that was why he was so keen to see her?'

—

Back in the office, late on the Saturday afternoon, Alice was determined to catch up on her paperwork. After six, with luck, she would have broken the back of it, then she could go to the cottage in Kinross-shire and take a look at it. Marvel at it and, if there was time, seek out Ian's friend too. If it was too dark to see properly her car headlights would do to light it up, and she would still be near it, could breathe the air around it, feel as if she had taken possession of it. In only three days the place would finally be hers, and already the previous owners had moved out.

Her mind elsewhere, daydreaming, the phone call from Aileen Tennant caught her off guard, and for a moment she could not place who the woman was. Fortunately, she added after her name 'counsellor', and a picture of her, pale as a ghost, sitting in her drab office in Windsor Gardens, appeared in the policewoman's mind.

'Mrs Tennant,' she replied, 'how can I help you?'

'There's one thing, Inspector Rice, which I've been worrying about. It's probably nothing at all, but I thought

I ought to tell you all the same. You can decide whether it matters or not.'

'Yes?' She stirred her newly-made coffee, wanting a drink, hoping the conversation would not go on too long.

'Miranda Stimms' notes were due to be filed away. For some reason I took a last look at them and, reading them again, something made sense. When you were in the office and I had them in front of me there was an abbreviation, but I couldn't for the life of me, at the time, remember what it stood for.'

'What was it?'

'TE.'

'And now you can?' She took a quick swallow of her coffee, burning the back of her throat and almost gasping out loud in pain.

'Yes. But I don't know if it'll get you any further. But she thought it was very important, and I had planned, I remember, when I first noted it down to look it up, but work's been very busy, my home life too, and I completely forgot. "The E", it was her religion. Like being a protestant or a Jehovah's Witness or something like that. She was one of "The Elect". Or rather she wasn't. She'd given it all up, but it still seemed to bother her an awful lot, be on her mind. Anyway, I thought I ought to tell you, in case it matters.'

'Thanks. I'll look it up myself, see what I can discover about it. Presumably the file will be simply stored somewhere, not destroyed? We might need it as evidence.'

'It'll go to our depository. It'll be safe there, for the next five years anyway. It's procedure. They keep them, all of them, for at least five years. I've no idea why.'

After she put down the phone, Alice googled 'The Elect' and numerous results appeared, ranging from a

Daily Mail headline '"The leader of the Elect molested me" shock testimony' and obscure American sites to assorted blogs, a 'Cult Documentary' on YouTube and Wikipedia. Sampling a selection of the links she discovered that the Elect was an offshoot of the Plymouth Brethren which had, throughout its history, been subject to frequent schisms, purges, mass excommunications and desertions. Over time the ever-decreasing rump (known as the Derby-Cornell-Waring sect) had become more and more withdrawn from the outside world, a place which was regarded as a zone of evil and corruption. Their current leader, who in similar style to his predecessors was known as 'The Chosen One', ran an agricultural machinery business in Wisconsin and, since his father had held the leadership before him, seemed to occupy an almost hereditary office similar to that occupied by the Kims in North Korea. The Elect themselves were subject to numerous prohibitions; these included eating or drinking with any person not in the fellowship, sharing a residence with anyone not in the fellowship (sharing even a semi-detached residence would breach this prohibition as the properties would share a common wall), sharing a sewer or driveway with anyone not in the fellowship, marrying anyone not within the fellowship, and joining any trade union or professional association. The Elect considered themselves exalted in the eyes of the Lord. Every day of the week, and several times on Sundays ('Christ's Day'), the Elect were required to attend meetings, whether for the 'Lord's Repast', worship, Bible study or reading, or prayer. If possible, the adherents, or 'holies' as they sometimes referred to themselves, schooled their children within Elect schools. Many had now been set up by them within the UK, including a fair number in

Scotland. Attendance at university was forbidden due to its potential for corrupting the students. Consequently, the community counted few doctors, dentists or lawyers within their number, and any of these were now elderly, having qualified before that particular prohibition was brought into effect. Ten years earlier, the church had lost a wrangle with the Charity Commission and its charitable status had been withdrawn on the grounds that it produced no benefit for the public.

As she checked out a selection of the blogs, many written by ex-members of the Elect or with contributions from them, one thing became very apparent. Many ex-members appeared to have been traumatised by their time within the sect, feeling the need to tell others of their experiences, seeking support from others whose memories of life within it appeared to be equally unhappy. One site, calling itself 'The Painful Truth', stated, 'The Elect who leave or are expelled from the faithful have often met with what non-members view as great unkindness, barbarity even. Leavers are shunned by members of the group because they are considered to have opted for the world and its works rather than God, and because they could bring members into contact with the sinful world and all its vices.'

According to her mother, Miranda Stimms had left the group, although whether her leaving was voluntary or not had not been mentioned. If she had indeed, as her mother had maintained, grown up gay or bisexual even, it seemed unlikely that there would be any place for her within the Elect whatever her choice had been. Picturing Mrs Stimms in her immaculate house, Alice had little doubt that she remained within the sect, and her slightly strange, frightened demeanour now seemed understandable. The police, being part of the corrupt world, servants of that world, would bring with them no comfort, no reassurance for her. They, too, would be contaminated, alien to the sect and its adherents. Hostile. And if Miranda Stimms had been brought up by them, she might well come across as old-fashioned and unworldly. In short, she would be odd.

12

As Alice was taking her coat off the back of her chair, ready to leave and go to Kinross-shire, Elaine Bell strode into the office. She was deep in thought, but catching sight of Alice she came bustling over to her desk. Parking herself on the edge of it, she settled herself down for a proper chat.

'What do you make of it?'

'What? Miranda Stimms, the deceased, being in the Elect?'

'What *are* you talking about?' came back the impatient reply.

'I've just heard from that counsellor in Musselburgh that Miranda Stimms belonged, or used to belong, to a religious sect called the Elect.'

'Did she, indeed. Whoever the hell they may be. No, not that. I mean about Hamish Evans being found. Are you off somewhere?'

'I don't know what to think yet. I've seen his parents, they identified the boy and had a few useful things to add. They'd never heard him mention Anna, didn't know much about any argument between him and Miranda. But there was one interesting thing. They told me it couldn't have been his baby, because he was sterile after an attack of mumps as a child. They speculated that that might have been the cause of any row between them. Have you spoken to Harry McCrae?'

'Harry? Yes, I spoke to him only about half an hour ago. He's pretty sure the lad died of those knife wounds to his back. I asked how long he reckoned he'd been dead.'

'And?'

'Patience, Alice. If you'd just be good enough to let me finish for once? As per bloody usual, the good doctor wouldn't stick his neck out. His "initial" or "preliminary" view, which may, of course, "be subject to subsequent revision at the mortuary" is that he'd been dead, in the water, for anything up to a week.'

'If he's been dead since last Saturday, he couldn't have argued with Miranda Stimms on the Monday, couldn't have killed her. That's when she was last seen, or, more accurately, heard. Him too. So we know McCrae's estimate's wrong to that extent at least. And we also know that the boy caught his London to Edinburgh flight on the Monday night. So, dead in the water for five days max.

'Maybe the blood spatters and so on in the common stair were his, not hers as we thought?'

'Could be, I suppose. We'll find out, although not soon enough. The lab remains as constipated as before. I doubt it anyway. Dr Cash postulated a fall from the start, specifically a fall backwards. That's what the head wound, knuckle abrasions etc. suggested. With those knife wounds to his back, the boy . . .'

'Would have bled like a pig in an abattoir, I know, but only *if* he was alive when they were inflicted. So?'

Seeing Alice doing up the buttons of her coat, Elaine Bell rose from her perch, and repeated, 'So? Are you off somewhere? Two murders within five days. Not two strangers but boyfriend and girlfriend, both dragged out of the sea. Connected, plainly *connected*. So, who'll be next? Get a move on, Alice. I don't want another body dredged up.'

'The boy being infertile is significant. Miranda Stimms' mother told us her daughter was gay – but Miranda had a boyfriend, him, or so her work friend, his parents and others have all told us. But we know she had a girlfriend, too. I suppose the existence of the baby just, to my mind, confirmed some degree of heterosexuality.'

'In this age of miracles and wonders – the age of turkey basters? I think you're being a little naïve there, Alice. You'll need to be sharper than that if you're going to catch whoever's responsible for these deaths. Have you anyone in your sights as the daddy, or the donor, for that matter?'

'Not at this minute. My point is, if it wasn't Hamish Evans' child, then whose child was it? I'd like to know, because whoever else's it was, it wasn't Anna's. There was someone before Hamish Evans, Irene mentioned him in passing. He worked at Co-op with her. His name is Sam Inglis. And I am off. I need to see somebody about something else, but something important.'

The chief inspector's mind being on the investigation, and the investigation alone, this explanation seemed to satisfy her curiosity. Alice did not feel the need to elucidate further, and to explain that the person concerned had nothing whatsoever to do with the Stimms case or the Evans case. Already they had consumed hours of her life, shortened it, and for the moment she had no more to give. This was important, to her. The Rice case also merited some priority.

—

Once at her destination in Kinross-shire, high in the Ochils, she got out of her car, stretched and gazed up at the night sky. Apart from the impassive gibbous moon which seemed close enough to touch, it was alive with numberless stars, every one brilliant, cold and flawless. Standing in the moonlight, bright as day, she exhaled slowly, allowing herself to relax for the first time in a week. All the tension in her body slowly began to drain from her. Here, she seemed to have entered another world, a cleaner, simpler one where the sounds of silence could not only be heard but also felt in the flesh, and she allowed the stillness to enfold her like a shawl. Completely motionless, conscious of her own breathing, her own heart beating, she was reminded of the huge gulf between life in the city and life outside it. It was as great, as wide, as that between a busy harbour, all ice-cream-carrying tourists jostling each other, yapping dogs, roaring motor boats laden with day-trippers in their sun hats, sea-gulls screeching from the chimney tops, on the one hand; and on the other, the great, wide expanse of the open ocean. One crackled with life, dazzlingly full of colour, electric with motion, fizzing with its own concerns, generating and nourished by ceaseless noise, and the other just *was*. Its grandeur was in its being. Humankind and all its affairs were as unimportant to it, as meaningless to it, as a single wave breaking on the shore. And without man and his schemes, plans and interventions, it would go on just being, changing at its own pace, ignoring the human blink-of-an-eye timescale, altering only in millennia or, in its perfection, not at all.

She closed her tired eyes and inhaled the chill air, savouring its sharpness in her lungs, revitalising herself with its icy purity. The cottage was exactly as she had remembered it, set on top of the hills, small, stone-built and with a view to the south unlikely to be bettered anywhere on earth. Below, in the plain, the loch shone like polished lead, the dark shadow of the Lomonds behind it and the lights of the settlements clustered around its shores winking across the water to each other. In the far distance, a plume of orange flame was visible, resembling the pillar of fire which comforted the Israelites in the wilderness, betokening God's presence. That would do for her, she decided. She preferred that view of it to the more mundane reality; it was the burning of excess gas at the chemical plant in Fife. With its image remaining branded on her retina, she turned back to examine the cottage.

As she had expected, no lights were on in any of its windows and she circled the place like a burglar, peering in, touching the stone, hardly able to believe that within days such a treasure would be hers. Even the double front doors with their faded green paint seemed perfect, and hidden deep in the hard ground below her feet would be bulbs, snowdrops, crocuses, grape hyacinths, daffodils, perhaps, and as the months passed they would reveal themselves to her along with all the other plants, and weeds, in her garden. 'My garden', the very words pleased her.

Less than two metres from the house's western gable lay the pond. A thin film of ice coated its surface, reflecting the moonlight, and as she walked towards it, her eyes scanning its far boundary, she made out the silhouette of a heron. It was standing on a single leg, in a bed of dry and broken reeds. On her approach it took flight, flapping its great wings in slow motion as it rose, majestically, above the roof, its long legs trailing behind it. When summer came there would be frogs, diving beetles and dragonflies, she thought, and for the first time since Ian had died she felt joy, pure, unadulterated joy, and recognising it, tears came to her eyes. Even if the roof of the cottage leaked, its plumbing failed and the place was overrun by a plague of rats, as some of her friends had predicted, he would have understood exactly why she had bought it. He would have seen all that she could see, and more.

—

The first thing that struck her on meeting Father Vincent Ross was the blueness of his eyes; the second, that he did not look like any priest she had ever encountered before. Her convent education had prepared her for a number of possible archetypes, but he fitted none of them. He was not Irish, for a start, had no pot belly, and did not exhibit the slightly self-satisfied and unctuous air that she had prepared herself for. Few clerics ministering to a convent of nuns, never mind the pubescent girls in their care, did not have their heads turned, whatever they looked like, believing themselves to be a peacock amongst eager pea-hens. Instead, she thought, looking at him across his own sitting room, he resembled a slightly dishevelled former pugilist, with his nose unmistakeably broken, and his pro-fuse sandy hair falling untidily all over his face. In boxing terms a featherweight, possibly, to her welterweight.

True to form, he had immediately offered her a drink, unable to stop himself from recommending a 2012 Sau-vignon Blanc Grande Reserve. Seeing him fussing about the place in search of a suitable glass, she was reminded of Ian's amusement at the fellow's notorious uneasiness over his hobby. Golf might be uncontroversial for a priest, but fine wines? And how many times had she heard him being teased over the phone, called Jancis or Gilly, being lambasted for his 'poncy', 'pseudish' winespeak. From the guffaws that usually followed such abuse he seemed to be able to hold his own.

Sitting opposite her in his armchair, he was so short that his feet hardly touched the floor, she noticed. A Siamese cat lay on his lap, purring, and sometimes, she thought, he seemed to be addressing his comments to it as much as to her. Despite the fact that she hardly knew him, she found his company restful, the few silences between them neither heavy nor oppressive. With the ease of an old friend he asked her what she had been doing that day, before she came up to see the cottage.

'I was looking something up . . . on one of your rivals, you might say. Another church. I needed to learn something about it for my work, for an investigation I'm involved in.'

'What church?' he asked, sitting back in his armchair with his nose hovering over his wine glass like a kestrel over its prey.

'The Elect.'

'Rivals? They're rivals to the Catholic Church in much the same way a mosquito rivals the National Blood Transfusion Service – or a lollipop lady the traffic division of the Met.'

'You've heard of them?'

'Certainly. There are a fair number in Kincardine, and no doubt others around the place. They are an offshoot of the Plymouth Brethren. They prospered in Scotland for a while, particularly in fishing and mining communities, until their leader was exposed as a "speaker with two mouths". That cut their numbers.'

'Sounds intriguing.'

'I thought so too. Do you want to hear about it? Have you time?'

'Plenty of time.'

While he talked she looked around the room in which they sat. It had been furnished sparsely, practically, without fripperies of any kind. No cushions or curtains, but there was a computer, a TV and books everywhere, overflowing their shelves, stacked on the floor. Photographs, all in a straight line, had been stuck along the entire length of a cream-coloured wall. One she recognised. It was of Ian, laughing, looking astonishingly young and holding a tankard up as if making a toast. Seeing it, she felt her heart turn over and looked away quickly, determined that her face should not give her away. A cardboard box caught her eye. It was filled with wine bottles, and had been shoved out of sight, or out of the way, below a desk. Three coffee cups, unwashed, were stacked by the side of his armchair. The place bore all the signs of someone living on his own, attending to the essentials and pleasing only himself. She should know.

'Well,' he continued, looking at her, apparently pleased that she was interested, 'it happened in about 1945. Their then leader, Timothy Cornell, was staying with a devout family, the Flemings, on some ministry matter. Unfortunately, Mr Fleming discovered the Chosen One naked in the marital bed with a naked Mrs Fleming. The pair of them were completely blootered – on an early Napa Valley white, apparently, if you can believe it. At that date, it will hardly have been drinkable pre-Robert Mondavi – if oak-smoked barrels . . .'

'What happened?'

'Well, the Chosen One explained that, despite appearances, he had simply been teaching theology to Mrs Fleming, and when challenged on their unlikely classroom and lack of school uniform, he added that the whole thing had been, in fact, a test, something designed to weed out the faithless from the flock. Mr Fleming, unconvinced, threw him out of the house, a semi in Mount Pleasant, Wisconsin, without clothes. A passing newsman took a photograph and it got into the local newspaper and from there into the national and international media.'

'Did any of the faithful remain?'

'You'd be surprised at the numbers who stayed on. Thinking about it, we are all, I suppose, credulous in our own ways.'

'Water to wine?'

'Rising from the dead sticks in the craw of many.'

'But not you?'

'If he was the son of God, why should it? Either he was what he said, the son of God, or he was a lunatic. "Love thy neighbour as thyself" doesn't sound to me like the sentiment, the words, of a lunatic. But we're straying from the point.'

'My fault. Are there any of them here, in Kinross?'

'Of the Elect?'

'Yes.'

'A few, probably, but I don't know for sure. Last year one of their oversized meeting halls sprang up between here and Stirling. They're unmistakable. More like a cash-and-carry than a church. They've got no windows, a huge car-parking space, high-security fencing, air-conditioning . . .'

'Air conditioning? Why on earth . . .'

'Because it's all centralised. They have to build them in accordance with a blueprint devised in Wisconsin, the home of their current "Chosen One". And it's always a Him. Hence the air-conditioning, obviously something largely superfluous in our lovely weather.'

172

'What else do you know about them?' she asked, impressed, amused by his enthusiasm for such relative arcana.

He sipped his wine, meeting her eye, then smiling widely as if at a private joke, 'Well, for a start, that you'd find them pretty difficult. In fact, I'd hazard you wouldn't last a day. Half a day even.'

'Why?'

'They're not keen on women in any form of power.'

'Oh, unlike the Catholic Church with its unbroken succession of female popes, not to mention all the she-cardinals and priestesses, you mean?' she retorted, sounding more heated than she felt.

'Satan!' he said, placing his hand over his cat's ears.

'Satan?' she repeated, bemused.

'I thought we were speaking about the Elect? My cat, Satan, probably shocked by your jibes, dug his claws into me. Anyway, what are you complaining about – wasn't one Pope Joan enough for you, an unforgettable double first, pregnant and papal?'

'We are talking about them, the Elect. Tell me more. Please,' she said, watching as the Siamese yawned, rose on the man's lap, arched his back, slid sinuously to the floor and then padded out of the open doorway.

'That cat's so easily bored! One of their tenets is that a woman mustn't put herself in "a position of authority" over a man, any man. Once married she can't look for paid work, and while working and unmarried she can't, for reasons obvious to them, rise to anything much above a receptionist or secretary. All in all, it's like life in the fifties, only worse. Madmen plus. You, I'm sorry to say, would probably be classified by them, using their terminology, as a "Loudmouth". As a Catholic, I'm one of the

Slaves of Satan – the Lord of the Flies, incidentally, not my cat. Although I am, of course, his slave too.'

'Thanks. And the "Chosen One", is he their Pope or what?'

'A sort of Mega-Pope. He's more like a cross between Jesus and the Holy Father, I'd say. His edicts have to be obeyed because, according to them, the Holy Spirit speaks through him. His word is law, whether forbidding the keeping of pets – creatures are to be eaten or used only – or banning mobile phones, TVs, computers and faxes, as "transmitters of filth". Thinking about it, maybe he has a point? Anyway, failure to obey his edicts can lead to excommunication.'

'Surely that's almost impossible nowadays, living without technology? Who would give them a job? No mobiles, no computers . . .'

'It did present them with a problem, although, luckily, most of them run their own small businesses. They're a highly commercial sect. You see, they aren't allowed to work for "worldlies". It must have been maddening for them, like running the marathon on one leg or knitting with one needle. Fortunately, in about 2005 things improved because, as their Chosen One put it, "the Lord saw things anew". Or, as you and I might put it, He changed His mind.'

'What happened to all of the faithful who had been excommunicated for sending a fax or whatever?'

'Sadly, they are still languishing in the outer darkness, on the grounds that God may move on but no one can "second-guess the Lord". Early enlightenment is not on, apparently.'

'The woman I'm interested in is no longer in the Elect,' Alice said, taking another sip of the Bergerac, noticing that his glass remained all but full. His nose still hovered above his wine, assessing it, but he did not drink.

'Do you like this white?' he asked.

'Very much, thank you.'

'Good, it has a lovely bouquet, I think. This woman, did she leave or was she pushed?'

'I don't know. I plan to go back and speak to her parents again.'

'Well, there's one thing you should know about them, Alice, for the purposes of your job. Their founding principle, their charter, to use business jargon, is the doctrine of separation. Hence no eating with "worldlies" like us, no sharing even of a common wall and all of that. As far as they are concerned, we live in a modern day Sodom and Gomorrah. Contact with us leads to contamination. We're iniquity, you and me; and me, obviously, more than most. So, when you're speaking to them, don't assume that you're both on the same side. Their loyalties are always to each other, their fellow "holies", not to any "worldly". Whatever crime she, perish the thought, might be investigating and whoever is under suspicion. Now, why not stay to supper?'

'I must get back to work, find out more about them. The ones in Edinburgh. Find out more about her,' she said, swallowing the last of her wine and putting her glass down on the table beside her chair.

'Stay. Please,' he said, and seeing her rise to her feet he rose to his own and added, 'if Ian was still alive you wouldn't be working non-stop, would you? Everyone has to eat. It's past nine. I'll lend you my book about them, that'll save you bags of time. There's a stew in the oven, ready now. There's more than enough for two. Please – you'd be doing me a favour.'

Looking into his anxious blue eyes, she saw he meant it. At that instant his cat returned, weaving itself lithely between his legs. Bending down to stroke it he smiled, saying, 'Slave that I am, there's only so much of Satan's exalted company I can take.'

13

On Sundays, as on every other day of the week, the Co-op in Pitt Street remained open. Mr Wilson, overworked, short-staffed and with the greenish hue of a man suffering from a bad hangover, accompanied the policewoman in the direction of the cheese counter, assuring her that she would find Sam Inglis there, somewhere among the stock.

'Please be as quick as you can,' he said, trotting beside her on his thick little legs, his nostrils flaring wide as they neared the fish counter, the air around it heavy with the aroma of smoked haddock. Unexpectedly, he stopped dead for a moment, a wave of bile rising in his throat, steadying himself and breathing laboriously. Who was it last night who had said that vodka acted like a tonic? Six, mixed with Coke, seemed to have had the opposite effect on him. Could heads explode? He leant against the end of the counter, closed his eyes and hoped to die quickly.

'Are you OK?' Alice asked.

'I must have eaten something last night that doesn't agree with me,' he replied, forcing himself onwards, but feeling desperate, on the verge of tears.

Around the corner, a stacked trolley at his elbow, Sam Inglis was busy behind the cheese counter refreshing and reorganising yesterday's display. He was arranging a batch of clingfilm-covered Stilton wedges artistically, if not appetisingly, on top of a wheel of French Brie. On the back of his head, at a jaunty angle, was a pork pie hat made out of white, plastic mesh. It was many sizes too small, and covered little more than the crown of his black, greasy hair. He looked as if he had been in a fight. One of his eyes was almost closed, the lid yellowish, swollen and bruised, and a gash disfigured the bridge of his nose.

'Sam,' the manager said, his hand over his mouth as he gagged at the sight of a slice of Dunsyre Blue, 'this is Inspector Rice, she's from St Leonard's Street Police Station. She's looking into Mandy Stimms' death. She needs to talk to you. Christ! What's happened to your face?'

'Talk to me here?' the man said. 'What does she want to know about Mandy?'

'No, not here,' Mr Wilson said tetchily, suddenly all but overcome by the fumes from a plateful of over-ripe Gorgonzola morsels which had been left on the counter for customers to sample. 'You can speak to her outside, where you go for your fag break.'

'What about the customers?' Inglis asked. A woman at the counter was waiting expectantly, obviously rehearsing her order in her head and about to speak.

'Where's Flo? Couldn't she take over?' the manager asked weakly.

'She had to relieve Ginny at the bakery. Ron's off.'

'What about Jane, is she not available? I thought she was supposed to be in this morning.'

As Inglis paused to consider where Jane might be, the woman pointed at a wedge of apple-smoked cheddar and announced, 'I'll take some of that – and some of the . . . what's it called, Stinking Bishop – yes, a bit of that too. I like it with chutney.'

'Stinking Bishop? What's that, when it's at home?' Sam Inglis said, looking inquiringly at his boss, unsure whether to serve the customer or obey his earlier instruction.

Shaking his head in his exasperation, thinking long-ingly of the Alka Seltzer tablets in his pocket, Mr Wilson gesticulated for Inglis to go. 'Right, right, right. I'll do it,' he said, tying the strings of a spare apron around his waist, a sickly smile on his face. 'Just one minute, madam, I'll be there in a tick. Some of the apple-smoked? We've no Stinking Bishop, that's . . . ah . . . something or other with herbs in it. Can I get you anything else instead?'

———

Leaning back against the wall of the Co-op car park, Sam Inglis wasted no time in lighting up. His roll-up looked ludicrously small between his large, nicotine-stained fingers and in seconds he was puffing away as if his life depended upon it. Off-duty, he undid the only button left on his white coat, sighing contentedly now his full belly was released from constraint. As he did so Alice noticed a mass of scratch marks across the back of both of his hands, now scabbing over.

'What do you want to know about Mandy?' he asked between deep draws on the roll-up.

'You went out with her?'

'Depends what you mean,' he said dismissively, remov-ing a strand of stray tobacco from the tip of his tongue.

'I heard from a colleague that the pair of you went out together, is that true?'

'Who was it?' he said, looking at her with narrowed eyes. 'John, was it John? No, I know who. Irene, eh? She'd not be able to keep her mouth shut. What if I did? It's allowed, isn't it? I'm fancy-free, you know. No ties. There's nothing wrong with that for a bachelor boy, is there?'

'How long did you go out together?'

179

Across the tarmac he spied a lorry driver getting out of his cab and, as if Alice was not there standing directly in front of him, he shouted over her, 'Hey, Dougie! How d'you get on?'

By way of answer the man gave him a double thumbs down, before heading for the back door of the store and going in.

'Hibs,' he said morosely, assuming she would be able to fill in the missing details herself.

'How long?' Alice repeated, looking into his dull eyes in search of a spark of intelligence.

'Oh aye. Mmm . . . a week, a fortnight. Not very long. She didn't suit me, you see. The search for Sam Inglis's lady continues . . . as they say on "The Apprentice". Luckily, the world's full of women, there's no shortage of them.'

'Why didn't she suit you?'

'You lot ask a lot of questions, don't you?' he said, with a hint of aggression.

'Yes,' she replied, unperturbed, 'it's my job. We're investigating a murder – possibly, a double murder. So I'll ask you again. Why didn't she suit you?'

'Did you ever meet her?' he asked, blowing his smoke upwards and watching it disappear.

'No. Not in life anyway.'

'Right. Well, you'd know if you had. If you'd spoken to her. She wasn't what she seemed – what she looked like. She was gorgeous, actually, really gorgeous to look at. But . . .' he stopped as if he had explained all that anyone might need to know.

'But?' she prompted him.

'But,' he repeated, suddenly looking angry, 'it was all "don't touch", "hands off". She was frigid, wasn't she? What d'you want me to say? She wasn't keen that way – to do it. Seemed shocked I'd even want to. What else did she think I'd want? She was a grown-up, for Christ's sake!'

'Did you ever "do it" with her? I'm sorry to ask, but I have a good reason for doing so.'

'I bet you do,' he replied, looking over her shoulder and waving at another lorry driver in his cab. Finishing his fag, he dropped it on the tarmac, and ground it with the heel of his grey lace-up shoe.

'So?' she asked.

'Naw,' he said. 'Her loss, I can assure you. Why do you ask, dearie?'

After a couple of seconds' thought, the policewoman replied, 'Because she was expecting a baby.'

'Never! I do *not* believe you. Oh, I get it, you thought it might be mine, eh? No, no, and no. You can forget it, just forget that. I never got beyond first base – not even to first base. Nothing to do with me. Her? I'd not have believed it. It must have been that wee shite, Hamish, eh? I'd not have believed it.'

'You knew Hamish?'

'Aha. I knew him. Smug wee bastard, he was too, showy, flashing his money about.' He leant back against the building once more, relaxed, hands behind his head.

'Did he take Miranda from you? That's what I heard.'

'Him? Naw, like I said, I dumped her. I'd no time for her.'

'Where were you last Monday night, say, from six or so onwards?'

'Monday . . . I don't know. At home, probably, in my flat. I'd be playing on my Xbox, something like that. I wasn't out, I know that. I was saving for a night out with my pals at Jackio's on the Wednesday.'

'Could anyone confirm that? Do you share the flat? Or

a neighbour, would a neighbour be able to say he or she saw you, heard you even?'

'I told you. I was on my Xbox. Raz was out, seeing his wee one. He spent the night there with Sharon and the wee one. I was on my own.'

Alice's phone rang and she turned to one side, to take the call.

'Alice,' said DC Cairns, 'we've just heard from that woman in Casselbank Street, in Miranda Stimms' tenement. The one that's been away in France. Since you're nearby, you may want to talk to her after the Inglis guy. Otherwise I could go.'

'No, I'll do it. Phone her back and say I'll be there in, say, half an hour. No, less than that –twenty minutes.'

Sam Inglis tried to interrupt the call.

'I'll need to be getting back soon. Mr Wilson won't be able to be on the tills *and* do the cheese counter. All the tills are short this morning.'

'Tell her twenty minutes, OK?' Alice repeated.

'OK,' DC Cairns replied.

'Like I said, I need to get back,' the man said, crumpling an empty Rizla packet in one hand.

'One other thing,' Alice said, 'what happened to your face?'

'You'd have to ask my mum and dad about that.'

'The injuries?'

'Raz and me had a falling out. You should see his gob.'

'And your hands?'

'What about them?' he answered, baffled.

'The scratches?'

'Oh, that,' he replied, holding them out in front of him. 'They're always there. I've a wee boat, just a dinghy. I keep it along the coast, near my parents' house.'

'How would you get scratches from a boat, I don't follow?'

'Not from the boat, from the brambles. Where I keep it, they grow all about the place. I get scratched every time I take it out.'

'Not really boating weather though, is it?'

'No, Inspector Rebus, you're quite right,' he laughed, good-naturedly. 'It isn't really boating weather, but it needs maintenance, varnishing and the like. This is when I do it, in the winter. So it's ready for the good weather.'

'Where do your parents live?'

'Limekilns. You know Limekilns? It's a wee place in Fife, just up from the bridges.'

A demonstration by cyclists against inconsiderate and dangerous motorists held up Alice's progress to Casselbank Street. Hundreds of them in their helmets and brightly coloured Lycra shorts were deliberately clogging up both carriageways of Leith Walk, riding four abreast or in single file in the middle of the road. They were spread among all the traffic, ensuring that no one could overtake or undertake them, barring all escape routes. Three of them cycled as slowly as they were able without falling off their bikes immediately in front of the policewoman, chatting to each other as they went, impressing upon all the car drivers backing up behind them that they, too, were entitled to use the public roads, demanding equal respect for their two wheels. The driver in the car behind Alice, an irate young woman in a red Audi, opened her window and shouted provocatively at them, 'Get out my road, you wankers! I've got a sick child in here – I'm on my way to the doctor!'

'Tough shit!' one of the cyclists shouted back, rising from his seat to give her a better view of his buttocks and waggling them at her. A couple of the protestors who had been blocking a Volvo in the next lane, dropped back to peer in her windows and check the truth of her claim. Seeing only her full shopping bags in the back, one rapped on her window and the other, a white-haired man in his fifties, inserted himself between Alice and her, somehow managing to go even more slowly than before, eventually coming to a halt and crashing to the ground in an undignified heap. Thirty minutes later, having travelled less than a mile, Alice finally ran up the tenement stairs to knock on the door marked 'Lavery'.

'Inspector Rice? Forgive me, dear, if I'm a bit . . . well, dopey, not awfully with it this morning,' the woman said, yawning, as she showed Alice through into her kitchen. The contents of her rucksack had been dropped in the middle of the floor, which was littered with dirty clothes for washing. A pair of muddy walking boots stood on a newspaper on the kitchen table, a half-empty bottle of milk peeking out of one of them. Over the back of a chair, like the discarded case of a giant pupa, was a bright green sleeping bag. Its orange lining was stained, and a pair of woolly socks was laid neatly on top of it. Next to it a fan heater was blowing at full power and the windows were all opaque, white with condensation.

'Maybe I should open one of them?' the woman said, wrinkling her nose, tugging at the nearest window but failing to break the seal of ancient paint that glued it shut. Defeated, she murmured, 'Sod it!' scrawled a double line with her fingers across the steamy pane and added, 'Sorry about the mess. I'm just back from my hols, literally just back, I was camping in France. We travelled back yesterday and all last night. On the ferry, on the train and then by bus. Christ, I can hardly keep my eyes open. There were no bloody seats on the train, we had to stand until Berwick. I had a bit too much to drink, too. Makes the time pass, eh, but you pay in middle-age, oh yes, you pay!' She ambled unsteadily towards a chair, kicking a canvas wash-bag out of her way and sending it flying against the skirting board, murmuring 'Goal!' under her breath.

'Camping?' Alice said, taking the seat to which she had been directed. 'Isn't it a bit nippy, even in France, being in a tent at this time of year?'

'That's what everyone says,' the woman replied. 'I'm Maisie Lavery, by the way, I know you've been looking for me. That's why I got in touch. Sorry, but on my hols I like to cut myself off completely. No one, and I mean no one, knows my plans. Not even me. No, but seriously, I don't tell my mum or anyone where I'm going. No phones, no newspapers, no nothing. Now, I'm going to have a cup of black coffee, I *need* one. Can I get one for you?'

'Yes, thanks, but white, that would be good. We want to talk to you about a neighbour on the stair, Miranda Stimms.'

'Randy Mandy? Is she in trouble or something?' Maisie asked, taking the milk bottle from the boot and pouring some into a teacup, then, tutting at her own ineptitude, transferring it into a little milk jug. Her head bent forwards, the double crown of her spiky, peroxided hair was visible. She seemed, Alice thought, more like a bear than a human being, her immense hips merging into saddle-bags making her resemble Yogi or Balloo's spouse. Some cartoon character, for sure. As she lumbered about, peering in the fridge and then searching in a cupboard, she hummed unselfconsciously to herself in a low monotone as if she was on her own.

'Biccies!' she exclaimed, turning round and beaming widely, a packet of custard creams now clasped in her oversized paw. 'And what about Miranda?' she asked, biting the packet open with her teeth.

'I'm afraid she's dead. We think she was murdered, that was why we wanted to speak to you,' Alice replied. At the word 'dead', the woman stopped in front of her, a single custard cream on her outstretched, calloused palm as if offering it to a horse, looking at her in frank astonishment.

'Christ on a bike!' she exclaimed, handing over the biscuit and then shuffling off to her own chair. 'If you'd said that she'd flitted without paying the rent, or been shoplifting or something like that – but *dead*! *Murdered*! You know, when I got your message I knew there must be something wrong. But Mandy – that would be like strangling a kitten! What happened? I didn't do it, by the way, I can assure you of that. Do I need a lawyer or something?'

'No. You're not a suspect. We're still investigating everything, asking everyone questions, trying to work out what happened to her on the Monday night.'

'Well, thank God for that,' Maisie sighed, lowering herself carefully onto her seat. 'That's me in the clear, then. Because I left on Monday afternoon, at four p.m. precisely. Caught the train to Kings Cross and spent the night in London with Katie. She'll vouch for me. I'll even have the ticket somewhere, in my money belt. On holiday I always wear one, then you don't need to worry, do you? Even at night, in the tent, in the bag, I keep it on. It'll be there, the ticket, I mean. D'you want me to get it?'

'Not at the moment, thanks. I need to learn about Mandy. Did you know her well?'

'Dead! That's awful! She only moved in, what, a month ago – a couple of months ago? You don't really see your neighbours that much, do you? I saw her a few times, said hello, went into her flat even, but just the once. It's not as big as this one. Furnished, unlike here, furnished with crap from a skip, courtesy of the lovely Mr Dowdall. Our landlord. Chosen by touch, I shouldn't be surprised. He's blind, you see. I brought my own stuff, apart from the white goods. Dead! It's unbelievable! Like another biscuit, dear?'

'Not at the moment, thanks. What sort of person was she? Randy Mandy as you called her?'

Mouth full, crunching a custard cream, Maisie answered as best as she could, holding a hand over her mouth to prevent any spray of crumbs.

'Timid. What else can you say? I was being sarcastic before. She was more Doris Day than randy anything. The poor little thing. She wouldn't say boo to a goose, and certainly not to a gander. I went to see her because some git on the stair had shoved her mail into my letter-box. I was shoving it through hers but she caught me at it, opened the door. She gave me a cup of tea.'

'Did you ever meet her boyfriend, Hamish Evans?' Alice asked, looking at the open packet of biscuits and stretching her hand towards it, having changed her mind. They were as good a breakfast as any.

'On you go,' Maisie said, 'take two, three. They're that small. No, but she told me about him. To be honest, you'd think men were buzzing about her like flies, the way she was going on. Fighting over her, or so she'd have it. Sam something, then this Hamish guy. The slightest attention turned her head. She was naïve . . . that's how it seemed to me, anyhow.'

187

The telephone rang and she rose, slowly and unsteadily, and lumbered towards it.

'Hello, Maisie Lavery. Monumental stonemason,' she said, hand on her hip, looking the policewoman in the eye as if she was addressing her.

Hearing the name of her caller, a broad smile spread over her face and she turned round, facing one of the steamed-up windows.

'Terry, my boy, you got home OK! Me, too, I can hardly keep my eyes open. Yeah, don't worry, we'll settle up later. Got to go . . . no, really got to go. Yeah, someone with me. No, I can't, the police. Tell you later. Byeee!'

'That's my pal, Terry. The one I went to France with.' She slumped back into her chair, helping herself to another biscuit.

'Now, this'll be my last one,' she continued, rubbing her eyes. 'What was I was telling you about? Mmm. Mandy's boyfriend, wasn't I? She showed me a photo. He was dark-haired, good-looking in a boyish kind of way. That's all I can remember . . . Sorry, but my brain's not really functioning.'

'What did she say about Sam?'

'Sam, Sam, Samity, a monster of depravity, according to her.'

'Did you meet Anna?'

'Anna? Was that her name? Her sister, d'you mean her sister, the one living with her?'

'I didn't know she had a sister. I thought she was her girlfriend,' Alice said. 'That's what we've been told, anyway. Did you meet her, the one living with her?'

'Her girlfriend? No. But her sister was in the flat when Miranda invited me in. She was there, but I went into the kitchen with Miranda. She was in the sitting room, watching the telly. Bloody loud, at that. I never actually saw her. More coffee?'

Alice shook her head. 'What makes you think they were sisters?'

'What makes you think they were girlfriends, more like? If you'd seen her going on, so pleased, about boys after her. Yeah, they were sisters, I'm almost sure of it. I don't know why I think that, though. Maybe she told me . . . she must have. Why else would I be so sure? Flatmates, maybe? No, sisters, she must have told me that they were sisters, that her sister was living with her. You've got me doubting myself!'

'Did many people, as far as you're aware, call on Miranda?'

'Visitors, you mean? Gentlemen callers? I haven't a clue. I'm never here anyway. I'm sorry, constable. I really am,' Maisie said, briefly covering her face with her hands, 'but I've got to get to my bed. I've been up for over twenty-four hours. My head's spinning. I'll be sick, I could barf for Britain right now. Come back, anytime – here or at my studio up Leith Walk – but I've got to get some sleep.'

The drive to Starbank Terrace took less than a quarter of an hour. For another five minutes Alice sat in her car a little distance from the Stimms' house, thinking, working out the best way to approach Mrs Stimms, devising the best strategy. It was all very odd. The woman had said nothing at all about any other daughter, never mind one that had been, supposedly, living with the dead girl. Why not? Surely some reference to her would have been natural, because she, too, would have lost a loved one? And if the daughters had been living together, why hadn't the remaining one reported her sister's absence? Perhaps she had witnessed her sister's death, could even describe her killer? Then why hadn't she come forward? Surely Hamish could not be jealous of the attention his girlfriend gave to her sister? Hearing of Miranda's death, would her mother not also, immediately, be concerned for the safety of her other daughter? In the circumstances, the woman's reaction seemed abnormal, difficult to comprehend. What the hell had been going on?

For a moment, her eyes drifted across to the sea, over its calm, grey surface to where it merged into a milk-white sky. She rolled down her window, inhaling the salt air, calming herself and preparing for her confrontation. There must be some explanation for this, and to get at the truth she must keep her wits about her. Mrs Stimms might seem like a shy, retiring person, a slightly inadequate one, but she had, for some reason, in extraordinary circumstances, managed to keep her self-possession, and quite possibly her secrets with it.

Outside the door Alice looked along the terrace of six houses, wondering whether all of them were occupied by members of the Elect. How did they first establish a bridgehead, without becoming polluted in the process? Maybe, years earlier, the whole terrace had been empty, had been bought up by them and thereafter only sold to their co-religionists. How else could they ensure that no walls were shared with 'worldlies' like her? To anyone passing it in ignorance, in a car or on foot, the street looked like many others in the neighbourhood. A row of stone-built, slate-roofed Victorian villas without gardens, fronting onto the pavement, and the public road beyond that. The only exceptional thing about the terrace was the magnificent sea view they all shared. And there were no spires, no crosses, no overtly religious signs or symbols, nothing to alert the sleepy, secular world to their presence, or to advertise their chosen form of apartheid.

The door opened and a man's head peeped out, the security chain still in place.

'Mr Stimms?' she said.

'Aye?' He had a high, light voice and sounded surprised by his own answer, meeting her question with a question.

'May I come in? I'm Inspector Rice. I've come to talk about your daughter, Miranda. I came before, as you'll know, I spoke to your wife. I was hoping to speak to her again.'

'Right, yes, she told me about you. Come in then, Inspector. She's out at the moment, seeing her brother in Glasgow – maybe I could be of help? I'm glad to meet you. I wanted to thank you, anyway, for your kindness – about our loss. I know you were very kind to her. I appreciate that, I really appreciate that.'

He opened the door fully, moved back into the hallway and indicated with a wave of his hand that she could come in. Following him, she walked into the spotless sitting-room once more. The man took a seat opposite her and, for the first time, she took in his appearance. Like his wife, he was well-dressed, wearing a dark pin-striped suit, his shoes gleaming as if newly polished. This little person, she thought, was not a bear but, rather, a mouse. It was partly his bright black eyes, partly his quick, jerky movements, and partly something intangible, indefinable, but unmistakeably rodent-like in quality. His whiskery moustache, perhaps? If he had twitched his nose then and there she would not have been surprised. But she must stop this; he was a man, not a mouse. Maisie Lavery was not a bear.

'So,' he said, overturning her mental image by taking the initiative, 'how can I help you, Inspector?'

'As I said, it's about your daughter, Miranda, I heard . . .'

Before she had a chance to finish her sentence he cut in, saying quietly, but firmly, 'I have no daughter, Miranda. She embraced wickedness . . . embraced unnatural relations, so I have no daughter called Miranda.'

'As you will. But you have another daughter . . .'

At her words, he leant towards her, looking puzzled, all his attention focused on her, concentrating fully, his dark eyes unblinking.

'I do.'

'And she lived with Miranda,' she continued.

'Aye, she did,' he said, 'for a wee while, for a holiday. Why are you asking about her? '

'In the flat in Casselbank Street?'

'Yes. What's the mystery?'

'When did she stop living there?'

'She never lived there. Like I said, she just went to stay with her sister for a wee holiday. I brought her home, back here, myself.'

'When did her holiday end?'

'I don't know the exact date but I could find it out for you, if you need it. It'll be in my diary, I put everything in there.'

'Was she still staying there last Monday?'

'No. I must have taken her home a good week, ten days, before that.' He looked at the policewoman and added, 'She'd had her holiday, a wee holiday, with her big sister. It was the end of her Christmas holidays. You see, they were close, very close. And with Miranda no longer . . . well, not being part of the family any more.'

'You didn't mind her going there? To stay with Miranda?'

'They're still sisters, aren't they? Family. It would be wrong to keep them apart.' He looked at his interrogator, smiled ruefully, and added, 'Have you a sister?'

'Yes.'

'Well, you'll know what it means then – to have a sister. Me, too, I've got one. I wouldn't harm their relationship, it's way too important, too special for that.'

'Where is she now?'

'Diana? She's upstairs, in her bed. The doctor was here only an hour or so ago. She's not well at all. She's got the measles, a high temperature. Her mother said she was on fire. The curtains are shut and everything. She's very precious to us, that's why I'm staying home with her. Extra precious now. As I'm sure you understand.'

'Of course, and I'm sorry she's not well. And that's that particular mystery solved, although we've still got the other woman unaccounted for – unless they're the same person. You see, I was told that your daughter, that Miranda was living with another woman. I've been trying to find her in case she knew anything about, or was even involved in, your daughter's death.'

'But she was living with a woman. Miranda was unnatural, homosexual, I told you. That's exactly why I had to go and pick the wee one up. I picked her up early, after she'd phoned me. I learnt about it on the phone. I was horrified . . .'

'How d'you mean?'

'Diana told me about . . . that woman, that she'd moved back in. I couldn't have that. I had thought – well, that Miranda wouldn't have the woman there – not when her wee sister was there too, but she did. I couldn't have that, nobody could tolerate that.'

'Anna? Did she ever mention the name Anna?'

'Anna?'

'That's what the woman who lived with your daughter was called, I believe. I need to speak to her, your daughter I mean, to get a description of the woman, Anna. We're trying to find her. I'll have to come back as soon as she's better, and get a description then.'

'Do you,' Mr Stimms asked, his voice breaking, 'think she did it then? Do you think this Anna person killed my darling – killed my Miranda?' Tears had begun to form in the man's eyes, and he turned his face away for a second, with a quick movement brushing them dry with his sleeve.

'We don't know. That's the truth, Mr Stimms, but we would certainly like to find her, to talk to her.'

'But, Inspector,' he said, his eyes still wet, shining with new, unstoppable tears, 'I saw her, I met someone called Anna. I can give you a description of Anna. I saw her, sat down with her when I picked up my girl. We didn't speak much. To be honest, I didn't want anything to do with her. You can understand that, I'm sure, but she insisted on talking to me – at me, when I was waiting for my daughter to pack her things. Miranda was helping her.'

'What does she look like?'

He hesitated briefly, looking heavenwards, summoning an image of the girl into his mind's eye, and then said, 'She'd be ages with Mandy . . . Miranda, I'd guess. Five-foot five, six or more, something like that. Average, nowadays? Not too tall for a woman, and she was dark-haired, yes, I'd say dark. Not black, but more black than brown, if you know what I mean.'

'What about her complexion?'

'I really didn't notice that, so I suppose it must be normal, just like you'd expect. She was smartly dressed, though, expensively. I can't remember what she was actu-

194

ally wearing but she was well turned-out, nicely dressed.'
He nodded his head several times, as if convinced of that.

'Is that her?' she asked, holding out the blurred photo
of the girl in the hat for him to inspect.

'That's her!' he replied excitedly.

'You're sure?'

'Sure as can be.'

'Did you learn anything about her, any details about
her, where she came from, that kind of thing?'

'I did, yes. Just a wee bit. I suspect that she wanted to
get round me, on the right side of me or something. She
kept talking while I was waiting for Diana to finish packing, prattling on like womankind do – sorry, like some
women, some women, do. Sorry . . .'

'What did you learn, Mr Stimms?'

He scratched his head, took a deep breath and said,
'Let me think. I just wish I'd listened better. I never
thought it would matter, you see. Well, she came from
Perth, originally, somewhere near . . . where was it? Could
it have been Scott Street? Yes, I'm sure she said her parents lived in Scott Street, somewhere near The Inch. I'm
sure she boasted about a flat, too, in Dundee, I think, but
don't ask me the address.'

'Her surname, did you happen to get her surname, do
you remember that?'

'Have you not got it?' He sounded taken aback.

'Not so far.'

'I do,' he said, quietly triumphant, 'I do. She was a
Campbell – to my shame – like my own mother.'

'Have you any idea what her job was?'

'Aye, she teased me, tried to charm me, asking me
if I could guess it.' He shook his head in disgust at the
thought.

'And?'

'She worked with flowers, in a garden centre, I think.'

'One other thing, Mr Stimms,' Alice said, rising to go. 'Have you heard of anyone called Hamish Evans, did you ever come across him?'

'Yes,' he said, accompanying her to the door, 'my wife told me all about him. She and I didn't speak, Miranda and me. He had his eye on Miranda, or so she told her mother, but . . . well, she was a lost cause, for any man, I mean. Anna Campbell didn't like him, I know that. He phoned her while I was there, and she called him all the names under the sun, blasphemous things. She went outside into the hall, didn't think I could hear, whispered it, but I heard quite enough in that matchbox of a place.'

'What were they arguing about?'

'My dau . . . they were arguing about Miranda.'

14

Back in her car, determined to make progress, she scrolled down her contacts until she found the pathologist's phone number. One thing was nagging her, and it was something that she could not find out herself. As the line rang through, she looked out to sea, marvelling at the size of a low, red oil tanker which seemed to take up about a third of the horizon. A cyclist flashed past her window, making her blink as he disappeared into the distance, head hunched low over the handlebars, his back curved like a cat's spine. Finally, a voice answered.

'Yes.' The tone was guarded.

'Dr Cash?'

'Inspector Rice, I presume. Do you never have a day off, a long lie? It's Sunday, for Christ's sake, the day on which God himself rested. So this had better be an emergency. There had better be bodies everywhere, and four-deep at that. And no, I don't have the result from the Evans boy's PM, if that's what you're after. It's tomorrow. Are you coming to it?' Dr Cash had just realised that the sickening stench she was aware of was coming from her own hand holding the phone. It was the chicken. Seconds earlier she had been massaging a bulb of garlic into the cold, clammy, pink skin of the dead bird.

Out of the corner of her eye she saw that the rhubarb she had stewing on the hob was about to boil over. Gesticulating frantically to her adolescent son, she mimed 'take the pan off!'

'I don't know yet,' Alice replied. 'I wondered, did you take any samples from Miranda Stimms' baby, the foetus you discovered at her PM?'

'No, Inspector, we did not. It's not routine and her PM's over. Nor am I going to. As I'm sure you're aware there is an offence – theft of DNA or something. So, no, I did not take any samples from the foetus and I'm not going to now. Get it off, Davie. It'll burn!'

'Sorry?'

'This is very inconvenient, you know. My lunch is getting ruined and I've got people coming. Guests. That's better, Davie's got the pan at last. Drain the excess liquid off – no, not in the sink, for pity's sake, into that cup! Yes, the blue one.'

'I need to know who the father of her baby was.'

'Do you.' It was a statement, uttered matter-of-factly and without enthusiasm, not a question.

'Yes. It's the missing bit of the jigsaw. I need the exact gestational age too, if possible. Before you just gave me a range. Your report's not yet come through.'

'I thought Hamish Evans, the body in the bay, was her boyfriend?'

'So did, so do I. But he had mumps, his father told me, which made him infertile – it couldn't be his. The baby. That's why I want to know whose it was. She had a boyfriend before him. Once I know, everything may well fall into place. So, tomorrow, could you take a sample? You've already said that you'll be in the mortuary.'

'Alice,' Dr Cash sighed, 'my son's busily whipping the cream into butter . . . Stop, stop! I can't speak now, except to say one thing and one thing alone. If you want a sample taken, I'll need written authority from Derek Jardine, I'm not doing it without the Fiscal's express written instruction. It's the Human Tissue Act, or something or other. Anyway, I'm not doing it without his say so, I'm afraid. OK, got to go. I've got a life to lead.'

'I don't think that's necessary.'

'A life? I think you'll find it is, Alice. And written instructions, too. If you're expecting me to take a sample for analysis, anyway.'

'If I get him to give you a call, would that do?'

'Yes, it would. Now, I've got to go, my guests are arriving.'

—

As she drove across the city to Raeburn Place, the woman's throwaway remark stung her, worked its way, burrowing like some evil worm into her brain. Had work become her life? If it had, it had not always been so, and the change must have taken place surreptitiously, gradually, imperceptibly, as far as she was concerned. She had been unaware of it. Certainly, when Ian was alive, and long before him, for that matter, she had had a home life, a full home life. Of late, it was true, nothing seemed as vivid, as stimulating, as important outside of work. But that was surely because she was unusually lucky – her job was interesting, often genuinely exciting. If she had been filling in forms, sweeping floors, clearing tables, then, obviously, home life would seem brighter in comparison, but only in comparison. Sod you, she said to herself, Helen Cash's words still needling her. Her life was not empty. But, thinking about it, she could feel the muscles in her back tightening, knew what the woman was getting at. It was true she had no one, no one 'special', but life was still good, fulfilling. It passed as speedily as everyone else's did, no slower than before. And, somehow, she had achieved a sort of equilibrium, a relatively pain-free state, a state in which she no longer ached for Ian, simply at the thought of him.

At that moment, her eye was caught by the sight of a troupe of students dressed as chickens cavorting on the pavement, weaving their way down Howe Street, their collecting buckets bouncing off their feathered bellies. Christ, she thought, realising that she had driven through Granton, through Trinity and Inverleith and somehow seen nothing, operating completely on auto-pilot, unaware of anything that happened throughout the entire journey. Had she gone through red lights? Up one-way streets? Over pedestrian crossings? Anything was possible.

The Forensic Team were ready, assembled outside the front door of the flat in Raeburn Place, impatient to get on with their respective tasks, in their gear, all their equipment around them, tensely awaiting the signal to start. Some of them chewed gum vacantly, staring at nothing; most chatted to one another, their white breath forming clouds in the cold air. A curious neighbour on the landing, wearing a striped flannel dressing gown, stuck his head out of his door, saw the strange crew and withdrew quickly.

'Like a big, frightened rabbit,' one of the SOCOS said, adjusting the elastic of his green hood in an attempt to stop it cutting into his chin.

'Have you seen yourself?' his companion chipped in, 'he probably thinks that the Ebola virus is loose in the place.'

Hastily donning protective clothing herself in case she needed to go into Evans' flat, Alice stressed to them all that they must treat it as a potential crime scene. Recalling the irate weasel-thin cleaner she had encountered there on the Thursday, it seemed unlikely that this was where the stabbing had taken place – impossible if Dr McCrae's estimate of the length of time the boy had been in the water was anything like correct. But if the doctor's estimate was way out for any reason, since Evans had been stabbed there could still be blood everywhere, spattered on the floor, walls, ceiling and furniture. Unless it had been cleaned the place would be like a slaughterhouse, and if it all had been cleaned up by the Wednesday, the weasel almost certainly would have let them know.

'On you go,' she said, opening the door and watching as they filed in, their feet sticking to the paper path as if it was the yellow brick road. While they were occupied inside, she would cast her eye over the stair. Some trace of violence might still be visible. As she was examining the grey-painted walls of the landing the neighbour opened his door again.

'What's going on? Where's Hamish? I took in a parcel for him, I need to give it to him. I'm always in, you see, I work at home,' he said, coming towards her with a brown paper package in his hand. He looked anxiously, first at the closed front door of the flat opposite and then at the detective. Since his last appearance in his dressing-gown, he had thrown on a jersey and jeans. He was a tall man, towering above her though she herself was six foot. He wore glasses with dark frames and a lock of black hair fell over one of his eyes.

'I'm afraid he's dead.'

'Bloody hell! No one told me. What will I do with it? It might be perishable . . .'

'When did you last see him?' she asked.

'When he left for London, the Thursday before last – would it be a Thursday? Yes, yes, it was. One of my choir days.' Brows furrowed, he swept the troublesome hair out of his eyes, twice, before giving up and pushing his glasses up the bridge of his nose instead.

'You never heard him return?' she asked.

'On Monday night, you mean? No, I was listening for him, that was when he was supposed to be coming back. I go to bed late. I'm my own master, thankfully. But he never came. I tried first thing the next morning, and the one after that, but I got nothing. I spoke to Rich, his cleaner. He said he hadn't been back. I thought about leaving it with him but, well, you know . . . I don't really know him, he hasn't been coming here that long. Hamish had an old woman before. What's in the parcel is anybody's guess, but it could be valuable. He was always getting stuff off eBay – iPods, cameras, that kind of thing.'

'Boss?'

A photographer, pale-faced and unshaven, had emerged from the flat and was now standing beside them.

'Yes?'

'You wanted a preliminary view? I'd say there's nothing. The place is spotless, everything in order. I don't think anything sinister's happened here. It's clean, but not because someone's been mopping away anything untoward, it's because it didn't happen here. '

'OK. Tell the boys to do the stair too, just in case. You never know, do you? And Mr . . . ?' She looked at the neighbour.

'McKellar – David McKellar.'

'I'll take the parcel, if I may. You'll get a receipt for it, so don't worry. But for the moment I'll take custody of it. There will be other officers coming along shortly to take a statement from you, and from the others, your neighbours. Just tell the officers, if you would, that I've got the package, tell them Detective Inspector Rice has it.'

While the police-woman was making her way down the stairs, resuming her superficial inspection of the tenement as she went, within the murder room of St Leonard's Street station, a process of elimination was taking place. Perth abounded with Campbells; Scott Street and the other addresses around the Inch alone produced twelve possibilities, and the phone directory for Dundee listed twenty-three of the name. DC Elizabeth Cairns, a slice of ginger cake in one hand and her phone in the other, continued for hours in her relentless chivvying of people, never taking no for an answer, bullying the uniforms who were doing the legwork, making sure that they tried to talk to everyone, Sunday or no Sunday. Of the six on her list, one, Trish Rennie discovered, already had a criminal record; one was incarcerated in Cornton Vale, one was now dead and another lost somewhere in the USA. DS Sharpe, leaving a trail of empty coffee cups wherever he went like the slime track of a snail, busied himself with garden centres, nurseries, B&Q and Homebase stores in or around Dundee and the capital. At four o'clock, feeling peckish, he patrolled the room in search of a snack. Seeing a plate near Elizabeth Cairns he rushed over to investigate.

'Have you eaten that *whole* cake yourself?' he said to her, dismayed, his eyes on a bit of grease-proof paper which appeared to be all that was left of the block of gingerbread that she had consumed, piece by piece, throughout the afternoon.

'Yes,' she replied, her attention still fixed on her screen, 'but at least I'm not an addict. Cake, I might remind you, is not a drug, unlike caffeine.'

'Then what's your excuse? And there are fewer calories in coffee,' he replied, puffing out his cheeks derisively.

'What exactly are you . . .'

'Sssh!' Trish Rennie exclaimed, her hand over the receiver, frowning at them as if they were naughty children. 'Yes,' she continued, 'I've got that. You're at Canal Street, Perth. Thank you very much for your help. Yes, don't worry, we just need to speak to her. Do you have a mobile number for her? No, I'm the same – can't remember my own, never mind anyone else's. If you do find it, would you let me know? Thanks, that's perfect and we'll be there with you within the next two hours.'

She put down her phone and breathed out, 'Result!'

'Result?' Ranald Sharpe repeated, 'Is our search over, then?'

'It is, I'm sure it is,' Trish Rennie replied. 'Not that I could hear myself think with the two of you at it like that. So, who's going to tell our esteemed leaderene?'

'Who were you speaking to?' DC Cairns asked, glaring at Ranald Sharpe and scraping the film of ginger cake off the paper with a knife.

'Her old dad. He's a widower, losing the plot a bit too, I suspect. Senile dementia or Alzheimer's or something. But his daughter is one Anna Louise Campbell, aged 19, now living in Gorgie.'

'Has she been in Edinburgh long?' Sharpe asked.

'The last four months, at least. She was at the university in Dundee before that, but dropped out – and guess what?'

'What?' Elizabeth Cairns asked, licking the bits of gingerbread off her knife.

'She's working afternoons only, he thinks . . . in a florist's shop.'

—

At eight o'clock the next morning, Anna Campbell opened the door of her boyfriend's flat in Melville Terrace, unaware that she had been the subject of a manhunt overnight. She was dressed only in an oversized T-shirt and pyjama trousers and, with sleep still in her eyes, let in the two detectives who had come to see her. In many ways, she fitted the description that they had been given, being dark-haired and of roughly average height. Still half-asleep, she left them in the cramped kitchen while she went to find more clothes. Returning with a man's black leather jacket over her night-clothes, she lit up a cigarette and attempted to get her mind into gear and to answer their questions.

'So, can I ask you why you weren't at your job yesterday?' DC Cairns continued.

'I only work afternoons on Saturdays, Thursday and Fridays at Bloomers,' the girl said, defensively. 'The rota's not changed. I haven't not gone to my work.' Then as an afterthought, she added, more confidently, 'You can check with Julia, my boss, if you like. Did Paul tell you I hadn't turned up? Paul's half-witted, he never knows the rota. It's a miracle they keep him on. He was in a car crash, supposedly he was normal before it. He's meant to be in charge, just on the days I'm off, but he's always in a muddle. He can't remember our shifts, his shifts, from week to week, day to day actually. But Julia will tell you. I can give you her number right now, if you like. Her home number. I've got it on my mobile. If I can just find it – I know it's somewhere in here or maybe I left it in my car. Or my bag, it might be in my bag.'

She stubbed out her cigarette on the plate in front of her and began searching in a red leather shoulder bag which had been hanging on the back of her chair. In her haste, she plucked out a lipstick, her purse, a make-up bag, another packet of cigarettes and a mess of paper hankies.

'Sod it, it should be there,' she said, staring down at her stuff as if mystified by the phone's absence.

'And you're sure you've never met anyone called Miranda Stimms – never lived, or stayed, in Casselbank Street?'

'I told you, I haven't a clue who you're talking about. I live in Gorgie, unless I'm here, with Roddy. This is surreal . . . like in a film or a nightmare or something. I don't get it at all. What am I supposed to have done? Why are you so interested in me, or whoever you imagine I am?'

'Do you know a man called Hamish Evans?' DC Cairns continued.

'No. No Hamish Evans, no Amanda . . . Miranda Stimms. I don't know any of these people you're asking me about.' Bemused by their questions, and frustrated that they did not appear to believe her, tears welled up in her eyes.

'Have you met a man called Mr Dowdall?' Alice persisted.

'No.'

'Margaret Stobbs?'

'No. No! Why don't you believe me?' she shouted, shaking her head violently from side to side as a very young child might.

'Can you tell us where you were last Monday evening from, say, six o'clock onwards?'

Hearing the sound of a key turning in the lock, she jumped up and, as a stocky young man came in, flung her arms around his neck, saying 'Roddy, thank Christ you're back! Get them off me!'

Gently, he freed himself from her embrace, taking in as he did so the two women sitting in his kitchen. Looking hard at them, he put down a bag of shopping on the kitchen table and said, belligerently, 'Who are you? What the hell are you doing in my flat?'

'It's OK, it's OK,' his girlfriend said, wiping her eyes, feeling less vulnerable with him beside her. 'They're the police, I let them in. But they keep asking me questions. Just tell them, will you, tell them where I live, tell them where I work. Tell them I was here, with you, all last week. Every evening . . . every night. I never went back to my flat all last week, did I, I was here with you every night, wasn't I?'

'Yes, sure, babe. Sure you were. Why are you asking her all these questions?' Roddy demanded, putting an arm protectively round her. The pair of them were about the same height, but next to his muscled bulk the girl appeared fragile, sylph-like.

'We're carrying out investigations relating to two people . . .' DC Cairns began, shifting on her seat, quailing slightly under his hostile gaze.

'So, what happened to them then? Were they murdered or something?' he asked sarcastically. But the sneer on his face vanished when he saw the glance exchanged by the two policewomen.

'They were, too!' he said, pulling the girl tighter to him, inadvertently squashing her face against his.

'This is a murder investigation,' Alice confirmed, watching as the remaining colour in the young girl's face slowly drained from it.

'Look,' said Roddy, coming towards the policewomen, 'you've made a mistake, honest. I don't know why you're interested in Anna, she's the softest person you'd ever meet, wouldn't harm anyone. Doesn't stick up for herself enough, she wouldn't harm anyone . . . not even a . . . what the hell is it? A fly, she wouldn't harm a fly. This is mad.'

'Just tell us, Anna, please, what you were doing last Monday evening?' Alice said, looking at the man as if to say that if she answered it this would be the last question.

'Tell them, Anna, then they'll go. We were probably here weren't we? Monday . . . Monday . . . weren't we here?' he said to the girl, pleading, kissing the side of her face by way of encouragement.

'No,' she replied quietly, looking into his eyes.

'No? Weren't you here?' he asked, unable to hide his surprise, and suddenly keen to know himself. 'I'd forgotten. Where were you, then?'

'I . . . I was seeing a friend.'

'Where does that friend live?' DC Cairns asked.

'In Musselburgh,' she whispered.

'Musselburgh?' the boy said, starting, taking his arm from her shoulder, standing back and staring at her.

'OK Anna,' Alice interjected, 'that's fine, what we were after. Could you tell us who you were seeing in Musselburgh? Just give us your friend's name and address and then we'll be on our way.'

'Yes,' the boy said, voice dripping with disdain, 'just tell us who you were seeing in Musselburgh and we'll be on our way. By the way, did you spend the night there?

You're right, you weren't here, now I think about it. So where were you?'

'It's not what you think, Roddy. I was just . . . seeing . . . just seeing him. I went home afterwards.'

'Who?' Alice asked.

'Simon . . .'

'Simon effing Shawton . . . residing at Fisherrow, Musselburgh,' Roddy said, staring at the girl and adding, 'You went home afterwards, did you? After what exactly? No, don't bother. You gave me your word. Your word! So that's it, Anna. We're history. Just get your stuff and go. I wish we'd never met . . . And leave my jacket behind. And I want my TV back, too. I never gave it to you, so you can bring that back as well. Leave the key on the kitchen table when you go.'

Elizabeth Cairns was the first to speak as the two policewomen walked towards their car, their footsteps ringing on the pavement.

'What do you think, boss?'

'It's not her. I'd bet my life on it. No one could fake that, and she's not much like the girl in the photo either, what you can make out of that blur. She'd no idea what we were talking about, genuinely. You could see the astonishment on her face. She's an Anna Campbell alright but not *the* Anna Campbell – if such a person exists. We'll get Simon Shawton checked out at that address, but she was there, with him. If she hadn't been so frightened, so bamboozled by us, she might have just let the boy go on saying they were together. He, obviously, couldn't remember, wasn't bothered, worried or anything. Instead, she told the truth. I'm sure it was the truth. We'll see if she'll give her prints, but it's not her. I'd bet my life on it.'

'What do you mean, "if such a person exists"? We know she exists, lots of people have told us about her.'

'No,' Alice said, stopping by the car, her hand on the door handle. She looked across the white, frost-hardened ground of the Meadows, watching as a couple of dogs frolicked together, their owners walking side by side.

'No,' she continued, 'we know someone exists – but not that she's Anna Campbell. Various things don't make sense. Mr Stimms, in particular, he doesn't make sense, and he's the one who filled us in about Anna Campbell. Last night I was reading a book a friend lent me that opens up a few questions. I think we'll go and speak to the Stimms again . . . to both of them.'

'How do you mean?' DC Cairns said, getting into the car, pleased to be back where some warmth from the heater lingered from their journey to Melville Terrace.

'He said he allowed his younger daughter to see her sister,' Alice replied, climbing in herself.

'What's odd about that?'

'For most people nothing – for them, everything. His daughter, remember, either left the Elect, or was thrown out. He suggested it was because of her lesbianism. They were the ones, the Stimms, who first started that hare running. The Elect abhor homosexuality. What we know is that she was no longer part of the sect, either because she left them or they had "withdrawn" from her.'

'"Withdrawn" from – what d'you mean?'

'It's one of their expressions. It's a form of excommunication; if it happens the sinner is cut off entirely from all family, church, Elect society – they're regarded as a pariah. The same happens if one of them leaves voluntarily. Then they're viewed as no longer "walking in the light", having chosen Satan's path instead. Either way, under the doctrine of separation to which they subscribe, from then onwards they'll have nothing to do with you – even if it means splitting spouse from spouse, parent from child, sister from brother, sister from sister . . .'

'So what?'

Alice's phone rang and she picked it up, fumbling for her safety belt at the same time. It was Trish Rennie at the other end.

'The DNA results have just been phoned in,' she said, 'I thought you'd like to hear them as soon as possible.'

'OK, fire away.'

'In Miranda Stimms' flat, they found DNA from Hamish Evans and, probably, her sister's DNA too. The rest of the stuff they haven't been able to identify. They can tell family members, as you know. Amongst a mass of unidentified stuff from the common stair, the blood and so on did come from Miranda. It looks as if she did get the head injury in the stair.'

'And the DNA in Hamish's flat?'

'His and hers, plus a mass of unidentified stuff.'

'I don't suppose they told you about the foetal sample, did they?'

'They did. Max muttered something about Helen Cash begging for it to be done, cashing in a favour or something – seems unlikely, I thought. He said she felt bad about some remark she'd made to someone. None of it made any sense to me. Anyway, thanks to her grovelling we do have an answer. He said to pass on "thirteen weeks" too, from Helen, whatever that's to do with anything.'

'Have they got the result?' DC Cairns asked excitedly.

Signalling for her to be quiet, Alice listened to the rest of what Trish had to say and then put her phone back in her pocket.

'They have. As I said, we're off to the Stimms – to talk to them about their daughters.'

15

The Mazda 6 was parked as close to the school's entrance on Montpelier Street as he could manage without drawing too much attention to himself. From his location by the school gates, he could see into the playground at an angle but was himself partially concealed by a roadworker's tent. Enclosed within its newly painted black metal railings, the Wargrove special school looked more like a museum than any kind of educational establishment. Tarmac had been poured right up to the walls of the turreted Victorian building and the place looked oddly sterile and uninhabited, except that large yellow litter bins had been placed at regular intervals round the yard. The staff car park took up the only area where there might have been play equipment.

He gazed at the building, examining it intently, staring at the windows, trying to see into it. Nothing. But it must be the one, he thought, there were no other likely candidates left on the list. This time he would succeed. He could not afford to fail again. This was it. The fiasco that had been Monday did not bear thinking about – the time wasted waiting outside in the icy air, worried that someone, somewhere, would sense, somehow, the fear that must have been oozing from his every pore, filling the air, infecting him and everything around him. Second by second, he had been convinced that he would feel a hand on his back, on his shoulder, ushering him gently or not so gently into the headmaster's office. And the police would be called to investigate him, this stalker, prowler or potential paedophile or whatever sort of monster they convinced themselves that he was. He could see it all. In one corner would be their informant, probably one of the smug mothers from the gates, explaining that she had seen him there before, watching the place, hanging about with nothing but evil on his sick mind.

And what about the business? So many hours lost, so many orders lost, and the takings were low already. He breathed in deeply, calming himself, reminding himself that it had not happened yet, and would not happen. Not least because that school had not been the one. But Lambie, Lambie's reaction had been all too real, unbearable, her scream when he told of another failure had pierced his brain, caused him to cover his ears. Looking at her, as he broke the news, he had feared for her sanity. But all of that must be lived through, endured, accepted and would pass. He had survived so far and she, whatever happened, she would do so too. She was not as fragile as she seemed, she understood him, understood what had happened, would understand him whatever happened. Despite everything else, and without the child, she had not lost her mind.

A lollipop woman walked past him, stopping at the school gates and planting the end of her lollipop stick on the pavement. At that moment, the near silence in the street was broken by the ringing of a bell, a harsh, electronic, inhuman ring. Why was that silly woman there? Did some of the pupils just stay for the first few periods or something, up until the first break and then go home? Mind you, if they did, so much the better. He might be able to lose himself in all the movement, the hustle and bustle, merge into a crowd and become invisible within it.

He rolled down his window, inhaling the welcome fresh air, wiping the sweat from his forehead, unpleasantly conscious that it was now running down his whole body as if it was midsummer or he was in a sauna or something. The flesh was weak, it always betrayed you. His eyes, like a predator's, were fixed on the school yard, looking for movement, alert for any signs that the children had been released and were about to come out for their playtime. A teacher, or assistant, moseyed out of the building, smiling at the lollipop woman then heading off in the direction of the staff car park. The doors remained open. Suddenly, their appearance heralded by raucous shouts, a stream of children flowed out, some with hands in the air, some mouths open shouting excitedly to each other, some running or hopping, some hobbling on crutches, a few holding back on the doorstep as if afraid of the outside world.

A girl, tall and fair, came to the railings and pushed her head between them, as if to see whether her face would fit between the bars. He watched her, studied her, noting the pale complexion and near translucent skin. She looked unwell, so thin as to be almost transparent. But it was her, unmistakeably her, and at the sight he thought his heart would explode. It was beating so hard he could feel it like a living thing within him, battering him, fighting for its own release. Adrenaline, like liquid fire, was now coursing through him, speeding everything up, exaggerating any sound, making the world too bright.

He took a deep breath, put his hand on the door handle and got out. Walking fast, confidently, he crossed the narrow cobbled street, entered the school gates and went straight up to her. Her back was to him, and he tapped her on the shoulder. Disengaging her head from the bars, she looked at him, registering who he was, and allowed him to take her hand in his. A boy, dark-haired and sporting an eye-patch, joined them, taking the girl's other hand and starting to walk in the opposite direction, pulling her towards the staff car park. Smiling widely at the boy, the man forcibly disengaged his hand, finger by finger, saying quietly, 'No, lad. Not this time.' Immediately, the child's expression changed, his face creased up, chin wobbled and tears began to pour from his eyes. In his frustration he began pummelling his thighs with his fists but, to the man's relief, he made no noise other than a strange, hissing, snake-like sound. Patting him on the shoulder, the man eased the girl around another child standing in their way and back towards the gates.

Just before they got there, a tall black youth spotted them and came hurtling over with a bag of crisps in his outstretched hand. Saying nothing, the man took it from him, immediately passing it to the girl, so that the donor would see the intended recipient had got it. Her hand still clutched in his, they strode through the gate.

The lollipop lady, seeing them, signalled for them to join her and the small band of parents and children waiting to cross. Grinning genially, the man shook his head to let her know they were going in a different direction.

The moment they reached the car, he opened the back door for the girl. As if everything was entirely as expected, she climbed in and immediately began to put on her seatbelt. Now in the driver's seat, he secured his own, checked his mirror and moved off.

'DDDadda,' she said, picking a piece of dry skin from her lower lip, then dabbing her finger in her own blood as if curious about its colour. Electrified at hearing her speak, he turned to stare at her.

—

Mrs Stimms, Alice noticed, appeared flustered before she had been asked a single question. Looking around the sitting room, the policewoman took in its near immaculate state once more, noticing that today one curtain remained partly drawn and that a tumbler, its amber contents only half drunk, marred the shining glass of the coffee table. A ring stained the cover of the uppermost illustrated book. Solace, perhaps, for a dead daughter.

Mrs Stimms sat opposite them, alone on her sofa, her legs as before folded primly to one side. The top button of her cashmere cardigan was undone but otherwise she was as perfectly dressed as on the previous occasion, all in navy, down to her matching court shoes. Looking at her face Alice noticed how drawn she seemed, with bruise-black coloration below her eyes, and fine lines visible around her narrow mouth. A new nervousness manifested itself in her hands, one always busy feeling the nails of the other in search of rough skin, something to pick, sometimes even to bite.

'You heard,' Alice began, 'about my last visit here? I came to see you, but as you weren't here I spoke to your husband instead.'

'Yes, yes, of course, he told me all about that.' She nodded, as if to corroborate her own statement.

'Did he tell you about Anna – Anna Louise Campbell to give you her full name? Has he told you anything about her?'

'Who?'

'Anna Louise Campbell. Apparently, she was in a relationship with Miranda, lived with her at Casselbank.'

'No,' the woman said, anxiously meeting the detective's steady gaze, 'I don't know anything about that side of things . . . of her life. I told you the last time, I don't want to know.'

'So, how did you discover that Miranda was a lesbian?'

A flash of annoyance crossed the woman's face and, shifting her legs to the right, she said, 'I don't see what that has to do with anything, but since you ask, my husband told me. Jimmy told me. That's how I know.'

'You never saw any evidence of it then, yourself? Your daughter never spoke to you about it, discussed it with you, her sexual orientation?'

'Of course not. And I didn't ask.'

'How did he know about it?'

'What is this? What has this to do with Miranda's death? What difference does it make now?' she asked. 'She's dead, isn't she. Does it matter any more who she . . . she . . . went with? It's all disgusting. Filthy. Why are you asking me all these questions?'

'How did he know about it?' Alice repeated.

'Oh, goodness, I don't know. He told me, it was all horrible, I know that. He told me that he'd come back from work that day and found her in bed with a woman. A young woman, they were both naked. That was proof enough, I'm sure you'd agree – enough for anyone. Too much for a father, too much for any father to have to see. I'm just glad I wasn't the one . . .'

'What happened when he found her?'

'What happened?' she raised her voice, shifting her legs again and smoothing down her skirt, 'what happened was that he told her to pack her bags, to get out of our house. She had made her choice – she had chosen Satan and all his ways. The other girl slunk out the back door. There was no repentance in her, no shame, not an ounce, for what she had done, for what she *was*. A disgrace. From that moment on she was dead to him . . . no, to us both.'

'Did you ever see her again after that?'

'No . . . not until last Wednesday when they lifted that sheet in the mortuary. I never saw my daughter again – not alive.'

'You never once saw her again from the time she left the house in disgrace?'

'No . . .'

At the thought, she began to weep, pulling a starched white handkerchief from her sleeve, unfolding it and dabbing her eyes.

'What about Diana, your other daughter?' Alice said.

'What about her?' the woman replied, swallowing hard, looking up at the policewoman once more.

'Did she see her sister? I mean once Miranda had been thrown out. Did she ever go and stay with her sister?'

'Once, she went there once,' the woman replied in a low voice.

'When was that?'

'I'm not sure exactly. She went there . . . I'm not sure, a couple of weeks ago, maybe less, something like that.'

'When did she get back from her sister's flat?'

'Last Monday night. I wasn't home that night, I was seeing my mother. But Jimmy brought her back, last Monday night, from Miranda's flat. I didn't see her until the Tuesday, obviously, but I know she got back the night before. She was very tired.'

'Where is she now?'

'Diana? She's upstairs in her bed. She's got measles. Jimmy probably told you. We've been that worried. It's quite dangerous, really nasty, they say. I had it as a child so I've no worries, Jimmy's the same, but if you've not had it before – well, you're not immune and no one would want to catch it.'

'I'd like to speak to her.'

'I'm sorry,' the woman said, eyes wide, 'but she's not well enough for that. You can talk to her later, tomorrow, or if not then, then the next day, but she's still ill, still feverish. She's only a child, too. Thirteen. I can't allow that. I'm surprised you'd even ask in the circumstances.'

'Fine. I'll not speak to her, but I do want to see her.'

'Now?' the woman said aghast, 'She's still infectious, you realise?'

'Now,' Alice confirmed, 'I'd like to see her now.'

'For pity's sake . . .'

'Now, please.'

Looking outraged, Mrs Stimms rose, and without a word left the room. The two policewomen followed her along the corridor and up the stairs. Outside a pink-painted door with a notice on it in purple letters saying 'Diana's Room', she glanced back at them, and then slowly turned the door handle.

Going in, she murmured, 'I'll just be a second, sweetie. In and then straight out.' She tiptoed up to the bed and gently touched her daughter's back. As she did so, she looked back at the two policewomen in the doorway, her eyebrows raised as if to say 'I told you so'. To DC Cairn's surprise, Alice marched in and went up to the bed. After a few seconds she pulled the curtains open and returned to the bedside. Slowly and very gently, she rolled back the covers. Beneath them were a couple of pillows in starched white pillowcases, carefully positioned to resemble as much as possible the outline of a human figure.

'She's very pale,' Alice said, looking at Mrs Stimms quizzically and signalling for her to return to the sitting room.

'Well?' she asked Mrs Stimms as soon as she had sat down again. 'Could you explain to me exactly what's going on here?'

'I had to do it,' the woman replied, smoothing her skirt against her thighs again, regaining her composure and both looking and sounding defiant.

'Why?'

'Because otherwise you'd keep her – or never give her back to us. It's happened before, so don't try and soft-soap me, tell me otherwise. I've seen it with my own eyes, experienced it for myself. "Not fit", the cheek of it! Worldlies, like you, telling us we're not fit! With your pornography, your lewd advertisements . . . *sex* trumpeted everywhere. But there it is, they've got all the power – you, worldly people, have all the power, have it all your own way. All I wanted was to get her back. But would you have helped us? Of course not, so we've had to do it all ourselves.'

'Get her back? I don't understand. I thought you said that your husband picked her up from the Casselbank flat on the Monday night, on the night Miranda died?'

'She didn't die on the Monday . . . it was the Tuesday – I thought it was the Tuesday. That's what the technician said in the mortuary.'

'No. We think she did die on the Monday. Her body was found on the Tuesday, but she died the day before, probably the night before. Did your husband not pick Diana up from the flat then?'

'He did. It took him a while to find her. Miranda, no doubt with the help of her new friends, the boyfriend, took Diana from us, you see. She snatched her from her school – took her without our permission. Jimmy knew he'd find her, and he did. One of the Brothers has a shop not far from there. He saw her on the street, phoned Jimmy and he went there and watched for ages, day after day. He followed her, discovered them in Casselbank Street, at her flat. On the Monday night he went there and picked Diana up, but she ran away.'

'But why did Miranda take her sister away from here? From you?'

'Jimmy says she did it because being out of the Elect herself, she wanted her sister out too. They were close, very close. Miranda was very protective of her wee sister, thought the world of her. I suppose, selfishly, she just wanted her with her – on the outside. She missed her, knew she'd not see her otherwise.'

'Where is Diana now?'

'She's . . . I don't know.' The woman looked her interrogators in the eye, letting them know from her expression that there would be no further co-operation.

'You must know,' Alice replied, 'and we need to know. We really do need to know.'

'Well, I can't help you there, I'm afraid. I don't see what any of this has to do with Miranda anyway. Diana is none of your business, is she? She's done nothing wrong. I haven't either. You've no right to come asking questions about her. What has she to do with you? She has nothing to do with you, that's what. Now, I've a meeting to go to so I'd be grateful if you'd leave. I do have a friend, you know. I could call her – or my husband. He'd tell you to leave. He'd take none of this from you.' To emphasise her words, she rose as if preparing to show them to the door.

'Mrs Stimms,' Alice began, 'I think you should sit down. We are interested in Diana. We need to speak to Diana, for her sake. Apart from anything else she may have been a witness . . .'

'Look, officer. I have not committed a crime, Jimmy has not committed a crime. You can't come here and bully people like this. We've already lost one . . . daughter. We'll get Diana back and that will be that, and we'll all get on with our lives. Now, I really do have a meeting to go to . . .'

'Mrs Stimms,' Alice continued, 'think about it. Diana may have been amongst the last people to see her sister alive.'

'How do you mean?' the woman replied, looking suddenly rattled. 'What are you saying, what are you getting at?'

'She may even have witnessed the crime, seen Miranda's murder.'

'Why should she have? Jimmy took her away . . . long before anything happened to Miranda, I'm sure of that. She doesn't speak, she's got a mental handicap. You wouldn't get as much as her name from her. You're just saying that to frighten me. Why should she have seen anything?'

'How do you know that Jimmy took her away before Miranda was murdered?'

'Oh,' the woman said, her face flushed, twisting her wedding ring on her finger, 'this is getting ridiculous. This is quite mad. Of course he did! What are you suggesting now? That Jimmy did it or something, that he killed Miranda?'

'It is possible.'

'Oh no, it's not, my lady. Not so fast. I can assure you that it's not. I know him, you don't. How dare you even suggest such a thing! Do you think I don't know my own husband? As if he'd ever do anything to harm one of his own children! His girls . . . He loved Miranda, they were as close as any father and daughter can be. If she hadn't . . . hadn't taken up with Satan, this would never have happened. She would have stayed at home with us. Diana would still be here . . .'

'Before she left home, did Miranda tell you that she was pregnant?'

'What?' the woman said, looking appalled, as if someone had just slapped her in the face. Alice repeated the question, word for word.

'No. I don't believe you. How do you know that she was? How could you possibly know that?'

'The forensic pathologist who carried out the post mortem on her body told us. And we have just discovered who the father of her child was.'

'I don't want to know. Miranda is no longer my daughter, I don't want to know who her lesbian person was, I don't want to know what man she had been sleeping with. She's nothing to do with me any longer.'

'The father of Miranda's baby was Jimmy, your husband, her own father. When she died she was thirteen weeks pregnant.'

'Jimmy?'

'Your husband, Jimmy.'

'Lies, all lies! I don't believe you – that's a disgusting thing to say!' the woman exclaimed, shaking her head, now white as chalk, looking at them and adding as if pleading for a denial. 'You're just saying that, aren't you?

It's not true is it? I'm his wife! With his own daughter?
No, no – no, he would never do that, I know him. That's
sick. Jimmy would never do something like that. No, tell
me it's not true! How could you even say such a thing!'

'I'm sorry, but it is true. Now will you help us find
Diana? She may be in danger. We need to find her as
soon as possible.'

'Jimmy – he wouldn't do that. He wouldn't . . . I never
thought . . . Miranda never said anything to me. She
would have, I'm her mother. How long – how long . . .
since when? How can you be sure? I don't believe you.'

'We can be sure,' DC Cairns said. 'A tissue sample was
taken from the foetus, analysed in the lab. The foetus
itself was measured. That's how we know.'

'Is Diana with Jimmy?' Alice asked.

'I don't know. He's found out where she is at last. A
special school. He's going to take her from there today,
bring her home to me today . . .'

'What is the name of the special school?'

'It's called the Wargrove School, somewhere in
Bruntsfield.'

'Get the number, now,' Alice said to DC Cairns. 'Is
he there now? When is he expecting to collect her?' she
asked the distraught woman.

'Oh,' she replied, still in shock at their revelation, 'at
. . . at . . . some time today. This morning, yes, he promised he'd try in the morning, first thing. At break time. If
he failed that would give him two chances, he said. I don't
know when, exactly. He always phones me after he's been
looking for her. He lets me know how he's got on.'

Typing in the number, DC Cairns handed Alice her
phone. She was immediately transferred by the receptionist to the Deputy Headmaster, Mr Rawson.

'Inspector Rice,' the man began, sounding strained, 'has someone been in touch with you already? It may all be nothing, we're still looking. This may all prove to be premature.'

'I'm sorry, Mr Rawson, but I'm not sure what you mean?'

'I thought that you were phoning about Susie . . .'

'No.'

'Are you not phoning about Susie, then? Are you not phoning about the loss of Susie?'

'I'm phoning to see if a man has removed from your grounds one of your pupils, Diana Stimms.'

'There's no pupil of that name here. No Diana Stimms. But we've got a girl, no one knows her real name because she doesn't speak. We were told to call her Susie, she seems to respond to Susie. It's her we're concerned about. It was her I assumed that you were ringing about. Our head, Mrs Griffiths, said she'd spoken to someone in the police.'

'What does this Susie look like?' Alice asked.

'She's tall, maybe five foot eight or so. Fair-haired and very slim, too slim, thin, scrawny even – and speechless. Until today none of us have managed to get her to say a single word, despite intensive therapy.'

The inspector turned to Mrs Stimms and asked her for a description of Diana.

'She's tall,' her mother said, 'taller than me and Jimmy, and she's got lovely blonde hair, dark eyes . . .'

'Slim?'

'Very slim.'

'What's happened to Susie?' Alice asked the teacher.

'Maybe nothing, that's why I was saying this is all pre-mature. But at the moment we can't find her. She didn't come back in after the break. We have searched high and low, in the school, in the grounds. I spoke to Miss Blair, a playground assistant, and she said she'd seen nothing, but Cass, our lollipop lady, told Mrs Griffiths that she'd seen a man take the child away, or at least one matching her description. At the time she thought it was the child's father, so she didn't do anything or think anything of it. To be fair, why should she? We do know he was driving a blue Mazda 6.'

'A blue Mazda 6?' Alice repeated, certain from Mrs Stimms' startled reaction that it was her husband's car.

'Susie,' she said to Mr Rawson, 'Tell me a little about Susie, if you would?'

'What do you want to know? I don't know much myself. She's living with foster parents in Blackhall. We don't know how long she'll be here because everyone is trying to track down her parents. She appeared, lost, somewhere in Leith about . . . I don't know . . . six, seven days ago. Somewhere round about Great Junction Street, one of the side streets.'

Holding the phone against her chest, Alice asked Mrs Stimms, 'Was it near Great Junction Street that your husband lost Diana?'

'Yes,' the woman said, 'at the garage on Great Junction Street. She got out of the car and wandered away. He looked for her but he couldn't find her. The police picked her up near there . . . I know they did. A man in a pub, when we were looking for her, told me that.'

Telling Mr Rawson to keep looking and let them know if the girl appeared, Alice returned her attention to Mrs Stimms.

'He's got her in his car. He's found her. We need to find her. For her own safety.'

'He may have done something . . . something awful, unnatural, horrible, with Miranda . . . and I never knew, truly, I promise, I had no idea – but that doesn't mean he'll harm Diana, does it? He'll just bring her back here . . . to me, won't he?' she replied, imploring them to agree, to restore some order, some predictability to her fractured world. She looked as if she was about to faint.

'He may,' Alice said, then she turned to DC Cairns and mouthed 'Tea' at her, indicating the shocked woman with her eyes.

'He may,' she repeated, 'but just to be on the safe side, I think you should give him a ring – see what he says. Then we'll be able to find them both, sort everything out. Once we know where they are.'

Using her landline, Alice putting it on speakerphone, Mrs Stimms phoned her husband's mobile number.

'Jimmy?'

'Yes, Lambie, my darling. How are you?'

'Have you got her yet? Have you picked up Diana from that school?'

'No. I'm going to go there this afternoon. I'll try this afternoon.'

'Why not this morning? I thought you planned to try this morning . . . at break time. You promised. I thought that was the plan?' the woman said, sounding desperate.

'Something came up at work, I had to do it. We have to live, don't we! We'd have missed a massive order otherwise – thousands and thousands of pounds. Jobs in the factory would have had to go. But I'll be there this afternoon and on the dot. Don't worry, my darling, she's almost home. Now, I've got to go – one of the other phones is ringing.'

'Are you at work, in the office then?'

'Yes, I am, and its pandemonium here. Got to go. There's no one else to answer it at the moment. Give you a ring later.'

'He's in the office,' Mrs Stimms said bleakly, putting the receiver down.

'No, he's got Diana, and he's not there,' Alice said, 'I'll show you.'

Getting Mrs Stimms to dial his office number, Alice spoke to the receptionist.

'Could I speak to Mr Stimms, please. I understand he's in his office this morning.'

'Sorry,' the woman replied, 'he's gone out this morning. He'll be back sometime after three at the earliest, he thinks. If not, he's supposed to be in the office all day tomorrow, so you could be sure to get him then.'

'He's definitely not in now?'

'Yes,' the woman replied, sounding mildly offended, 'that's right. I saw him leave myself earlier this morning, he's definitely out. Do you want to speak to someone else instead?'

'No . . .'

'Give me the phone,' Mrs Stimms said to Alice and, obediently, she handed it over.

'Rhona, it's me,' she said, 'Amelia Stimms. Put me on to Jimmy, please.'

'Mrs Stimms . . . I'm sorry, I didn't realise it was you asking. But he's not here, honestly. He left here, I don't know – a couple of hours ago. I don't know where he is. He crossed his diary out, cancelled the appointment he had for this morning. He told me he wouldn't be back in the office today. Have you not got his mobile number?'

Amelia Stimms put down the phone. When offered a cup of tea by the young constable she pushed it away, staring, for a moment, out of the sitting room window, seeing nothing and saying nothing. She no longer sat straight-backed. Slowly, her head bowed until her chin almost rested on her chest. She closed her eyes.

'We'll need,' Alice said gently, 'a photo of him, a photo of Diana and the registration number of the car he's in. Can you manage that?'

'Yes.'

'There's one other thing, too. We know he's got Diana . . .'

'No, *we* don't *know*,' Mrs Stimms replied, rousing herself one last time, and turning round to face the policewoman.

'I do, and he hasn't come home with her, although he could have done so. He's lied to us about when he picked her up from Miranda's flat, probably about the existence of Anna Campbell, probably about your daughter's lesbianism. He's lied to you, too. I need to know where he's likely to take her.'

'How do you mean, to take her? He'll bring her back here eventually, he's going to bring her back to me . . .'

'No, Mrs Stimms, he isn't. Miranda is dead. We know he saw her shortly before she died. He may have killed her. Diana may have seen him doing so, witnessed something. Miranda's boyfriend is dead, murdered and deposited, like Miranda, in the sea. Now, please tell me where your husband would be likely to take Diana. Is there anywhere on the coast of the Forth, upstream from the bridges, that he knows well, that he goes to?'

'One thing,' she said in a monotone, 'this Anna Campbell person, how do you know about her?'

'We heard about her from your husband. He was the one to give us the details about her. Others in the tenement in Casselbank Street had only heard her name. A few had seen her – well, someone who might have been her.'

'Jimmy said nothing to you about our Anna? You see, that was what Miranda called Diana. Anna. When Miranda was wee she didn't like Diana's name, don't know why – she called her "Anne" or sometimes "Anna". Afterwards she used it as a pet name. It stuck. Only Miranda, no one else, called her Anna. You giving the name as Anna Louise Campbell put me off, but Jim would know, immediately, who Anna was.'

'Where would he go?'

'I don't know . . .' She was distraught.

'Think. Diana's life may depend upon it.'

'This is ridiculous! He'd never kill her!'

'Mrs Stimms,' Alice said, looking steadily at the woman, 'is this a gamble you want to take? He would. I don't seem to be able to get this across to you. I'm quite sure he was responsible for Miranda's death. We know, from you, that he was with her that night. We know that she was involved in an argument in the stair. I had thought it was with her boyfriend, Hamish. But thinking about it this minute, afresh, it will have been with him. There was no lesbian lover, no flatmate – there was just Miranda and Diana. Your husband comes to the flat to get Diana back, they fight over her and Miranda is found dead the next morning. I'm pretty sure, now, that he was involved in Hamish's death too.'

'This is pure fantasy!'

'If only. Tell me this, on your return from staying with your mother on the Monday night did you notice anything different about the house – was it in a mess, for example?'

'No, it wasn't different at all, not in a mess. In fact, Jimmy, God bless him, had cleaned up everywhere in the kitchen for me. Specially, as a welcome home for me. He'd cleaned it top to bottom. I had to re-do it, of course, he's a man, can't clean to save himself. I had to wipe down all the surfaces again and mop the floor. But it's the thought that counts . . . I was touched, particularly as he's always so busy at work. You've nothing against Jimmy – no evidence that he killed this Hamish you keep bringing up.'

'You judge. We know that Miranda's last phone call was to Hamish. Suppose she phoned him about her father, about his visit. Perhaps, she saw him coming from a window or something – told him, let Hamish know that her father was coming. She would know why he was coming, would not give Diana up without a fight. After all, I'm pretty sure that your Jimmy abused her from puberty onwards. Diana was thirteen, you've told us. Hamish, on his return from London, goes to see her. She's not there, Diana's not there, where would he go next?'

'To her father's house,' DC Cairns said, as if the question was aimed at her.

'Exactly. We know he caught his flight to Edinburgh. Suppose that finding no one in Miranda's flat, he goes to see Jimmy. He's never seen again. Then, like your daughter, Miranda, he ends up face down in the Forth. He died, not of drowning, but of knife wounds. And what you've just told us is that on the Monday night, Jimmy cleaned up the house.'

'The colour of the water was . . .' she began, then looking stricken, she added, 'he's got a knife. He must have used a knife. One's gone missing, it's missing still from the block. I never said anything to him about it, never thought he'd have anything to do with it – but he's got a knife!'

'Where is he?'

'I don't know! I don't know! How would I know? He's always on his travels, he sees people all the time, selling the cards, speaking to the Brothers, holding services, he's never off the road. There are thousands of places he could be – thousands of places he could go!'

'Is there anywhere on the coast, quite near here, anywhere that he knows well nearby on the coast of Fife or the Lothians?'

'On the coast?'

'Yes, somewhere very close to the sea.'

'There is a spot, West Lothian way. It's right on the Forth, near Hopetoun House. When the kids were little we'd all go there all the time, have a picnic. Jimmy loved it, used to go there himself sometimes, walk about, relax . . . He knows that little bit of countryside like the back of his hand. We haven't been there for years, but . . . it's the only place that I can think of like that, on the coast.'

'Will you come with us? Show us exactly where it is?'

16

'Dddaa . . . ddaa . . . ddaa . . .'
'Dddaa . . . ddaa . . . ddaa . . .'

She sang it again and again, as if it was a lullaby and she must send herself to sleep. Familiar with the ins and outs of Bruntsfield Place, he took another quick look at her reflection in the rearview mirror, watching her mouthing it, repeating that single word obsessively, polishing it like a jewel on her tongue. It was only seven days since she had gone, but to him it felt like several lifetimes. To his tired eyes, her beauty had blossomed whilst they were apart. She must have lost weight, a good stone, and now she had an unearthly fragility, appearing more doll-like, closer to an angel than any flesh and blood girl. How had she survived in that horrid world of theirs, remained pure and innocent, untouched by the filth of the place? In a Hell on earth, somehow, she had walked through that fire and remained unscorched, unscathed, with her virtue as her only armour.

The traffic was bumper-to-bumper on Lothian Road. In the offside wing-mirror as they crawled along, he caught a glimpse of a marked police car in the nearby lane, only a couple of cars back from his own. Its blue light was flashing. He held his breath. The instant the traffic lights changed, it accelerated past him and turned right into Morrison Street. He relaxed his grip on the wheel, began to breathe normally again.

Hardly conscious where he was going, he crossed the west end of Princes Street into Charlotte Street and started heading out of the city northwards, as if pulled magnetically in that direction. The phone in his pocket rang, his nerves jangling in time with each of its piercing trills, but he ignored it; he would not speak to anyone about work, and could not bear to talk to Lambie again. Cutting through Ainslie Place, he followed the curve of the gardens into the corridor of Great Stuart Place as if tied to the car in front of him, then continued, equally blindly, onto Queensferry Road, as oblivious to the traffic whizzing past him as he was to the rest of his surroundings. In the bubble of his own consciousness, with his eyes fixed on the road ahead, the only noises which penetrated his brain were the occasional words uttered by his daughter as she practised her new skill.

'Yes.'

'No.'

'Yes.'

He could make them out alright. As each one emerged, she giggled in surprise and delight, thrilled with the sounds she was forming, impressing herself with her own virtuosity. Listening to her, he realised that despite her sojourn away in an entirely unfamiliar world she had retained that strange, characteristic self-absorption, that fascination with her own internal landscape, that lack of curiosity about his and everyone else's world. She was still like a budgie in a cage, in love with its own reflection. He had waited long enough. Now sweating profusely, desperate to see how she would react, if she would react, he said in a loud, booming voice, 'Diana – where's Miranda?'

In the mirror he caught it. A wide-eyed glance thrown back at him, one of undisguised fear. Time had washed nothing from her memory. Oh, if only things had been other! Because, silent, at home with him and Lambie, everything about that night might have faded, slowly erased itself and, with his help, turned itself into a dream. It would have melted like snow on a summer's day. And if, by chance, any busybodies from the police came before then, who would have listened to anything she had to say? Say! She did not speak like a human being. The noises she produced were still more like grunts. Most of what came from her mouth was strings of meaningless sound more likely to be found in a farmyard or a zoo than a civilised Christian home or school. At least, that had been true up until now. None of these newly recognisable syllables, newly recognisable words, had ever passed those dry lips before. So, all credit to the therapists in the special school in Bruntsfield. They had worked a miracle, and in doing so, he thought ruefully, brought about his downfall. And hers with it. When Anna Campbell proved untraceable, as she surely would, the police would scurry back to Starbank. Once there, they would want to speak to him; and far more dangerously, to Diana. Now that she could talk, in some fashion at least, how would she respond to them, what exactly would she say? She could answer questions. Darling Lambie would have had no reason to question her, she would have been content just to put her arms tight around her, never let her go. And, dutiful wife that she was, she would have let all the sleeping dogs lie. Like she always had, like she always did.

Overcome with anxiety, he could not resist trying again.

'Diana, where's Miranda?'

There it was again. His answer. That look, that look of blind fear, terror even. And it was aimed at him, at the back of his head. It was far more eloquent than any of the broken words that might spill from that pert little rosebud mouth of hers. Simply at the mention of that name, all that had happened in that cold tenement flooded back into his mind's eye. And, plainly, the same happened to her.

Miranda standing at the top of the stairs, on the landing, shouting at him like a fishwife, threatening him with the jail. Calling him foul names, the foulest names, and all in public to boot. And there was Diana, too, cowering behind her sister, clutching her around the waist, tears streaming down her beautiful face.

'Incestuous paedophile!'

'Child-molester!'

'Monster!'

He would never have touched Diana, not in that way, whatever that slut might have thought. And how dare she! He was the head of the household, and he had never done a bad thing to her either – certainly nothing that she had not wanted. Right to the end. It was all very well now to run away, pretend that she had not desired him, pretend that she had been scared, revolted, disgusted . . . but he knew better. He had always known better, from the very first. He had seen it in her eyes, read it as if it was print. But what could he do? This was a girl intent upon rewriting history, distorting things, and turning him into a villain in the process. She should remember; know her scripture, as he did. It was Eve who had tempted Adam, not the other way round. And on that Monday night, if she had not fought him, tussled with him, had simply allowed him to take his own daughter away, then he would not have had to push her, she would not have fallen. 'Fallen'! She had fallen long ago, long ago, years ago, and now was intent on taking him with her. Her aim was to pull him down. And that boy, her follower – insulting him, accusing him, threatening him with the police and all in his own home. In crossing his threshold he had brought the filth of the world with him, the arrogant little bastard. But now it was clean again, washed away in the blood of the Lamb.

The prolonged blast of a horn made him jink back suddenly onto his own side of the road, abruptly aware of the excessive narrowness of the Dean Bridge. Shaken by the near miss, he determined to concentrate on his driving, slowing down and deliberately watching the cars around him, expelling everything from his mind bar the traffic and the road ahead.

Vigilant once more, he passed through the Barnton roundabout, the derelict hotel on his right with its pagoda tower and boarded-up windows. A string of green lights greeted him as if fate was favouring him, sending him a fair wind for his journey. No, it was not fate. As ever, the Good Lord was looking after his own, levelling the very roads for him. And now he, too, understood where he was going, had at some deep level known from the start where he was headed but had not cared, or been able, to acknowledge it. He had a mission to carry out, and had come prepared for it. To reassure himself, he glanced down at the side-pocket of the car door, at the butcher's knife tucked away in it, its ebony handle poking out. On the straight road once more, he allowed his eyes to wander back to the rear-view mirror. Unaware of his scrutiny, his daughter was looking out of the window, her face vacant as they travelled through the bleak winter landscape. In those long days away from home, what horrors had she seen, what had she been feeling, thinking about? While her mother suffered, wore herself to the very bone, cried a lake of tears, what went through that strange, unreachable mind? Had she missed them at all?

The corridor of drab, grey-harled houses at the west end of South Queensferry seemed to go on interminably, the wheels of his Mazda rattling into the potholes of extensively patched tarmac time after time, making him wonder for a moment if he had taken a wrong turning. Then, just as he had begun to doubt himself, they emerged onto the coastal road, the water bright beside them with the tide in, the mouth of the river merging with the open sea. The long wall of Hopetoun House estate, a forest of black, leafless tree-trunks rising high above it, comforted him, cradled him, told him that there was not much further to go. And no one, no one was about, not even the ubiquitous walkers in their red socks who used to patrol the roads like pilgrims of old. Just before the sign for Society House, he turned right onto the dusty track leading to the knoll of trees, their picnic place, and slowly brought the car to a halt. He would try one last time.

'Diana, do you know where your sister Miranda is?'

There it was. Unmistakeable, that look of sheer terror, directed at him, telling him all he needed to know. She had forgotten nothing. Her eyes still on him, she started picking her lips, distracting herself, soothing herself in the only way she knew how. In the silence he looked at her sorrowfully, unable to get over her radiance. She was as beautiful, no, more beautiful, than her mother had ever been, but they had the same delicate features. And that same ethereal quality, more spirit than flesh, more fairy than woman. Miranda had had it too when she was little, not as she got older and more lumpish, teenage and difficult.

In life, he mused, his eyes never leaving her face, choices had to be made. But they were not free choices. He had not chosen that Miranda should die, that the boy should come looking for her, hounding him, threatening him. If she had not snatched Diana, none of this would ever have happened and life could have gone on as before. But no, she could not keep quiet, had to 'rescue' her sister from her own parents, her own father, and involve a stranger in all their affairs. As if he, a Worldly, would, could possibly, understand anything of their lives.

Anger at the thought of all he had endured now coursing through his veins, he rose, left the car and walked through a glade of bare trees towards the sea, feasting his eyes on its immensity, calmed, momentarily, by its peacefulness, the perfection of the straight lines made by the horizon and the two bridges superimposed across it. This was a tranquil, a blessed place. How many times had they brought the girls here, watched them paddle on the warm sands, searching for empty razor-clam shells, cockles, cowries and other treasures.

Seeing for a moment in his mind's eye Diana in her first, red-and-white striped swimsuit, bucket and spade in hand, toddling towards the water, tears came to his eyes. But she must go. Otherwise, he would have nothing. Lambie would understand about Miranda. A fall is a fall. No one is to blame for that. But the boy? No. That would be too much for her, even though he had had no alternative. It had *not* been a free choice. The boy would have told her, everyone, about . . . it, the so-called sexual abuse. As if she had not asked for it. As if any of it was any of his business.

With Diana gone, it could all be an accident and nothing else need ever trouble Lambie. Or, by any means, could Diana disappear again somewhere into their closed world, never to surface again? No. Not with this new gift of hers: words. Today there were only three or so, but how many tomorrow? 'Nothing must trouble Lambie,' he repeated to himself, walking back towards his car, his resolve renewed. As Abraham had been prepared to slay Isaac, he would be doing what was required of him. Doing it not for himself but out of love for her, and for the Lord.

Inside the car he could see the silhouette of his daughter, now in the front passenger seat, her head slightly bowed. He pulled on the door handle. Nothing happened. The door did not move. He pulled again. Again, nothing happened. Inside, he saw Diana's face staring back at him, her eyes only inches from his own. Peering into the interior, he noticed her leaning over, her hand tickling the key fob dangling from the ignition. The stupid little vixen must have pressed it, locking herself inside, him outside.

'Diana, dear,' he said, watching as she looked up at him, 'unlock the car door, please.' She was not deaf, and would understand his words perfectly.

In response, she shook her head mulishly.

'Diana,' he repeated, louder this time, 'I said unlock the car door, please. Now. And I mean *now*!'

Again she shook her head. This time he squatted on his haunches down beside her so that their eyes would be exactly on the same level, ensuring that she would look into his. But like a dog, she hung her head, choosing to stare instead at the dashboard, studiously avoiding his gaze.

'Diana, missy, open the door now. I said *now*!'

Looking straight ahead, she raised her head and, for the third time, shook it, her lips compressed in her resolve. It was as if she wanted him to appreciate that she was defying him and his orders. He watched her, unable to believe that she would treat him in this way. This was not his child of old. Surely, in a matter of seconds, she would weaken, relent, press the key fob and allow him to yank the door open. But, no, her hands remained on her lap, her profile presented to him.

Maybe, he mused, this was her fear at work. Maybe she was too frightened to open the door. Deliberately moving away, he strolled to the front of the car and leaned over the bonnet. From his new vantage point he forced his mouth into a warm smile, and waved both his hands simultaneously at her. That got her attention. Despite the rain beginning to fall, and determined to keep her attention, he blew her a kiss and then waited, playfully, as if she might reciprocate. She did not do so and in a comical manner, as if to tease her, he thumbed his nose. Then, still smiling, blinking away the raindrops running into his eyes, he said in what he believed was a jovial tone, 'Diana, lovey, open the door would you? It's pouring! Your old dad's getting soaked out here.'

Impassive as a log, she kept her gaze on him but made no movement to obey.

He held up his hands in a dumb show, letting the drops bounce off the palms, then shaking himself, rubbing his shoulders to let her know that he was not just wet but cold.

'Please, darling. Open the door for daddy, eh?'

She remained still as a statue as if he was not there, immune to him, ignoring the fact that he, a man, was begging her and demeaning himself in the process. Suddenly, something inside him snapped. Enraged by her disobedience, her blatant refusal to bend to his will, he raced round to her window and banged hard against it with his fist, watching her start in her seat. Fleeing him, she slid across into the driver's seat. As he continued battering the window, she bowed her head, clamping her hands over her ears and rocking to and fro in her distress.

'Open the door, you stupid little cow!' he roared, beside himself with rage, hammering on the window with both his fists, then aiming a furious kick at the car door. Bending further forward as if to escape him, her face almost flat against the steering wheel, the girl began to tremble uncontrollably.

She would not defy him. If need be he would smash the car window to get at her, come up with an explanation to satisfy Lambie about that later. Despite the rain now hammering down, he saw a few metres away a ring of soot-blackened boulders used by some past picnic-maker for a barbecue. Pushing a straggle of wet hair to one side, he strode over to them, already hearing in his head the satisfying noise of window glass shattering.

As he picked the largest one up, the Escort with his wife and the two policewomen drew up behind a straggle of trees, unseen by him. While they fumbled with their seatbelts, desperate to get out as quickly as possible, he brought the rock down onto the driver's side-window of his car, turning it momentarily opaque, into a mosaic of a million pieces, before shattering. His wife, the first one out of the police car, shouted, 'Jimmy!'

He turned instinctively towards her voice, smithereens of glass falling all around him like drops of water. Immediately, the child in the car rose up through the shattered window and plunged the ebony-handled knife into his chest. Seconds later, a flicker of a smile transforming her features, she withdrew the blade.

Slowly, the man swivelled back towards his daughter, a look of amazement on his rain-spattered face. The boulder in his hand thudded to the ground and, gradually, he began to sink, his legs no longer made of flesh and bone, collapsing as if shaped out of sand. A fountain of blood jetted in all directions, and as it sprayed over the girl's face she began to scream, a high-pitched river of sound flowing endlessly from her open mouth.

Mrs Stimms raced towards the car, looking frantically first at her fallen husband, then at the screaming child. Carefully stepping over the man's still shuddering body, she opened the door of the vehicle and bent inwards, immediately cradling the child's head against her breast, murmuring softly, 'There, there . . . everything's going to be alright, Diana, my darling! Everything's going to be fine.'

Silent, body-racking sobs replaced the piercing scream and in the ensuing quiet all that could be heard above the pitter-patter of the rain was the cry of the gulls as they circled overhead, blowing around like flakes of ash in the storm-darkened sky. Gently, the woman manoeuvred her child out of the car, over the prostrate body of her father and into the shelter of the trees.

Once they were away, Alice Rice knelt down beside the man on the wet grass and took his hand in her own. DC Cairns approached them, her head bare and her hair drenched in the downpour.

'Is the ambulance coming?' Alice asked, fumbling urgently on the man's slippery wrist in search of a pulse.

'It's on its way – I gave them instructions on how to find us.'

'The forensic team for the car?'

The constable nodded, then seeing that the door of

the Mazda was still hanging open, she carefully pushed it closed with her elbow.

'Have we anything in the car to put over him in the meanwhile?'

'No.'

'Can you take Mrs Stimms and the child to the station? I'll wait here with him until the medics and back-up arrive. We'll need to go over the house in Starbank as soon as possible, although between his cleaning and her cleaning God knows if any traces will be left.'

—

Elaine Bell was shaking her pedometer when Alice entered her office. The device seemed to have stuck, recording nothing of her return journey from the ladies as if she had travelled on a cushion of air like a hovercraft, or flown. 'Cheap tat!' she muttered crossly, dropping it in her drawer and transferring some of her attention to her subordinate. Something radical would have to be tried, as despite sticking to a diet of air, ounces were being gained not lost. Sport of some kind might be the answer.

'Is he still alive?' she asked.

'He is. He lost a lot of blood, she nicked an artery. The ambulance crew saved his life, the doctors reckon. He was well enough to confess – only too keen once he understood it might have an effect on his sentence.'

'And the child? How's she?'

'Alright now. She was terrified when we picked her up, wouldn't let go of her mother, moaning incessantly. The medics checked her out, and she's with her now, at the granny's house. Everyone accepts it's for the best, for the moment at least. A counsellor's on hand.'

'Why didn't the child's school report her missing?'

'It was run by the Elect, one of their schools, and Mrs Stimms told them she was off ill, appendicitis or something.'

'OK. What have you found otherwise?' the DCI inquired, looking out of her window as if taking in the view, all the while slowly raising and lowering herself on her toes, using her calf muscles.

'Quite enough. We've got the knife. Ranald phoned from Stimms' office, he's been checking out the factory. There's a lock-up there and Hamish Evans' car was in it, so that explains why we never managed to find it. I reckon he transported his daughter's body in the boot of his own car. There are traces of blood and a woman's shoe, just the one, was behind the spare petrol can. Her mother reckons it was Miranda's shoe. The back seat was soaked through with dried blood – all he'd done was lay a couple of rugs over the mess. I'm pretty sure it'll turn out to be Hamish Evans' blood.'

'Where did he dump the bodies? Presumably it was him who put them in the sea? Mind you, did he not have help?'

'Have you a sore neck, Ma'am?'

'No. Why?'

'You seemed to be moving your head from side to side – I thought maybe you had a stiff neck.'

'No . . . I'm simply taking in the whole of the view.' The woman turned round to face her colleague, her head now completely still.

'He's adamant that they were both dropped into the Forth from the same place, the place we found him with Diana. That makes some sort of sense for her location, but for the Belhaven Bay body it is odd.'

'How do you mean?'

'Well, he says he dropped Miranda in the water on the Monday night, then went home. That's where Hamish found him. The boy was stabbed, he says, because he threatened him. Obviously, knowing what he knew, the boy was a threat to him full stop. Supposedly, Stimms dumped the body in the same place early the next morning. Somehow in only, what – less than five full days? – the body travelled all that way down the coast.'

'Too far?'

'Far too far, taking into account the changing tides and the speed of the currents round about. I spoke to the Leith harbour master and he had a possible explanation. He thinks that whilst the body was floating about somewhere near the bridges, some ship with a bulbous bow may have caught him on it – over it. Apparently, it's happened to small whales before. In the Forth, there are lots of such craft – the ferry, some of the tankers and container ships coming down from Grangemouth.'

'Why didn't he end up in Zeebruge, Ostend or wherever they're going, then?'

'It's all speculation, of course, but his explanation is that it tends to get rougher out of the river, out of the lee of the land. The transition point is often round about the Bass Rock – you get south-easterly gales blowing up there, making the boat pitch more. That's not so far from Tyninghame, from the bay.'

'Well, it all sounds a bit far-fetched to me, but we needn't worry ourselves about it. Not if Stimms has confessed to the killings anyway . . .'

'You're doing it again, Ma'am. That neck-bending thing.'

'It's my neck, Inspector, and I can do more than one thing at a time.'

'A 360-degree turn next, maybe. The lift-hitching theory is the only one we've got. If you're interested there's a Youtube video of a whale, trapped across the projection on a ship's bow.'

'Have you put your theory to Dr Cash?'

'It's not my theory. Needless to say she didn't have a moment to spare to consider it, being "busy, busy, busy", but in the tick she allowed me she seemed to concede that it was possible. The best I could get out of her was that it would not be inconsistent with her findings.'

'What the hell. As I say, he's confessed anyway, wherever the dead bodies were disposed of. Others can puzzle that one out if they have to. So you're satisfied that there were no accomplices amongst the Elect helping him to move the bodies, putting them in the water?'

'Yes, I don't think he had help. I'm not sure he'd have needed it. Jimmy Stimms is small but fit as a fiddle, whippety-thin, wiry. I honestly think he'd manage on his own. That's certainly what he maintains. His house was brimming with trophies for cycling.'

'Whippety-thin? Cycling, you say? That's interesting . . . of course, you have to wear Lycra for it, don't you? I'm not sure I could get away with that – too skin-tight. Now, I gather you're off for the rest of the day. Got anything planned?'

'I'm collecting some keys, Ma'am, nothing more.'

—

The lock on the faded green front door was old-fashioned but functional. With the turn of the key, the dog rushed straight inside. His tail was wagging furiously as if he was on a hunt, his nose twitching, ready to explore every room and then race out into the garden. Hannibal's approach was less whole-hearted, more subtle and cautious. Freed from his cage, he patrolled, in a sedate fashion, every available inch of her new property and then lay down in the patch of sunlight on the bare wooden floorboards, rolling onto his tummy in apparent ecstasy. Alice simply breathed in the air, still unable to believe her good fortune in acquiring such a jewel of a place. In time, she would move some furniture, pictures, and crockery there, but in the meanwhile a sleeping bag on the floor would do, plus a few feeding bowls for her companions. She stood in the doorway, looking out over the loch and the lavender blue Lomond Hills in the distance, marvelling at the silence and the newness of it all.

For a second, her pleasure curdled as a pang of sorrow hit her, coming from nowhere, at the thought that she, and she alone, was enjoying, experiencing, such a wonder. Had Ian been there he would have been pacing about the place, considering where an additional window ought to be situated, designing the layout of the kitchen in his head, mulling over likely colour schemes. And talking to her all the time. Change stimulated him, brought all his creativity to the fore. In his absence, she would have to make do with his pictures, and her memories. This place would not be an amalgam of their tastes as the Broughton Street flat had been, but her undiluted taste for good or ill.

The sound of car wheels on the sparse gravel leading to the cottage put paid to her musings and she went out to see who had arrived. Maybe it was just the post, or someone lost, in search of directions to somewhere else. Instead, she recognised the small figure climbing out of his slightly battered Polo, a bottle of red wine clutched in his hand.

'Alice,' Father Vincent Ross said, almost apologetically, 'I happened to have this rather good Cabernet Sauvignon at home and it suddenly struck me that you might enjoy it. As a house-warming present? Also, if I'm honest, I'm dying to know how you fared with the Elect, my so-called "rivals". Pah! By the way, is that an elderflower bush by the gate? In the summer we could make the most exquisite champagne from its blossoms. My last attempts exploded in their bottles, I don't like to think how Satan escaped the shrapnel, but I've learnt my lesson. It's just an idea. What do you think?'

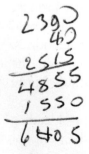